Light Reading

ALIYA WHITELEY

Light Reading

MACMILLAN NEW WRITING

First published 2008 by Macmillan New Writing
an imprint of Pan Macmillan Ltd
Pan Macmillan, 20 New Wharf Road, London N1 9RR
Basingstoke and Oxford
Associated companies throughout the world
www.panmacmillan.com

ISBN 978-0-230-70062-8

A CIP catalogue record for this book is available
from the British Library.

Typeset by Intype Libra Ltd
Printed and bound in Great Britain by
MPG Books Ltd, Bodmin, Cornwall

This is a work of fiction and is the product of the author's imagination.
Any relationship with real events, places or people is entirely coincidental.

For Mum and Dad

One

It was December, a Wednesday morning, and I was standing in the flower bed outside the front window of Flight Lieutenant Sharp's house, having the usual thoughts of how children gathered around a television screen resemble aliens waiting to receive instructions from the mother ship and whether it was too early to have a third gin and tonic.

My best friend Lena was the only smoker in our group, and whenever she was banished outside to protect the delicate lungs of the offspring I went with her. We had just heard that the men would not be coming back home from the desert for Christmas this year, and she was on her fourth cigarette in a row.

'You smoke too much,' I said. I watched her reflection in the window. She took slow, calculated puffs; it was too cold and too early for such languor. 'You must have got enough nicotine into those yellowing arteries by now.'

'Shut up, Pru,' she said. 'It's this or eating something.'

I picked paint off the window sill and watched the other wives sit on the black leather sofas with their knees together.

They watched the children who sat on the floor with their legs tucked under them, watching the Teletubbies, who were taking it in turns to watch each other's stomachs.

Flight Lieutenant Sharp and all our husbands collectively made up the officers of 24 Squadron. They flew C-130J planes by night and sunbathed in deckchairs by the runway during the day. At dusk and sunrise they drank Stella out of cans. Every morning during the men's absence we would assemble at a different house on the married patch and debrief to the noise of CBeebies and the taste of Mess gin.

'Where's Yvonne?' Lena said.

'Don't know.' I scanned the living room. 'Not in there. And they're getting ready to cut the coffee-and-walnut sponge. She never misses that.'

I stepped out of the flower bed, happy that I had ruined Tracey Sharp's bulbs. Tracey organized the wives' social events, and put slips of paper printed out on her home computer through our letterboxes to detail what kind of cake we were expected to bring and whose turn it was to supply the gin. For all her organizational skills, she still didn't know something we all did: that her husband was having an affair with the redhead who worked behind the Mess bar at weekends.

Lena dragged her cigarette butt along the brick wall before dropping it in the grass. 'I'll just ring Yvonne's doorbell.'

'Leave it,' I said, but she was already crossing the road, throwing her long grey scarf over her shoulder. I followed.

Yvonne used to be a good friend, but all that changed six months ago when she gave birth and joined the clan who compare notes on the contents of nappies. Her new-found devotion grated all the more because she didn't know something we all did: that her husband and the most senior member of the unit, Squadron Leader Patten, were having an affair in the desert.

Squadron Leader Patten was Lena's husband.

Lena walked three doors down from her crossing point and up the gravel path, and I caught up with her just as she pressed the doorbell. She held it down for a second or two. Then she turned to me, squinting against the weak sunshine.

'You should get some exercise.'

'Over my fat dead body.'

'It's your funeral.'

I stepped back from the door and looked up at the main bedroom window. It was ajar and I thought, for a moment, I heard a high, thin sound; maybe a baby crying.

She pressed the bell again and held it for a good five seconds before giving up once more. 'Perhaps she's out.'

'The tank's here.' Yvonne had one of those ridiculous off-roaders, four times the size of my own VW Golf. She said she needed it for the baby. I heard the noise once more, and this time there was no mistaking it. The baby was crying.

We exchanged glances.

Lena looked up at the window. 'I'm shinning the drain-pipe.' She unzipped her knee-high boots and stepped out of them to reveal grey socks that matched her scarf. Then she bundled her skirt up between her legs and put her long fingers around the pipe.

'Get real,' I said, but I have to admit I was impressed. She climbed it like a cat burglar, hand over hand, thighs clenched,

3

making delicate grunts of effort until she reached the window, pushed it open with one hand, and slithered inside.

I clapped, not only in approval but also to keep warm. The wind had picked up and my previous gins had just about worn off.

It took an age for Lena to appear at the door. She swung it wide and pushed past me to run to the end of the path, where she bent over the gutter and spat. It was the most unladylike thing I'd ever seen her do.

'What is it?'

'I'll get some help,' she said. She didn't turn round, or straighten up.

'Get real,' I said again. She had a strange sense of humour sometimes.

'Go in and get the baby.' And then I knew something was wrong. Lena would never tell me to pick up a baby unless I absolutely had to. She walked off, still in her socks, crossing the road in the direction of Tracey's house.

I looked into the shadowed hallway.

Two

I stepped inside, ignored the crying of the baby from upstairs, and let my feet take me to the second door on the right.

The lounge was magnolia, dotted with photos of the baby, with two large blue leather sofas placed around the blaring television. I took the remote control from the arm of one of the sofas and silenced the Teletubbies. Then I walked through the archway into the dining room.

It was the first time I had come across that smell; the smell that arrives with just-admitted death, like old leaves scraped into a pile and beginning to rot. It wasn't unpleasant, but, given time, it would be.

Yvonne was lying on her new walnut veneer dining table. She had been so glad when it arrived in time for Christmas. I remembered her telling the wives it would seat ten.

Her arms were crossed over her chest and her eyes were closed. She was half-wearing a wedding dress that had refused to stretch over her baby-expanded bust. The veil was over her face, as was a small dribble of a yellow substance that I supposed was vomit. It was the only detail marring the overall effect: that of the undertaker having been and gone.

On the matching sideboard, also new, were a half-empty bottle of gin, a tumbler, an empty pill bottle, and a piece of A4 paper with a ballpoint lying on it.

The baby kicked its crying up a notch, assuming a note of command as if it was aware I was listening, but the lure of the note was too strong. I tiptoed around Yvonne and craned my head so that I could read it without touching it.

How could I have been so naieve. The only way I could find out my husband is gay was to overhear those twittering cows. I was coming back from the kitchen with a knife to cut the coffee and walnut sponge. They were saying that I must know my husband is gay, I must know he's bumming Squadren Leader Patten in the desert, and that the baby can't be his.

Well it is his, and I didn't know.

Thanks very much girls.

As suicide notes go, it was the usual. A couple of spelling mistakes, a mixed metaphor, a little bit of blame, and a touch of self-pity. The usual.

I heard the other wives approach, at least three of them judging by the noise they were making. They came into the house and ran up the stairs to the baby. A moment later, it started to quieten down, and soothing sounds floated back down the stairs. They were saying it was going to be all right, and other such lies.

'Where's Pru?' I heard Lena say over the hushing. Feet were on the stairs again.

I had only one more moment to myself. In that moment, I made a decision that was the start of a lot of trouble.

I moved the pen to one side. I picked up the note. I folded it twice, and put it in my back pocket.

It had become part of my collection.

Three

'I can't believe it,' Tracey Sharp said. The baby wriggled in her arms, probably keen to escape the cloud of Dior and the harsh wool of her herringbone jacket. Tracey adjusted her hold on the little body to a grasp that resembled a half-nelson. 'I can't. Yvonne. Yvonne, of all people, with so much to live for. I just can't believe it.'

I pointed to the open doorway. 'You can go in and check if you want. She's on the dining table.'

She ignored me. Lena gave me a glare, which I returned. A lot had happened in three minutes. I'd telephoned 999, then the guardroom from Yvonne's hallway, and both an ambulance and the RAF police were on their way. I've always refused to join the ranks of blank-eyed text junkies, but this was the first time I've ever wished to possess a mobile phone. Three minutes can seem like a very long time when you're standing a few feet away from a dead body that used to be part of your social group.

In the meantime, Lena had rallied the wives on to the pavement outside Yvonne's house, ostensibly to look after the baby, but I suspected pack behaviour was the real driving force. We had the look of startled meerkats on alert. At a foot taller than everyone else and with her eyes searching for a sign of the emergency services, Lena was the chief watch. I was waiting for her to tuck her paws up to her chest and squeak.

I felt the suicide note in my pocket. It was the one thing Yvonne had ever done that I could relate to.

'It's this little one I feel sorry for,' Tracey said. 'She'll never know her mum now.'

Melanie Watt, dressed appropriately in an ankle-length black raincoat with a sprig of holly in her lapel, burst into tears. Rachel Pinkett searched frantically under her hand-knitted poncho for an embroidered handkerchief, then gave it to her. 'Poor little Jasmine,' Rachel said. 'Poor thing.'

Jasmine managed to squirm her upper half out from Tracey's half-nelson in order to solemnly point at me. 'I think she likes you,' Tracey said with surprise in her voice. 'Maybe you should give her a cuddle.'

'I don't do babies,' I told her.

'Not even in her hour of need?'

'This isn't her hour of need. Her hour of need will come the first time she gets bullied at school, or the first time she gets her period. The last hour before the bar shuts, when she realizes her mother left her and ends up blotting the pain out by going home with some twat who doesn't care about her but said all the right things on the dance floor – that will be her hour of need. She can give me a ring then if she wants.'

'Big of you,' Lena said. She kicked at the grate over the

drain and rubbed her upper arms. 'But that doesn't change the fact that someone needs to look after Jasmine right now.'

The wives exchanged uncomfortable looks. 'What about Karen?' said Rachel. Karen Mitchell was particularly fond of children. At least, that's what we assumed, considering she had given birth to three of them over a period of four years. She was with them now, having volunteered to stay behind and watch everybody's offspring, keeping an eye on them as they kept both eyes on the screen.

'Ummm . . . she's got a lot on,' Tracey said. 'It's the afternoon nursery play this week and her eldest is playing Moses. Plus it's her youngest's Baby Ballet recital, and her middle one is moving up a class to Advanced Toddler Tumbling.'

Lena held up one finger. 'I'll take Jasmine.'

'But you don't know anything about babies!' I said. A baby would throw up on her immaculate clothes, and put dark shadows under her green eyes. A baby would stop her from drinking gin with me.

'I think Pru has a point,' said Tracey. 'No, I'll take Jasmine for now, at least until Yvonne's parents can be reached.'

'The police – are – here,' Melanie said through loud sobs. We all looked up. I had been expecting sirens, speedy vehicles squealing round the roundabout, tall men leaping into action with resuscitation kits and determined chins. Instead there was a slow procession of two cars, bearing the blue and yellow stripes of the RAF police. They came to a quiet halt beside us. One short old man and three lads who looked barely out of school, all wearing crumpled blue uniforms, reluctantly climbed out.

'At last, the A Team is here,' I said. 'We're all saved.'

'Shut up, Pru,' said Lena.

'Which one are you?' I said to the old one, who was standing nearest to me. He had no hair and was fiddling with his belt. 'Mr T?'

He grimaced at me. 'Is she in there?'

'On the dining table.'

'Right, well . . .' He shifted his feet and looked at his colleagues. 'And the ambulance is on its way, right? Should be here in a minute, I'd think. I suppose we should go in. Have a look round.'

'I suppose you should.'

He led the way without enthusiasm, for which I couldn't blame him. Once we were alone once more, Melanie's taste for melodrama kicked up a notch.

'We should have done more . . .' she sobbed. 'We should have talked to her more . . .'

'We saw her every day,' said Tracey. 'She knew we were there for her.'

It was amazing how quickly people could bounce back from a brush with death to start thinking about their own shabby consciences and petty lives again. Since we had reached the point of talking about how Yvonne's suicide would affect us, I decided it would be acceptable to voice a thought of my own. 'Do you think they'll send the men home now?'

There was a disapproving silence all round. Melanie put the handkerchief under her nose as if I had just made a smell.

'Not that I care, really,' I defended. 'It's not like Steve and I are love's young dream any more, that's no secret, is it? I just thought they might . . . Fine. I'm the selfish one for bringing up what you were all secretly thinking. I get the picture.'

'They'll send Derek Fairly home, obviously,' said Lena. She rearranged the loops of her long grey scarf. 'But nobody else, I wouldn't have thought.'

The other wives slumped. They knew the RAF as well as I did – the organization was far too understaffed to allow troops home for something as trivial as the suicide of a wife. Derek would be back for a few weeks. Longer, if he wanted it, but then it would be a return to the desert. Perhaps it was for the best.

It was a shock to realize I was disappointed too, but not about missing out on the chance to see my own husband. No, I was disappointed because it meant there would be no change to routine. Things would go on as before. The only difference would be the absence of Yvonne. At first her space on the sofa would seem like an accusation, but that would soon pass. Someone would start to take her slice of sponge, and her name would get mentioned only in the occasional maudlin mood that grew from one too many glasses of gin.

'Poor Yvonne,' I said softly. 'Poor Yvonne.'

Nobody heard me. They were busy dealing with Jasmine, who had decided that now would be the appropriate time to start screaming for her mother. Her cries mingled with the distant siren of the ambulance, drawing closer, getting louder and louder.

Four

'Bye, Yvonne.' I raised my glass. 'We'll think of you.'

Lena followed suit, and chinked her glass against mine. 'So long, Yvonne. Good luck in the next life.'

I breathed out. 'I'm not going to the funeral.'

'Why not?' Lena said. She necked her gin and reached for the bottle. We had been sitting since early afternoon, facing each other, cross-legged on the burgundy carpet in my living room, a box of Milk Tray and a bottle of gin between us. The television was on a low volume – the all-night news channel was reporting an explosion in the desert. I had long become used to such things.

'Because Tracey will be shouting instructions and singing hymns at top volume, Rachel will be crying relentlessly into a hanky she embroidered specially for the occasion, Mel will have arranged the flowers – and probably spray-painted them black, knowing her melodramatic streak – and Karen will have baked one of her horrible sponges, which we'll all have to eat. And not one of them will be thinking about Yvonne, so it defeats the point of the service anyway.'

'You're not wrong,' Lena said, pouring herself a generous measure and taking a gulp. She was drinking faster than me. That was unusual, and a bit scary.

'What's up?'

'Don't think I can face Derek,' she said.

'Oh,' I said, not wanting to say any more until I knew what was going through her mind.

'Don't play bloody dumb with me, Pru. I know you know,' she said. 'He's humping David out in the desert. They're sharing a tent. You can't tell me it isn't common knowledge. I know what this place is like.'

'Oh,' I said again.

She put down her glass and looked at her hands, hunching over, her long brown hair over her face.

'How about a cuppa?' I said.

She didn't reply for a few seconds. Then, in a fairly normal voice, she said, 'Yeah, go on.' We stretched and got up from the carpet, and I led the way into the kitchen.

All RAF kitchens look exactly the same. The lino is grey and the cupboards are light green with thin metal bars for handles that were last popular in 1976. The cookers were apparently a job lot the DHE got from Poland, with the grill at eye level and the oven door reaching a temperature designed to take the skin off your knees if you dared to turn the knob to the on position.

As I filled the kettle, Lena examined one of the cupboard doors, her eyes looking a little unfocused.

'Can I ask you something?' she said. It was a day of firsts – the first time I had seen a dead body, the first time I had stolen something, and now the first time I had seen my best friend get drunk enough to want a real conversation with me.

'Okay.'

'Why did you take that note?'

That was the last question I had been expecting. I was thinking she wanted to talk about death or God, the two issues that always rear up when our equilibrium is disturbed. Those I could have handled in a general way, with no specifics needed.

'What note?'

'Don't give me that. The note. The note that was on the sideboard when I found Yvonne, and wasn't on the sideboard when I came looking for you. The one that still hadn't turned up by the time the police left.'

'Did you tell them it was missing?'

'No.' She stared me out. 'Because it isn't missing. You've got it.'

'Do you need a cigarette? Go outside if you need a cigarette.'

But she had a one-track mind. 'You're so selfish, Pru.'

'Me?'

'Don't you care about her family at all? Don't you think they deserve to know why she killed herself?'

'You think that note would tell them why she killed herself? That note tells them why she was pissed off with her husband, and nothing more. It doesn't say why, instead of having a good cry or having an affair of her own or getting a divorce or flying to the desert and punching him out, she chose to top herself. There hasn't been a suicide note written that manages a decent explanation for a suicide.'

Lena looked at the floor. When she raised her head, there was trouble in her green eyes. 'How do you know?'

I hesitated. It was the kind of hesitation that made it obvious something big had been stumbled upon. She was way too astute not to notice a hesitation like that.

'How many suicide notes have you seen?' she asked me.

I don't know why I told her.

'One hundred and eighty-eight.'

I told her about my collection; how I'd started it at seventeen; that I wasn't obsessed by any means, but every now and again I acquired another one and filed it away with the others. They were easier to get hold of than she might have imagined.

It's true. Most of mine come from auctions on the internet. There's quite a few of us collectors out there, and competition for the high-profile notes can be intense; I have to admit that I like those last ten seconds online, when I'm second-guessing four other bidders to win. Sometimes I go way over the price I had in mind, caught up in the moment, one might say, but Steve never seems to notice.

'Sod the cuppa,' Lena said, once I had finished my explanation. 'I'll pour us something stronger and you fetch the notes.'

So I left her rummaging through my drinks cabinet while I went upstairs and pulled my old suitcase out from under the bed, laying the wedding dress within to one side so I could get to the filing tray underneath.

I looked under 'M' and removed the one note I didn't want Lena to see. My jewellery box, containing my engagement ring and the mess of unworn necklaces Steve continued to buy me on birthdays and anniversaries, seemed the best place to put it. Then I took the filing tray downstairs and put it on the dining-room table. It felt like the appropriate place.

Lena walked through from the living room, carrying two fresh tumblers filled with a murky brown liquid. She pulled out the chair at the head of the table and settled herself, turning the tray to face her. I sat on her left.

'You are bloody strange, Pru,' she whispered, examining the 'A' slot and lifting out the first note between her thumb and forefinger. She put it down on the tabletop. It was a small piece of light blue paper with a sheen of glitter, and the words were in a rounded script, written with a green felt-tip pen.

Daz sez he doesn't like me any more, he likes Becky, and I'm so fat and so ugly. It's never going to get any better. The world is better off without me.

In a couple of places the green ink had expanded and lightened in a splatter, as if a solitary tear had fallen upon it. It was far too artful an effect for me to consider it to be a sign of real despair.

It was one of the first notes I had bid for, and I had made the novice's mistake of not asking about the case before buying. There's no interest for the serious collector in this type of note – a teenager crying wolf and managing to top themselves for real in the process. It was obvious that this girl had wanted to scare her parents, and maybe get Daz back in the process. Personally, I thought Daz, and the world, was better off without her. Suicide should be treated as a serious business.

Lena slid the note back into the tray. 'That's so sad,' she said. 'Such a waste.'

I picked up my glass and swallowed away my automatic response. A bitter mouthful told me it was whisky. Whisky always gave me a hangover. I didn't care.

She pulled out another note, this time from the middle of the tray. A quick glance told me it was one of the jewels of my collection; I had no other notes that were written on the back cover of a cheque book in a thin, barely legible scrawl. It took Lena time to decipher it.

sod this 4 a game of solders

'Nice. Who wrote it?'

'T. K. McVey.'

She laughed, as I knew she would. T. K. McVey won the Booker Prize with his debut novel and threw himself out of a window twelve months ago when his long-awaited second book was mauled by the critics. It was big news at the time and, of course, the book sold thousands because of it. Funnily enough, the press had chosen not to promote his final excursion into the land of the written word.

'A spelling mistake, and a cliché.' Lena clicked her tongue between her teeth. 'Plus, I see what you mean. It hardly gives you an insight into his decision to bail out.'

She was really getting into it. I was caught in a rare tide of enthusiasm. 'Look at this one,' I said, leaning over her to reach the 'T' section. 'It's my most recent. You're going to love it.'

I pulled out a clear plastic folder that contained a piece of hotel stationery and a folded newspaper clipping. Those two items had cost all of Steve's detachment pay. I put the folder down in front of Lena, sat back in my chair, and folded my arms.

She removed them both from the folder and examined the stationery first. The letterhead showed a dark blue coat of arms, and underneath, in swirling typescript, 'The Royal'. At the bottom was the printed address, also in dark blue. In the centre of the page, written in black capital letters, very small and neat, was one word.

FRIPL

'I don't get it,' Lena said.

'Read the article.'

She unfolded the clipping, laid it flat on the table, and scanned it as she sipped her whisky. The carriage clock on the mantelpiece, a wedding present from her husband's Great Aunt Alice, beeped 2 a.m.

It must have been a combination of things – the late hour, the events of the day, the gin, the whisky – that got me thinking at that moment. As Lena read, the silence of the dining room wrapped me in a shroud. I looked at the tray in front of me, and remembered a time when the notes had not been glamorous objects to collect, but representative of real moments, real despair. Every one was written by a closed-down mind; a mind finding the only solution in giving in to the black.

I don't believe in an afterlife – I haven't done since I was a teenager – but it seemed that if those lost souls did have some way of watching over the living, this room was the place they would congregate. Maybe they were looking at me and hoping I'd see something personal, something unique in their last lines that would bring them back to life, just for a moment.

But, to me, all the notes looked the same.

'You're kidding,' Lena said. She straightened up and looked at the note once more, touching the top corner with one finger. 'Seriously?'

'Seriously.'

The article revealed the writer of the note to be none other than Crystal Tynee.

Crystal was a household name. She had been a home-grown star since the age of six, when she won a televised talent contest with her rendition of 'Singin' in the Rain'. This led to a short stint as The Nation's Sweetheart, a title which was removed when Crystal hit puberty and started gaining weight. In 1998, at the age of twenty, she made national news once more when she was arrested for the manslaughter of her manager. She served a five-year jail sentence. On her release she became the advertising face of a cosmetics company, having slimmed down on prison food and uncovered a pair of cheekbones to die for.

Then she discovered how chocolate masks the taste of regret, put on weight, lost her contract and retired to obscurity, never to be The Nation's Sweetheart again. Maybe that was what she was thinking about on the night she killed herself in a Devon hotel five months ago. She was twenty-six.

She was one of those celebrities who meant nothing to any other group of people but the British: not big in Europe, unheard of in America, and yet representative of something to us Brits, something to do with the dry sense of humour and the conviction that what goes up must come down.

And so the press had chosen to see it as a modern tragedy caused by abuse within the penal system. I have to admit I had seen it as an opportunity to own a slice of modern history. I had watched her win that competition on television, back in 1983. She was a little younger than me, dressed in a sparkling pink raincoat and matching wellies, and I can remember seeing my mother smiling at the screen. Crystal Tynee had been the interesting, exciting, happy little girl I wanted to be, right up to the moment she took the easy way out.

I had started searching online for the note an hour after I heard about her death, and, after various wrangles, it had come into my possession two weeks ago.

'What does it mean?' Lena said.

I looked at the note again. Fripl. It was one hell of a word. I shrugged.

'Have you tried a dictionary?'

'Yeah. And I Googled it.'

'Maybe it's a code.' She swallowed the last of her whisky. 'Maybe it means something. Or leads to something.'

'Like what? Buried treasure?' But she was feeling the same as I had upon first seeing the note – an excitement. That had soon died when no immediate answers were forthcoming. Now, close to her enthusiasm, my own interest began to build inside me again. 'How could we check if it was a code?'

'I don't know.' She ran her finger along the header of the note. 'What are you doing tomorrow? Do you want to do something? Go somewhere different?'

'No.'

'Like go here?' She tapped the hotel crest.

'No. What for?'

'For clues.' There was a keen, greedy edge to her words. She was like a literary sleuth, more Nancy Drew than Miss Marple; gleaming eyes despite the alcohol, glowing skin despite the cigarettes.

'Do you really want to find out?'

Her excitement transmuted into frustration. 'What difference does it make? What's so great about being here that we need a really good reason to leave? If you want to call this an escape attempt, fine. If you want to call it avoidance, that's fine too. It's all fine. I'm still going, whether you come or not.'

'You know that's not true.'

She glared at me. 'Oh really?'

'You don't drive. And you hate public transport. So, actually, if you want to do this, you need me. And my car.'

I think at that moment she realized I was close to saying yes.

My only excuse is the optimism I saw in her then. It led me to believe that maybe solving this mystery would lead somewhere. Even though I knew she just wanted to escape the funeral and her gay husband's lover, I bought the idea that we might get to the bottom of this suicide.

'Am I Holmes or Watson?' I asked.

Five

The Diary of Lena Patten
9 December, 6.47 a.m.

I'm meant to be thinking about how this diary is a necessary step in my training to be a psychiatrist, or how it might help me to understand why I fucked my gay husband, but there's only one thing I'm thinking of.

The yellowed lace of that puffed sleeve, slipped over the still black veins of her arm: it was a sight as sharp as broken glass. And her fingernails. Dirty, of course. Pale pink varnish and that rim of grime, like she'd been trying to scratch out a life from the dirt on the standard issue linoleum on the kitchen floor before deciding it wasn't worth it any more.

What could make a woman leave her baby? That's not normal, is it? Isn't that missing a vital component of bio-logical and genetic necessity? Your baby is born to you through pain and perseverance, and as a reward nature gives you a shot of love potion number nine, like seeing light for the first time, a wash of completion that soaks into your soul and leaves its stain on you.

Or is this making it obvious that I've never had a baby?

My vision moved from the fingernails, up the arm, over that lace edge with the ivy pattern sewn in silver thread, along the knob of the elbow, across the grassy knoll of the neck, and then it slowed to a crawl, like a meandering ant, over the lips, tickling the merest mention of bleached facial hair to tackle a mountain of a nose and finally alight upon an eye. An open eye.

Yvonne Fairly's eye – an eye I knew well. I've been looking at that woman for a sign that she knew the truth about our husbands for the past three months. Her eyes always contained a wink of suspicion, always, as if her heavy blue mascara was forcing down those lids to wary slits.

Dead in her wedding dress. That was what told me she had known about our husbands all along, before I ever saw the note, and before Pru decided to take it to indulge her personal weirdness.

I didn't have a wedding dress for my special day. I had a suit, white linen, Chanel, beyond beautiful, cool against my burned wrists and thighs even in that tropical meltdown. The local boys sold frozen bananas from a yellow fridge they'd dragged out on to the sand, and even they complained about the heat that day, but it didn't bother David. I remember being amazed at how the rays of the sun sank into him, were absorbed into his core to become part of his personality; for evermore a golden man. His mother used that word to describe him – golden – when I first met her and we sat side by side on her small floral sofa with scrolled wooden arms.

A photograph album was open on her lap; a distraction, so we didn't have to look at each other and see if we both knew that bringing a girl home to meet Mother was a lie.

Her name was Trina. She died seven years ago. David misses her, I think.

I've always wanted to be a psychiatrist. I want to be able to write down thoughts and take meaning from them; to jot it all down on expensive cream sheets in a blue leather notebook that slips in and out of my crocodile handbag with a firm gold clasp. And now I'm going to do something about it, without telling anyone, without giving them the opportunity to talk me out of it. I've enrolled in night school – a course in counselling. Classes start next September. I've got books out from the library on all sorts of subjects: death, pain, regret, sex, love. I've read everything I can get my hands on about the training needed, and all the books say the same thing.

To understand other people, you must first understand yourself.

For instance, you might assume, dear Diary, that I married a gay man because I'm afraid of sex. I'm not afraid of it. I love it. And I've had plenty of it, or at least, I did before David came along. But I've always thought of it as a recreational activity, like crazy golf or going to the theatre. Maybe as a form of stress relief, sometimes. Certainly I've never considered it to be an essential part of a good relationship, and David and I have the best relationship. Had the best relationship.

Yvonne Fairly didn't change that. Neither did her husband. I remember being pleased that David had found someone to perform that service for him; he needs people to idolize him so he has a reason to keep up that brave strong face, to hold that pose as if cast in bronze, from an age where Gods and Heroes were one and the same thing. I used to do the job of crowd admiration, it's true, but all that changed six weeks ago, on his last visit home.

He came through the front door after midnight. I was in my dressing gown, painting my toenails and listening to Debussy. I was waiting up for him, and he didn't disappoint. The desert had taken weight from him and left him with a stance of readiness, and white lines in the corner of his eyes. He brought energy into the house, and I found myself stirring from my cocoon for the first time since his departure. He could always wake me. If I'm left alone, I tend not to feel much.

I made him an omelette and poured him a large gin. He ate and drank, and talked between mouthfuls, mainly about the mess out there in the desert: the tents they live in while the Americans have air-conditioned prefabs, believe it or not; the real people and the culture that's disappearing under the weight of our idea of bomb-blasted democracy. I asked a question and he nodded vigorously; I remember sand fell out of his hair and on to his empty plate. He scratched his leg through his desert fatigues and told me not to empty his bag until he'd checked it for spiders. He laughed at my expression and I walked away in mock annoyance to load the plate into the dishwasher. That was when he came up behind me and started to talk about love.

He said he had found comfort in Derek Fairly, through the bonds of danger and fear, the strangeness of war, not knowing what will happen so you start to live for real, instead of living to collect memories to polish along with your medals when you're a retired old soldier with only shaky hands and a tin of Brasso for company.

Don't you know you'll never be alone? I said. *No matter what happens, you'll always have me.*

He took my hands and looked at my lips. *I've always been alone*, he said.

But we've been through so much. And we're still together. We love each other.

We love, yes. That's true. But we don't . . . And he winced. *We don't connect. We are untouched.*

And I knew he was thinking about the time we'd visited the National Gallery early on a Tuesday during one of his unpredictable holidays, and the place had been empty; empty rooms of red walkways and gilt poles holding long arcs of ropes in place, the cold paintings marshalled behind them. We'd stopped in front of Van Gogh's *Two Crabs* and I felt the pull of the circles of thick paint on the carapaces. I told David, in the quiet voice we all use when we feel that God or a uniformed attendant may be close enough to hear us, that in many ways I was one of the crabs in the painting. People walked past me. Some stop and look. Some admire me, and some shrug, not getting it, and move on. I've been behind red ropes and gilt poles for as long as I could arrange it.

Do you think, he said, *that sometimes paintings want to be touched?*

But the uniformed attendant, an older woman with large breasts strapped down to a neat line, level with the brass buttons on her purple jacket, had come into the room and taken up the corner seat. If I had answered she would have heard every word, and so I said nothing. We walked on, the

27

funereal march of the cultured amidst the works of the dead. I thought the conversation had been left for ever, but now it seemed that David had been thinking about it, maybe as much as I had.

We are untouched, I repeated to him as he hugged my hips and I faced the dishwasher. *Even in love, we are untouched.*

We don't have to be.

He fucked me, there, in the kitchen, bent over the counter with the dishwasher door rattling and the striplight buzzing, he fucked me. No love. No romance. Just connection, and I knew he wasn't thinking of anyone or any place else, not the desert, not the muscled buttocks of his married gay lover. My breasts, my thighs. He entered me. Like a 1950s expressionist artist who thinks the act of creation is more important than the painting itself, he put his hand into the paint and moved the colours.

If I didn't know he was capable of fucking me I would still be a happy woman, because it created something we couldn't talk about. Before, he would tell me how he felt about men, what he wanted to do with them, how he brimmed with destructive urges: the need to rape, to kill, to hold a weapon, to tear down the happy-clappy bullshit that gets put around about gay men and their nurturing instincts. Honesty.

Then it occurred to me, in the aftermath of sex with my dressing gown glued to my bum and his slow tilt of the bottle to pour more gin into his glass as if this was a normal homecoming; it occurred to me that he had been telling me what I wanted to hear. He said things that brought the voracious edge of adoration to our relationship because he liked to be the centre of somebody's world.

Possibly he never liked me. He just liked attention.

A wife should never doubt her husband in that way.

After a silent week in separate rooms, he went back to the desert, I slid back into my cocoon, and that's how things have stayed. I can't help thinking that he'll never say anything of meaning to me again. And even if he did, he'd say it for the wrong reasons.

Here in my bedroom, with the expensive sheets on the bed and the clock on the bedside table ticking away its battery power, listening to the dustmen make their way down the black-windowed street with only the earliest birds for company, I find I have to ask myself if I'm still in love.

Yes, I'm still in love.

But that doesn't mean I can do this any more. Not if I'm being manipulated.

There's only one person I've met throughout my life who hasn't tried to use me as a symbol or a shield, and that's Prudence: the fat, ugly, closed tome with lumpy binding that somehow became my best friend. The one person I want to talk to, and the one person who will never let me.

David says there is nothing – no fact, no problem – that can't be overcome by telling it to someone else. He believes in honesty. I believe in happiness, and I used to think that was the same thing.

Soon I'll get up and pack to go to Allcombe. There's a mystery to be solved there, and that's a lot more exciting than anything that's going to be waiting for me here, in this place where women make faces behind each other's backs and don't know what the truth is, let alone how to tell it.

Six

Case 476: Mrs Prudence Elspeth Green
Transcript of conversation recorded Thursday,
    9 December 2004, 1.52 p.m.
Location: M5 motorway, junction 19

PATTEN: What I don't get is why people sell these notes
    in the first place.

GREEN: Dunno.

PATTEN: You've never thought about it? Don't these last
    words mean anything to people? If David . . . you
    know . . . I'd want to keep the note.

GREEN: Not everyone has a tequila sunrise of a relation-
    ship, do they? Perhaps people end it because they
    think they aren't loved any more. And you can put
    that cigarette away. You're not smoking in here.

PATTEN: I'll wind down the window. Don't be such a
    Nazi.

GREEN: I'm serious, you fag hag.

Lena sighed. 'All right. Pull over at the next service station.
I'll have a smoke and a wee there.'

'Right.' I pulled into the inside lane, looking forward to getting off the motorway. The afternoon traffic was heavy, the weather was freezing, and driving was not my forte. 'People don't always get along,' I said. 'And a suicide note is hardly the happiest memento, even if you did love your dear departed.'

'So why do you collect them?'

I ignored the question. 'This is what happens. Someone decides to bump themselves off. They write a little note, usually about how rubbish everything is or how someone else is to blame for all their problems. Then they sign off using pills or a razor or a rope or whatever method they've taken a fancy to.'

'Do you have any emotions at all, Pru?'

'Up yours. Eventually someone finds them, and the police get involved. Suicides are always investigated, so the note gets taken as evidence, and examined thoroughly. Which is interesting, because it's something all the jumpers and pill-poppers never think about, isn't it? That their precious last words will end up in a plastic bag in a police station for six weeks, with Sergeant Twatface poring over every little spelling mistake.'

'I suppose not,' she murmured.

'Okay, so, when the police have done their investigation and declared it a suicide, the note gets returned to the next of kin along with any other possessions that had been taken as evidence. And then what they do with all that stuff is up to them. Why not sell it on? Make a bit of money? After all, they won't be getting any insurance money. Suicides aren't covered, you know. Do service stations sell alcohol?'

'You can't seriously want a drink. You're driving.'

'Well observed, Watson. But a couple of units is still within the law. Besides, a gin would steady my hands.'

'You're addicted, you know that?'

I glanced at the cigarette and lighter in her hand. 'You can talk.'

'I could stop any time,' she said, with no conviction.

'Go on, then. Show me the extent of your willpower. Impress me.'

'Tell you what. I'll stop smoking if you stop drinking and swearing.'

'Fuck off!'

'Not up to it?' She took advantage of my inability to back down. 'Just for this trip to Allcombe. Maybe we'll annoy each other a little less that way.'

The exit for the service station came into view. I indicated and pulled off the motorway. 'That seems highly unlikely.'

She sighed. 'Just this once, we'll give an idea of mine a whirl and step outside your incredibly small comfort zone for a few days. Maybe you'll even rediscover the old Pru – the one who could occasionally be pleasant company.'

'You're such a b— . . . daughter of a Rottweiler.'

'Ditto,' Lena said. She slid her cigarette and lighter back into her handbag. It seemed she'd made the decision for both of us.

I parked up and we got out of the car. The air was freezing. The car park was fuller than I had expected for a Thursday morning in December, and there were people climbing out of cars all around us, fiddling with their hair and pulling down their jumpers, doing the things people do when they get out of cars.

It looked messy. I was used to houses that all had the same interior layout, and men in uniform guarding perimeter fences. This place felt out of control. Exposed.

Lena pulled at the bottom of her wool cardigan and ran her hands through her long hair. Then she fiddled with the clasp of her handbag.

'No cigarettes, remember?'

'I know. Are you coming?'

'Actually, I might just wait in the car. Get me a burger, will you?'

'I'll get you something healthy,' Lena said, and walked away before I could tell her to forget it.

I got back in the car and put my hands on the steering wheel, resting my head on my knuckles. Had I once been a pleasant person? I couldn't remember. It seemed both Lena and Steve were in agreement that I was no fun to be with any longer.

I think I fell asleep for a while. I woke to the sound of the passenger door opening.

'Where's my burger?'

Lena got in and threw me a sandwich. I read the label: egg and cress.

'If you don't want it, Pru, throw it away.'

'Didn't you get your own sandwich?'

She shook her head. 'I got this instead.' She pulled open the paper bag and revealed a paperback, turning the title towards me. It read, *Crystal: Smilin' in the Rain.*

'We can swot up,' she said. I hadn't heard that expression in years. 'It might provide a key to her personality. Listen to this . . .'

33

She opened the book to a page she had earmarked and began to read.

'It was at the tender age of eighteen months that Sally, still five years away from taking the stage name of Crystal, showed signs of stardom.

'"She sang . . . before she could talk," said her mother, Julie Smithson, in a rare 1998 interview. "She danced . . . before she could walk. She was like Judy Garland, but . . . better."'

'Thrilling.'

'Oooh . . . this bit's good. About how her close relationship with God got her through her prison experience? "I know I did wrong, but I'm going to spend the rest of my life making it right."'

'Does it say why she bumped off her manager . . . what was his name again?'

'Tony Gamberetti. Ummm . . .' Lena flicked through the pages. 'Not in so many words. I thought it was manslaughter. It does say that she used her experiences to help her relate to victims of crime. She saw through her selfishness and decided to help others instead. "She's a wonderful person," Christopher Biggins said in 2003.'

I started the car. 'From here to Allcombe is a two-hour journey,' I told Lena. 'If you carry on reading from that book, I'm going to do it in one.'

Seven

It took an hour and forty-five minutes.

Lena filled the entire trip with anecdotes and snippets from her new purchase, and by the end of the journey I was sick of Crystal Tynee. I may have felt a connection with Crystal once: that illusion had been destroyed. I heartened myself with the thought that these celebrity books never tell the truth anyway.

It was dark, late afternoon, by the time we arrived, giving us no opportunity to look closely at Allcombe as we drove past the squat, grubby shops of the high street and turned the sharp corner to the promenade. There was a row of tall, elegant houses that looked out over the still sea, punctuated by regularly placed iron streetlights and benches. The Christmas lights were on, and only a third of them were broken, I estimated. Strings of reindeer dangled in the air between the lampposts, and a giant Santa with a wink danced at the entrance to a rickety pier that jutted out into the still blackness of the harbour. A few small boats lay attached to the moorings, all of them low in the water as if about to give up the struggle to stay afloat for good.

The Royal Hotel was towards the end of the row of promenade houses, with a blue porch light that picked out the green points of the ivy leaves in the hanging basket below. A miniature plastic tree with no adornment sat in a plant pot by the front window. I parked the car between a dirty white Ford and a dark blue Mini that looked like they had long since rusted to the road.

'Bit of a dump,' Lena said.

'What are you on about? It's stylish. Old-world chic.'

She leaned past me to retrieve her ubiquitous huge crocodile handbag from the back seat, dragging it past my head and out of the car. I took my purse from the glove compartment and stepped out.

Lena sniffed, facing the sea. 'Great air.'

She was right. It had a freshness to it that hit the back of my tongue like orange juice. But the wind, bouncing off the waves, was freezing, and the windscreens of the parked cars were already iced over. I took my small black rucksack from the passenger seat and passed Lena's large blue travel case, bulging and heavy, to her.

I walked up to the porch and looked through the glass-paned front door. The reception area had varnished pine floorboards that contrasted with the dark wood of the main desk. I could see the first seven or eight steps of a grand, curving staircase.

Lena pushed past me, hitting my leg with her case, and threw open the door. I followed her inside, embarrassed by the clatter of her heeled boots on the floor. By the time I closed the door, she had reached the desk. A tall young man pushed through the orange beaded curtain covering the archway to the right. He walked over and took position on the other side of the desk, his eyes fixed on Lena. There was something about his gaze on her chest that made me want to punch his spotty maw until it bled.

'Have you got a room available?' she said.

I joined her at the desk. 'Twin beds, if you've got them.'

He was a bit too thin to be considered handsome, with sunken cheeks and dark patches under his eyes. Nineteen, maybe early twenties, and keen on staying out late, drinking too much. I knew how people got those dark patches.

'Can do, ladies. Do you want to include breakfast? It's served from seven to nine, and you get the full English – sausage, bacon, eggs . . .'

'Do you have cereal?' Lena asked.

He eyed her up. 'We have a weight-watcher option, like yoghurt, for the slimmer lady like yourself.' He gave her a smile which revealed that he thought of himself as a bit of a catch. Lena gave a small laugh, which she stifled with the back of her hand.

'Aren't you a cheeky chappie?' I said in my hardest voice, but it wasn't enough to dent the grin; not after Lena's encouragement.

'Call me Phil. Credit card?' he said.

I opened my purse and produced my plastic, sliding it along the desk. Phil appeared to be determined to complete the transaction as slowly as possible. He jotted down my card details on a white form he produced from under the desk.

'Mrs P. Green,' he read. 'Nice. You look more pink to me.'

'Very clever. You'll have us all in stitches, won't you, sonny?'

'Here on holiday?'

'Yes.'

'You're a bit out of season.'

I didn't reply. Let him think what he wanted.

'Last-minute thing,' Lena said into the silence, giving Phil the kind of smile people usually reserve for job interviews. I wished there was some way I could tell her not to encourage him.

He gave me back my card and reached under the desk once more, producing a silver key attached to a large rectangular wooden fob. 'It opens the front door as well. I've put you in room 4.' He handed it to Lena.

'Ummm . . .' she said. 'This isn't the room that – that ummm . . .'

As usual, subtlety was beyond her.

'Nah,' he said. 'That's number eight. It's taken at the mo. I never would have put you two down as tiny pilgrims.'

It was a moment or two before I realized he meant Tynee pilgrims.

'We're not,' Lena said, touching her chin with the key fob and looking up at the ceiling.

'Of course not,' Phil said. 'Bags.'

'I beg your pardon?' I said.

'Bags. Do you want me to carry them?'

'No.' That was more than enough conversation for me. I took the key from Lena. 'Where's the room?'

'First floor. Turn left.'

'Bye,' Lena said, and I heard her following me up the stairs, her handbag banging against the banisters.

On the first floor the carpet had faded to a dirty green, and the off-white walls showed dark rectangular marks where pictures must once have hung. The wall lights were yellow, as if the dirt from the walls had crept over the bulbs in the brass tulip lampshades.

Room 4 was the first door on the left. I inserted the key into the lock. Lena waited, breathing heavily. She might have been slimmer than me, but she wasn't fitter: smoking had seen to that. I wondered if she needed a cigarette right now in the way I needed a drink.

The room had been infected with meadow-print. There were meadow-print duvet covers on the single beds, and an identical meadow-print picture framed on the wall above. The same pattern was on the lampshade, the curtains, the pillowcases and the shower curtain.

'We're in floral hell,' I said.

Lena placed her bag on the bed nearer the window, then pulled the curtains. They didn't meet in the middle.

'Give it a rest, will you?' she said.

'What's your problem?'

'I was getting information from Phil—'

'I don't think we should be on first-name terms with the boy—'

'*Man*,' she stressed. 'And you were your usual self: rude, arrogant . . .'

'Don't be so melodramatic.'

'Well, I found out more than you did,' she said.

'Yeah, and you couldn't have been more obvious about it. Right, come on.'

'Come on where?'

I opened the door and let my eyes adjust to the dimness of the hall. 'Room 8.'

The hotel had a strange numbering policy – there was no 3, 5 or 7. It turned out room 8 was on the second floor, directly above us, between rooms 9 and 12.

We stood outside the door, in a corridor identical to the one on the floor below.

'What now, Sherlock?' Lena said.

I knocked on the door.

'You knocked on the door!'

'Give that woman a prize.'

'What if someone answers?'

I snorted, but I admit I had absolutely no idea what I would do if somebody did answer.

But nobody did.

'Nobody's answering,' Lena said.

'I'm going to use your head as a battering ram in a minute!'

Her eyes challenged me to try.

'Look,' I said, 'just try to think of a way to get the door open.'

She did something that hadn't occurred to me. She tried the handle.

It was locked.

I have to admit to feeling smug. 'Just getting warmed up, are we?'

She spun round, flinging her hair over her shoulder like a

shampoo commercial, and started back down the stairs. I leaned over the balcony and watched her right hand slide down, all the way to the ground floor, and then caught a glimpse of her long skirt as she walked away.

'Ummm . . .' I said. I couldn't muster the courage to call out to her.

It must have been ten seconds before her left hand appeared on the stair rail below. It was closed into a fist. Poking out was a wooden key fob.

She reached the top, caught her breath, and put the key in my hand. 'Phil wasn't around. I took it from the reception desk.'

I nodded, slid it into the lock, and turned the handle. The door opened a few inches and I slid my hand in, casting around for the light switch. Yellow light sprang through the gap. I pushed the door open, and stepped inside.

Eight

There was a black briefcase by the side of the bed and, visible through the half-open wardrobe door, a matching suit-bag. It had to belong to an organized man – an unlikely guest in such a cheap hotel. On the bedside cabinet were three hardback books.

I moved over to them and scanned the titles as Lena poked around in the bathroom. There weren't any familiar names, and they didn't look particularly interesting. I wondered what sort of man would finish off the day by reading a passage from *In Search of England* by H. V. Morton, *No Highway* by Nevil Shute, or *Words for the Faithful* by Reverend John Smythe. Maybe it helped put him to sleep.

'Found anything?' I called to Lena, who was in the bathroom.

'Nope. How did she . . .?'

'Took pills. I think that's what the papers said.'

Lena appeared in the bathroom doorway. 'Are you sure?'

'Nope.'

'How would you do it?'

'Ummm . . .' I pulled back the wardrobe door and examined the interior. It was solid, oak maybe, and looked like it had stood in that spot for years. Inside was a thick metal bar from which the suit-bag and a few wire coat hangers were suspended. I put my hands on the zip of the bag.

'Can I help you?'

I turned around. Lena was in my eyeline, facing me, her eyes huge. She stumbled across the room to stand beside me.

The man in the doorway was of average height, a little taller than me. He had a polite yet guarded quality to his voice. His grey suit and blue tie completed the image of a conservative man. There was something defensive about him, about his way of standing. He held his hands in front of his thighs, as if he was expecting life to knee him in the balls. Maybe, like me, he was used to assuming the worst about people. I took an immediate liking to him.

'We're the chambermaids,' Lena said.

'We're not the chambermaids,' I said.

He didn't move from the doorway. 'So what are you doing?'

'We're . . .' Nothing came to mind. I improvised. 'Did you know someone died in this room?'

He gave a tiny smile. Perhaps he thought it was a joke. Lena laughed, the most annoying defence mechanism ever invented.

'Perhaps I should call someone,' he said, his smile growing. I felt the hairs on my upper arms rise.

'Look, we really do have a valid explanation,' I told him. Absolutely nothing was entering my head apart from panic signals. I could not think of a single reason why we should be going through this attractive man's room and standing around his wardrobe.

'They're carpenters.'

Phil came into view, his head visible over the shoulder of the man in the doorway, who turned and stepped back.

'I beg your pardon?'

'I asked them to have a look at the wardrobe. The door doesn't close properly. You probably noticed that yourself?'

The man looked back at us. I made a show of examining the wardrobe door. I don't know what Lena was doing, but given her track record in stressful situations she was probably blushing and looking nothing like a carpenter.

'It's no good. You'll need a new wardrobe,' I said, rattling the door handle.

'Yeah, right, well, come on, you two,' Phil said, waving his hand at us. 'Let Mr Tunnell have his room back.'

It must have been Phil's confidence that did the trick. Mr Tunnell took another step back and made a space for us to pass. I took the opportunity, giving Lena a shove and following her out. I kept my eyes on the floor, and didn't stop until I'd passed Phil and reached the staircase.

'Right then, Mr Tunnell, I'll see you at breakfast,' Phil said. 'Let me just remove my key from your door . . .'

'Yes. Thank you. And thank you, ladies,' he said. I risked a look at him. No, he hadn't fallen for the carpenter story for one moment. The quirk of his lips showed amusement, with a trace of puzzlement. I was left with no idea as to why he'd let us off the hook.

'Goodnight,' he added, when he got no reply from either of us. Then he walked into his room and shut the door.

I felt my breathing begin to return to normal.

'Thank you,' Lena said to Phil under her breath, her eyes huge. He put one finger to his lips and ushered us down the stairs until we were once again on the first floor, outside our own door. There wasn't enough room for the three of us to stand there comfortably. I backed against the door as Lena took a tiny step forward, her body curving towards Phil. She thanked him again – she really was a stuck record – and he shushed her again.

'The pub on the corner. Seven,' he said in a low voice.

'Pardon?' Lena said.

'What's it called?' I interrupted, hoping to speed up the conversation.

'The Slaughter. See you there.'

This town got weirder and weirder. 'Seven. The Slaughter. Will do.'

He walked away downstairs, to his desk, no doubt. Lena watched him go before daring another whisper in my direction. 'Why does he want to meet *both* of us?'

'Don't know.' Then the tone of her words hit me. 'Do you mean why doesn't he want to have a drink with just you?'

'Of course not,' she said, fidgeting with her fingers. She was the worst liar in the world.

'Get over it! He just got us out of a situation. Now he's going to inform us of why he got us out of that situation. He wants something. Probably money.'

'Of course,' Lena said. 'What time is it now?'

I checked my watch. 'Coming up for six.'

'Open the door, then. I need to have a shower and do my hair.'

'You are a seriously deranged woman if you think he helped us because he's hot for you.'

She gave me an uncharacteristically stern look. 'Pru – I've been married to a gay man for ten years, and it looks like that marriage is over. As far as I'm concerned, this is not only an investigation into a suicide, but a chance to work on my incredibly rusty flirtation techniques. Open the door and keep out of my way.'

'Okay, so you are a seriously deranged woman,' I said, sliding the key into the lock. 'Seriously f-flipping deranged.'

Nine

The Bosworth Slaughter turned out to be a locals' pub.

The place wasn't exactly full of grizzled fishermen comparing tattoos and singing songs about Spanish Ladies, although the barman had a patchy grey beard and was wearing a crew-neck sweater. But when we walked down the stone steps, through the low oak door and into the main bar, everyone turned simultaneously and stared at us. I could have sworn they were all on automatic timer.

I waited for them to get over the shock of seeing an out-of-season stranger as I looked around for Phil.

The pub was one large, dark room. Sitting on the wooden benches near the door was a group of long-haired teenage lads, dressed entirely in black, nursing what appeared to be half-pints of cider. Standing at the bar, given a tanned glow by the orange fairy-lights strung up over the optics, were the hardened drinkers – three middle-aged men in T-shirts stretched tight over their bellies. They were leaning back, elbows on the bar, giving the casual eye to the girls who were forming a line for the ladies' toilet. The girls looked underage to me: dyed hair, miniskirts, and tank tops with multi-coloured bra straps hanging out. They nudged each other as they returned the men's stares with frank and amused eyes.

The far end of the room was split into a dance floor and a stage. A range of musical instruments were placed on stands, waiting to be played.

There was no sign of Phil.

Lena shifted her feet beside me; I could understand her discomfort. We looked like we were attending two entirely different social events. She had pulled a little black dress out of her case, along with make-up and earrings. I was still wearing my jeans and jumper, and was not smelling fragrant after a day of travelling and unexpected confrontations with strange men.

It seemed the locals had finally had enough of eyeing us up. They turned back to their drinks and conversations, and I took the opportunity to walk across the dull brown carpet to the bar.

The stalwart drinkers ignored me, but the barman peeled away from them and wandered over in my direction, giving me a nod.

'Two gin and tonics, pl—'

Lena interrupted me. 'No, that's two orange juices, please.'

The barman rolled his eyes. 'What's it to be, ladies?'

'Orange juices,' Lena repeated. He sighed and turned his back on us, busying himself with glasses.

'But I'm gasping for a drink!'

'Yeah, well, I really need a smoke, but we've decided not to.'

'Can't we decide not to not to?' I said, feeling ashamed of my own weakness.

She held my gaze as she shook her head. 'Not this time.'

'Ice and slice?' the barman interrupted, his hands on the handles of flesh where his hips used to be.

'I'm getting a seat,' Lena muttered, leaving me to deal with the request. I told him yes and paid him a sum that was astronomical compared to Mess rates. When I turned, drinks in hand, Phil had materialized and was sitting opposite Lena, facing me, at one of the wooden benches. He looked up and gave me the international 'bottoms up' gesture for a pint. I ordered the local bitter for him, ignoring the sighs of the barman, and performed a balancing act to get the drinks over to them.

'I was just telling Lena—'

'That's Mrs Patten to you,' I said.

'No, he can call me Lena. You can call me Lena, Phil.'

'Right, well, I was just telling Lena that I've realized I've picked a bad spot. Thursday night is the local band night. They'll be starting in a minute and it gets a bit loud.'

'Why is it called the Bosworth Slaughter?' Lena asked.

He shrugged and took a mouthful of foam from the top of his pint. I felt my mouth fill with saliva in response, and I didn't even like bitter. 'Some king stayed in the town once or something. It's like a grockle thing now.'

'Grockle?'

'Tourist,' he said, his lips twisting.

'Did they stay at the Royal?' Lena said, leaning over the bench, turning a strand of her hair with her fingers.

'Nope. My dad named it the Royal when he leased it.

Before that it was called the Devon Cream Rest Home. A lot of those big houses are charity write-offs for mental or old people now.'

'Oh dear.'

'Look,' I jumped in, before they could land on another topic and pound it into submission. 'Just tell us what you want.'

'It's not what I want. It's what you want. And how I can help you.'

'And for what price?'

He pulled an innocent face, widening his eyes and pouting.

Lena leapt back into the fray with her usual misreading of the situation. 'Thanks so much for covering for us earlier – with the carpenter thing.'

He tapped his fingers on his glass. 'Like I said, didn't put you two down as Tynee pilgrims. Thought they had all dried up by now.'

'So why do you care what happens to a couple of Tynee pilgrims?' I asked.

He gave me his charming smile again. He was definitely a big fish in a very small pond. In the city nobody would have given him a second glance, but here, he was probably the most attractive thing in a fifty-mile radius, judging by the teenage lads at the next bench.

'Are you only interested in the Tynee myth?' he asked. 'Or do you want to find out the truth?'

I pushed my untouched orange juice away and folded my arms. 'Spit it out.'

'Let's just say that Crystal's last visit to the Royal was not her first.'

Now we were getting somewhere. 'Go on.'

'She had a long-term interest here in Allcombe. I know that's hard for someone like you to understand, but there it is.' I noted he didn't include Lena in his insult.

'What kind of an interest?'

He picked up his pint glass and drained it with four swallows. There was something lascivious about the movement of his mouth and Adam's apple as he gulped. I stole a quick glance at Lena. She was watching him, her lips parted, her cheeks red.

'Oh look,' he said, 'I've finished my pint. I could do with another.'

I steeled myself. 'What kind of interest?'

He gave a dry laugh and made the pint gesture again.

I didn't move.

There was a rumble from the far end of the room. A trickle of applause began, and petered out. I leaned back to see past Lena's head and looked at the stage. The band had arrived and were picking up their instruments, fiddling with their amplifiers. Three lads, all stick thin, all in black; I turned round to check if they were the same guys who had been on the bench next to us, but no, those teenagers were still in place, the levels of their half-pints of cider no lower. There was obviously a plethora of heavy metal pubescents in this town.

'We're Dead Vegetation,' the lead singer said in a squeaky voice. 'Hear us roar!'

The guitarist struck a mammoth chord on his bat-wing

guitar, and the glasses on the benches trembled. He played a riff that, after concentration on my part, revealed itself to be the opening to 'Whole Lotta Love'. It was impossible to talk over it so I put my fingers in my ears and resigned myself to waiting it out. Lena had other ideas. She nudged me in the thigh with her elbow and jerked her head towards the door.

I stood up and, after a glance towards Phil, who was transfixed by the band, left the pub. Lena was right behind me.

The ferocious night air hit me as soon as I opened the door. I walked up the stone steps and crossed the road to stand in the doorway of a fish-and-chip shop, breathing in the aroma of grease and feeling my stomach tighten. 'What now?'

Lena stood in front of me, apparently untouched by cold or hunger. 'Let me handle Phil.'

'What are you going to do?'

'Let me handle him.' The wind took her hair and whipped it across her face. She pushed it back. 'Go for a walk, or back to the hotel, or something. Just leave me to deal with this.'

'You think you can do better than me? Who do you think you are, Mata Hari? You think Phil will settle for a cosy chat with you? He doesn't strike me as the type to give it all up for a bulimic pansy-lover. He'll want another pint, then another, then whatever he thinks he can get.'

'Just . . .' She took a step towards me, her arm raised. I took a step back. There was something about her that I didn't recognize: something that almost scared me. 'Just shut up, Pru.'

She crossed the road, descended the stone steps, and disappeared from view.

My stomach grumbled. I walked into the chip shop and ordered a double fishcake and chips. Then I walked to the corner and sat on the freezing iron bench as I ate.

To my right was a road dotted with small stone cottages, leading to the rickety pier. On my left was the tall Victorian terrace and the benches stretching onwards, running parallel with the sea. There wasn't a person in sight. I couldn't even see a light in a window, and the streetlights provided only a tired orange haze. My eyes became accustomed to the darkness, and my ears began to tune out the constant swish of the sea. I looked over my shoulder. Apart from the neon sign of the chip shop, the only other light was coming from the lamps outside the Bosworth Slaughter.

An illustration from a childhood book that my mother used to read to me slid into my mind. A group of woodland animals – foxes, squirrels, badgers, mice – had been dancing together in a cosy space under the roots of an old gnarled tree. They had been waiting out the winter as only fictitious creatures could, hiding from its vicious breath. It had looked so cosy in their den, with cakes and sweets stored and the band playing merrily. I remembered how sorry I had felt for the animals who hadn't managed to make it before the door was shut. There must have been some who remained outside, freezing and lonely.

The last few chips looked grey and unappetizing, but I ate them anyway. I put the polystyrene tray in the bin by the bench, and then started a brisk walk down the promenade before the last of the warmth in my stomach faded.

With dark-accustomed eyes I saw the effects of neglect on the grandeur of the terraced houses. I hadn't noticed earlier that one house in five was boarded up and covered in graffiti. The bandstand halfway along the promenade was rusting, and barbed wire had been erected around it in a failed attempt to keep people out. I counted at least seven empty cider bottles on its floor as I walked past.

I read the names above the doors of the houses. Many of them were in faded script with outmoded designs, and the boards were rattling in the wind: Raffles, The Gloucester, Sea View, Avalon . . . This place must have been a thriving resort once, perhaps before package holidays came along, but now these buildings were the bones of the corpse of the local tourist industry. The only difference was they would take longer to disappear than the holidaymakers.

For a moment, in between gulps of fresh air, I caught a familiar smell. It was the smell I had come across in Yvonne Fairly's dining room yesterday morning. It was the smell of the end.

Why would Crystal Tynee choose this place to kill herself in? It had made more sense to me when I thought Allcombe was mysterious; I could see her, gazing out to sea, making the decision in a *Sunset Boulevard* kind of way. Now I had uncovered a new puzzle. She had ended it all in this dump. And, apart from that, she had visited regularly.

Maybe Lena was getting to the bottom of it. Maybe she was artfully leading Phil into revealing the truth. Or maybe she was in a filthy cubicle in the men's toilets with her knickers around her ankles, her fingers in his greasy teenage hair, discovering the cheap thrill of sex with a stranger.

I looked up and found myself at Royal, with its hanging basket of ivy, lonely naked Christmas tree and blue porch light. There was nothing to do but go inside and put myself to bed.

Ten

The tap dripped. The sound reverberated around the bathroom and over me.

The man in the room above was pacing.

Lying in the dark, staring at the ceiling, I searched my memory for his name. What had Phil called him? Mr Tunnell. He hadn't believed our excuse but he had let us go. I pictured him in my mind: trimmed moustache, smart clothes; the briefcase, the dark hair, the suit-bag. I could not imagine what business he had in Allcombe in the dead of winter. He didn't fit.

The mattress springs were soft; my bottom was a few inches lower than my head and feet. The duvet was too light for the weather, and the gap between the sash and the window sill allowed the wind to dash past my forehead. It had to be gone midnight.

I looked at the empty bed beside me.

Tunnell paced regularly, the squeaks and croaks of the floorboards adopting a rhythm that melded with the dripping tap. He must have had a lot on his mind.

Or maybe it wasn't him.

Once that thought had sneaked in, others followed, and the tone of the night changed. The dark corners of the room began to look like shapes rather than shadows. The regular creaks and drips took on the tone of music, and the sea was an unfamiliar percussion.

I was scared.

And it wasn't an issue of loneliness. I've been alone for so long that it really makes no difference any longer. In fact, I find company difficult to accept, as a rule. I've preferred my own space since I was seventeen.

But Yvonne's death was having an effect on me, even though, when I had stood in her dining room with her body, I had felt nothing but pity and curiosity. Maybe even disgust. But not fear.

Even if I could have slept, I was afraid to. I didn't want to see that wedding dress: the bare shoulders and the dirty white bra straps hanging loose, the veil pulled down, the toes of her white satin ballet shoes pointing up like exclamation marks.

I wanted something else to think about. Something real.

Tunnell paced on.

He was good looking: broad shoulders, dark hair, a way of looking at me as if he knew me. He reminded me a little of Steve; of how Steve used to look to me before we got married.

Perhaps that was why Tunnell had not challenged our blatant lies earlier. It was possible he had sensed my attraction, wasn't it?

His pacing took on a personal note. Did he know that I

was only one floor beneath him? Maybe my closeness was keeping him awake, keeping me in his mind just as he was in mine?

Couldn't it be that, for once, it was someone else's job to want me?

I ran it through my mind. I could simply get out of bed, put on my clothes, walk upstairs, and knock on his door. He might frown, and ask me what I wanted. I could cry; I could be crying and, as he answered, the tears would spill down on my cheeks and he would take one look at me and lead me into the room, his room, Crystal's room.

The pacing stopped.

In the new silence, the sound of a key in the lock downstairs was loud, as were the footsteps crossing the wooden floor. The snap of high heels told me it had to be Lena, but she didn't have a key. I had the key.

Then I heard the low thrum of voices, and the image of Phil came into my head. Phil and Lena were talking to each other at the bottom of the staircase, sharing the idea that they must lower voices so as not to disturb.

It was a long conversation. I was on the verge of getting up, leaning over the banister and shouting at them to flipping well stop whispering, when their voices dropped away to silence. I counted to ten before I heard the sounds of two separate sets of feet going in two different directions.

I slid out of bed, tiptoed to the door, opened it a crack, got back into bed, lay on my stomach, and closed my eyes. By the time she entered, I had slowed my breathing to a regular pattern.

I heard her shut the door. Then there was the squeak of

the leather as she removed her boots. She crossed to the foot of my bed.

'Pru? Are you awake?'

I considered not answering, but there was an edge to her voice that made me roll over on to my back and cross my arms over my chest. 'What do you want?'

'Don't be like that.'

'Like what?'

She expelled a breath and sat down on my bed, inches from my right foot. I could make out her bowed head, her hair across her face.

'Phil's dad found her. Hanging in the shower cubicle. Her own belt was tied around her neck.'

'That's weird. I thought the papers said she took pills.'

She shook her head. 'No. Hung herself. Must have been a horrible way to go.'

I was surprised by the sadness in her voice. 'Did Phil see her?'

'His dad called him to help cut her down. His parents run the hotel, but they're on holiday at the moment, so he's taking care of things.'

'So who found the note?'

Lena shifted her weight. 'Phil did. It was on the bedside table. It doesn't mean anything to him either.'

I picked at the seam of the duvet cover. 'So that's it, then. We should go home tomorrow.'

Lena stood up and pulled her jumper over her head. Her gleaming white lace bra was the brightest object in the room. I moved my gaze to the gap in the curtains. 'There's something else,' she said.

'What?'

'Phil said . . . wait a sec . . .' I heard the creak of mattress springs coming from the other single bed, followed by the rustle of a duvet. I decided it was safe to look round. She was in bed, facing me, resting her head on one elbow. 'He said there was no way she could have done it by herself. She was small, only five feet something, and she couldn't have looped the belt over the shower head on her own. Phil said there wasn't a stool or anything she could have been standing on when he saw the room.'

'So she had help?' I'd come across suicides where other people had been roped in, so to speak. On the surface, I wouldn't have put Crystal down as that type.

Lena shrugged, her eyes locked on mine. 'Maybe . . .'

I dared myself to say it. It came from my lips as a whisper. 'Maybe it was murder.'

She whispered back. 'Phil said he overheard the police talking about it when they were cleaning out the room. They said it looked suspicious. They took . . . the body and the note away, and interviewed him and his dad, and then everything went quiet. Not one word was ever said, not even in the newspapers, about it maybe not being suicide. About it being . . . murder.'

Now we had both said it. It was out there. It was a possibility.

'Sounds like a conspiracy,' I murmured. It was impossible to raise my voice any louder than that; the air in the room seemed to have thickened.

'I don't know. I suppose so. I can't think about it any

60

more,' Lena said. 'Why would someone do that to her? In the biography it said everyone loved her.'

I feigned surprise. 'You mean . . . the book might be wrong? Heaven forbid that someone should publish something that's not one hundred per cent accurate about her life!'

'Fine, Pru, have a go at me.' She rolled on to her back and tilted her chin towards the ceiling. 'But if it could happen to her . . . I mean, anyone could just go. Could just die. I could die. I've been thinking about it since Yvonne . . . What does it take to push someone to suicide or murder? How do you get there? Maybe we're closer than we think, you know, to the edge. When I found out David was cheating on me, with a man, I felt something . . .'

'You've been thinking too much,' I said.

She was silent for a minute or so. Then she turned her back on me.

Not having to look at her face made it easier to talk. 'I meant that you . . . you can't think about this stuff all the time. Push it to the back, somewhere. Where you put the worst things. And then they only come out occasionally. I mean, they always do, on bad nights. But the rest of the time you can go on.' I ground to a halt. 'I'm not explaining this very well.'

'I understand,' she said. 'That's what you do.' *But not me*, she was thinking. I could tell. The unspoken words were thick in the airless room.

Everything was too serious. 'We'll make an early start tomorrow if you want.'

'To do what?'

'I told you. Go back home.'

Ice frosted her voice. 'So we can get on with filing this experience under "U" for Unpleasant? Don't you want to find out how bad it can get?'

'I think it's got bad enough, don't you?'

'I never put you down for a coward, Pru.' She sat up and stared past me, at the gap in the curtains. 'I'm not going back yet. I'm not going to Yvonne's funeral, to shake hands with her husband and offer my sympathy. And I don't want to push this whole thing to the back of my mind and hope the gin keeps it under control.'

'You're just a child, really, aren't you, Lena?' I put my hands behind my head in an attempt to appear in control. 'You have no idea how bad this could get. Flirting with strangers, playing with murder. I never realized how innocent you are.'

She didn't reply. She got up from the bed, wrapped the duvet around her, slung her handbag around her neck, and waddled to the door.

'Where do you think you're going?'

She didn't turn round or take her hand from the door handle as she said, 'To get rid of my innocence.'

'But I . . .'

'I'll see you at breakfast,' she said.

The door closed behind her with a click.

I didn't sleep at all that night. Neither did Mr Tunnell. The pacing started up again and did not stop until five in the morning. All my thoughts of creeping up the stairs to him had been revealed as dreams with nowhere to go. They belonged to a different kind of person: one that still believed in escape.

Eleven

The Diary of Lena Patten
10 December, 2.32 a.m.

As far as I'm concerned, dreams don't mean anything.

Your brain is a vat, a bubbling bowl in which your thoughts ferment, and inevitably scum forms on the surface of that churning liquid. Dreams are that scum. They are the dregs of the miasma you call a personality. There's no message to be taken from their existence.

Saying that, why would that old dream come back to haunt me last night, of all nights?

I was falling from a high cliff, plunging so fast my cheeks were grabbed by the wind and pulled back behind my ears, and below me was a desert, a blank expanse, and the only object I could see from my astronomical viewpoint was a single black dot, which formed into a green splodge, which grew into a cactus with the sharpest prickles you've ever seen in your life and guess what? It was directly underneath me.

I fell for an age, knowing what would happen, thinking

about how much it was going to hurt and how wonderful it would be if David came to save me in his Hercules, swooping down in the sky and catching me, like the giant grey hand of God. But he didn't appear.

And then, at the moment of impact, just before I was about to be punctured in a thousand places and my neck and wrists were snapped back, and my skin burst open like a tomato hitting a wall – I woke up.

I must have flinched, but Phil slept on with the assuredness of a teenager who hasn't regretted a thing and doesn't care if anyone else does either. I was glad he didn't wake up.

Is this the point where I write: What have I done?

I'm not going to. I know what I've done. I can stand in this reception room, lean against this desk, scratch these words out with this pen: The new can be accepted into my life without a fuss . . . I can choose not to give way to emotion for the things I leave behind.

Phil is asleep in his parents' bed, his face buried in the pillows that smell of his mother's hairspray. Their picture is on the dresser beside him. Mother smiles out from some captured moment that means nothing to Phil; I can tell that because he didn't bother to slam her face down or turn her around before he slid off his Calvin Kleins to free a springy mound of pubic hair that nearly hid his erect dick from view. He stood there, over me, over her, without any emotion but excitement. He was an animal.

I don't mean that in a complimentary, *he was an animal in bed, oh my, what a rogering he gave me*, type way; I mean it in a programmed, ceaseless way. He was obeying the oldest imperative by fucking me. Nothing, no pretence of emotional interest or his mother's happy face, was going to get in the way. He lay on top of me, bent his knees, tensed his bum, and attacked me as if that small dick of his was a clumsily wielded battering ram.

Maybe it lasted three minutes, and I certainly didn't have a good time in the orgasmic sense, but it wasn't about that. It was about renewing something in me, about not being the emotionally entangled, physically empty Lena Patten any longer. Instead I was unmarried Lena Mackie once more: a seventeen-year-old in an Essex town who discovers that her desires can blot out everything else, and so follows those desires every Friday and Saturday night with the help of cheap vodka and smiley-faced pills.

We should all obey our bodies and leave the future alone, I think. I wonder what people would do if they didn't have any thoughts to get in the way of their desires: hungry, thirsty, hot, cold and horny – these are the real laws we live by, aren't they? I wonder if Yvonne Fairly would still be alive if she'd dropped the baby off with a sitter and wandered off to town for a fuck instead? Maybe if she'd been capable of that I might have liked her more in the first place.

People say rules are made to be broken but they don't really mean it. I know, when I read this, years in the future, I'll say that I didn't mean it either. Maybe the words *melodramatic* and *fantasist* will be how I will characterize my younger self.

Just thinking about these things makes me feel sexual.

Pru will be angry with me. I don't believe she feels desire. I think she's worked hard to be that way, maybe because of something in her past. She's like me. She has secrets.

Something happened, something that changed her. I wonder what she was like before it happened, and before she married Steve in order to have a lifestyle she hates simply because it offers the opportunity for daily inertia. I wonder what she was like before she started collecting suicide notes so that she had something to do other than drink gin and eat slices of coffee-and-walnut cake.

I'm not sure I enjoy writing down this sort of thing. I'd better get back to him. He'll be awake soon, and ready to fuck, I would think. I hope so.

Twelve

The dining room was in the basement. At quarter to nine in the morning, with all the overhead striplights on, it was a cold, damp place. It would be the same even in the middle of summer – something about the eternal meadow-print wallpaper did nothing to brighten the windowless walls. The matching tablecloth on the white plastic table was sticky under my fingers.

I could hear Lena's voice through the archway that led to the kitchen. She was laughing. Then Phil's voice cut over her giggles. A moment later, while the sound still reverberated, she appeared, wearing yesterday's clothes, her hair unbrushed, her lips a naked pink without their usual slick of lipstick.

'Do you want the full breakfast? Phil! One full breakfast!'

Phil's head appeared around the archway. He grinned. 'Coming up in a sec, pigeon,' he said.

They were doing couple things. So there was no way we were going home today.

'Since we're staying here for a while longer, can we please

stop going gooey-eyed and get on with solving the mystery behind the note?'

'Don't you mean *finding the murderer*?'

She said it so casually. She'd obviously got used to the idea overnight. 'Well, I suppose since we're solving one, we might as well do both.'

'Phil says they might be related.'

'It's probably for the best if, just for the time being, you don't mention Phil around me.' I rearranged my cutlery. 'It's a silly little problem, but hearing his name makes me want to reach over this wobbly plastic table and spear your vocal cords with my bent fork. Call me tetchy.'

She snorted with contempt and cut her banana into wafer-thin slices on a meadow-print side plate. 'I think you need a drink.'

'You're so right. And you need a cigarette.'

'Nope. I've given up artificial highs. Discovered something much better. I don't think I'll need another cigarette for the rest of my life.'

'I sincerely hate you, and I want you to know that,' I said.

Phil chose that moment to erupt from the archway. He carried a jug of milk in one hand and had balanced a large plate on the other. After manoeuvring around the other tables with agility, he placed my breakfast in front of me with a flourish.

'Enjoy,' he said. Then he placed the coffee pot in front of Lena, gave her a wink, and sauntered away. I nearly vomited on my sausage.

Breakfast was passable, and we ate in silence. It was almost as if things were back to normal. When I'd finished mopping up the egg with the fried bread, and Lena was done with pushing her banana around her plate, I sat back and took a deep breath. My jeans felt tight and grimy around my stomach.

'Bet you want a ciggie now,' I said.

She gave me a half-smile, half-grimace. So much for the healing power of sex.

'So tell me about the long-term interest.'

Lena looked blank.

'Crystal's interest? In Allcombe?' I prompted. 'Tell me you've got some kind of lead to go on, or this is going to be the shortest murder investigation in history.'

'Right. Yes.' Her eyes fixed on the ceiling, she recited, 'Number six, Long Row. By the pier. Small cottage. White front door.'

'Meaning what?'

'Julie Smithson.' She huffed at my drawn-together eyebrows. 'I told you about her yesterday? Crystal's mother?'

'Oh.' It didn't ring a bell at all. 'I never thought she actually came from Allcombe.'

'Well, I'm supposing not everyone moves every eighteen months like us RAF wives.'

'Obviously not, Mr Spock. Right, come on.' I pushed back my chair.

'Not another knock-on-the-door-and-see-what-happens-next type deal!'

'Nope. This time I've got a plan.'

'Right.' She hesitated. 'Would you wait outside for me? I've got to make myself decent, change my clothes.'

'And say ta-ta to your bang-buddy?' Her smile confirmed

my guess. 'Okay. Okay, just as long as I don't have to hear about it.'

As I crossed the basement, it occurred to me that none of the other tables were laid. Obviously our Mr Tunnell was not a breakfast man. I wondered if he was still lying in bed.

I shook my head as I took my first steps into the brittle daylight of Allcombe. I had other things to worry about. I had to come up with a plan for getting information out of Crystal Tynee's mother, and I had to do it fast.

Thirteen

Case 476: Mrs Prudence Elspeth Green
Transcript of conversation recorded Friday,
*   10 December 2004, 9.10 a.m.*
Location: Allcombe promenade

GREEN: I'm just saying, don't you feel anything for David any longer? Aren't you thinking about him at all? I'd be thinking about Steve if I'd just shag— cheated on him.

PATTEN: No, I'm not thinking about him. He doesn't think about me when he gives it to Derek Fairly. As far as I'm concerned my marriage is over and I'm getting on with things.

GREEN: But why throw away a perfectly convenient marriage for the sake of—

PATTEN: It isn't convenient. I mean, it wasn't a marriage of convenience.

GREEN: You mean you loved him? You didn't know he was gay?

PATTEN: I love him.

GREEN: I can't believe you love him.

PATTEN: Why did you marry Steve? For the joys of RAF
        life? You couldn't get enough coffee-and-walnut
        sponge?

GREEN: Well, yes, at first I was in love. Now it just
        works. Steve gives me his money and we leave each
        other alone.

PATTEN: Yes, you do, don't you?

GREEN: What does that mean?

PATTEN: Six Long Row. This is it. Tell me what the plan
        is.

GREEN: Watch and learn, Watson. Watch and learn.

I composed myself to knock, and in that moment I heard a
sound, rather like a crunch, coming from the side of the small
cottage. The first crunch was followed by a second.

'Digging,' Lena said.

Gardening in December: interesting. I walked around the
side of the cottage, stepping over a collection of stone frogs
strumming guitars, and a wicker basket of seashells on the
path. It opened out to a small patch of brown grass with a
border of dirt. Beyond that, the view sloped away to the grey
of the sea and, finally, the white horizon.

There was a woman holding a spade at the far end of the
garden. The crooked line of her back showed her age. As she
scooped the soil from the pile beside her, tensing her muscles,
her breasts moved in her woollen jumper like bowling balls
in their carriers.

I stepped on to the grass and, as if sensitive to the bending of the stalks, the woman turned her head and stared at
me. I had the same feeling as in the Bosworth Slaughter the

72

previous night. It was as if that strange word 'grockle' was tattooed on my forehead.

'Got nothing to say, miss,' she said.

She turned back to the soil, moved the last of it to the border of the garden, and tamped it down with the back of the spade. Lena took a step forward and coughed.

The woman drove the spade into the dirt with a crunch and looked up.

'Mrs Smithson?' Lena said.

'At least you didn't call me Mrs Tynee. Some of the bloody thick ones call me that.' She looked at my filthy jeans and greasy hair, then at Lena's immaculate grey trousers and knee-length leather coat. 'You don't look the part. Although trespassing's about right.'

'We wanted to talk to you.'

'About Crystal,' I added.

Mrs Smithson leaned on the spade handle. 'Who do you think I am?'

I looked at her. She had bleached blonde hair that was grey at the crown. Her sheepskin coat had dirt on the elbows, and her corduroy trousers were baggy at the knees and thighs. I would have guessed that she had lost a lot of weight in a short amount of time. 'I think you're someone with a lot on their mind.'

'You're not as stupid as you look,' she muttered, but the insult didn't appear to come easily to her. She must have learned to talk big recently. I remembered going through a similar transformation myself once.

'You look bereaved,' Lena said, her voice soft, 'and we don't want to intrude on your loss . . .'

'Don't play your games with me.' Mrs Smithson walked towards us and I decided to seize the moment as best as I could.

'Do you think your daughter was depressed?'

'What do you think?' She passed within inches of me, and I caught the smell of sweat on the breeze.

'I mean, did she tell you she was depressed?'

Her hand was on the back door when she stopped. She didn't turn round. All her attention seemed to be fixed on her fingers, closed around the handle. 'Did she tell me? No. She never mentioned it. She never mentioned anything. We hadn't spoken in years.'

Lena stuttered something that was cut off by the slamming of the back door. I heard the key turn in the lock.

I started back down the side path, and listened to Lena stewing behind me. As we came to the front of the cottage, she asked the most obvious question.

'So if Crystal wasn't close to her mother, why was—'

'I don't know why Crystal was in Allcombe.'

'There's no need to be so abrupt!'

'Well, don't ask such obvious questions then. The woman is either lying, or there's some other reason why Crystal came here.'

'Like what?'

I increased my pace, walking in the direction of the Slaughter. 'Incapable of thinking for yourself? Has sex destroyed your brain?'

'I resent that,' she said, breathing hard as she made the effort to keep pace with me.

'Why are you asking me to explain everything? Do I look like Buddha?'

'Getting that way,' she said, 'if you carry on having the full English.'

We reached the corner. I stopped next to the steps that led down to the Slaughter. The fish-and-chip shop opposite was closed, but that was really the only major difference from the night before. There was still nobody in sight, and the sky was only minimally brighter. At least the wind had dropped, making the temperature bearable, but I had a feeling it wouldn't stay that way.

Lena flapped her hands and struggled to catch her breath. 'So – what now – oh enlightened – one?'

I pretended not to hear her. 'You know, I could really do with a drink.' I glanced down the stone steps to the squat wooden door of the Slaughter and wished it were open. It would be warm in there, at least.

'How about a coffee? There's a department store in town. Brand new. Phil told me about it. It's got an internet café.'

'So that's what you did last night? You talked about shopping opportunities in Allcombe?'

A knowing look spread across her face. 'That's not all we did.'

'Don't tell me,' I said as an automatic reaction. Lena's smile grew wider.

It was a stroke of luck that I looked past her smile to the seafront, otherwise I would have missed the sight of Julie Smithson striding along the promenade, her shoulders hunched, her scowl visible even from a distance.

'Look,' I whispered.

Lena grabbed my arm, squeezing it hard. 'Where's she going?'

'Hang on, I'll use my telepathic ability and find out,' I said, pulling myself free. Mrs Smithson didn't look up from her course. I watched her hurry away, sure she hadn't seen us.

'Okay, since you're desperate for me to make a decision, here's the plan,' I told Lena. 'I'll follow her. You go back to her house – see if you can get in, have a look round . . . play detective, Watson.'

'Hang on . . . why don't *you* do the breaking and entering?'

'Too late. You asked me to take charge. I'll meet you in the café in the department store. Don't be longer than half an hour, okay?'

I left Lena wrestling with her conscience on the corner and set off.

Fourteen

This was the second time I had tailed someone.

Once, about a year before I got married, I became suspicious about the amount of social functions Steve claimed he had to attend. He was always moaning about the amount of time he had to spend in uniform, eating five-course meals and raising his glass to Her Majesty. It seemed ridiculous to me then, as a university student, that a job could take up so much of anybody's life. So I followed him when he left my flat to return to the Mess one Friday night, through the back streets of Bristol and up the motorway to the RAF base. I parked up on the other side of the main fence, with a view into the entrance of the Mess, and waited.

He appeared in the doorway just as the sun was setting. He was in his Number Ones, his waistcoat buttons gleaming, a pint glass in his hand and a gang of mates surrounding him.

So he wasn't having an affair. But he wasn't having a horrible time without me either.

That was the moment I realized he was in love with his career, and he thought it was necessary to lie about his devotion to duty. How could a woman understand that there was something else, something vastly important other than love, in a man's life?

At the time, I found his inability to explain it endearing. I used to smile to myself as I commiserated with him about having to go to yet another party without me, or visit yet another foreign country. And when he asked me to marry him a few months later I immediately said yes, confident that I understood him better than he understood me. But knowing someone's faults does not mean being able to put up with them indefinitely.

Of course, on that occasion I'd had a car. On foot, it was much more difficult to play detective, particularly as the promenade was, as usual, deserted. If Mrs Smithson had as much as glanced over her shoulder she would have seen me. I was only fifty yards away and trailing her like a duckling.

It was sheer luck that she didn't turn round.

We passed the bandstand. The possibility that she was going to the Royal occurred to me. Perhaps she had something to say to Lena and me. But how would she know we were staying there?

There was only one answer: Phil. I didn't understand what he was trying to achieve, but all the information pointed to his involvement. I knew there was a reason why I had taken an instant dislike to him.

I stopped behind the nearest iron lamppost and breathed in as she drew level with the Royal, but she didn't even turn her head. She took twenty more steps and came to a halt at the next house.

She stood outside for a long time, staring at the front door with such apparent concentration that I forgot to hide. I watched her quickly clench and unclench her fists. Then she walked into the building.

I ambled up to where she had been standing, and pretended to admire the architecture. The house, the last and largest on the row, was in a bad condition. The gateposts were adorned with oxidized green concrete pineapples, and peeling palm trees grew on either side of the double doors. Hanging at a slight angle was a sign, written in a florid grey script that was not easy on the eye. After a fair amount of staring, it revealed the name of the hotel to be the Paradise.

The double doors were open, and the reception area seemed to follow the same layout as the Royal. I could see faded yellow wallpaper and a large oval desk, on which sat a brass bell, a blotter, and a pen in a black holder. The staircase curved upwards, as in the Royal, but this one had a stair-lift. The metal chair looked incongruously modern against the dark wood of the banisters.

Mrs Smithson wasn't in sight. I took a few steps into the reception area and listened. Her light voice, with that local twang, was coming from my left, through another set of open double doors. I craned my head, and caught a glimpse of a battered upright piano pushed against the wall, with a selection of random threadbare armchairs surrounding it.

Her voice got louder.

After a quick check that nobody was around, I got down on my hands and knees and crawled, careful to make no noise, to the lip of the doorway. I curled up to the right of it and stuck my head around, giving myself just enough vision to see that the armchairs continued, scattered in no discernible pattern, into the deep room. Halfway down, Mrs Smithson's head and legs were visible around the sides of an armchair. She was sitting at ninety degrees to my hiding place, facing a bald man who sat in the chair opposite her. He had full lips and long ears, and immediately reminded me of a child's toy – Mr Potato Head. I estimated that he was on the short side. Mrs Smithson was tilting her head downwards to meet his eyes.

'So this is the final instalment towards the costs incurred,' he was saying. He had no discernible accent. 'You can consider our arrangement terminated.'

'That's a relief,' Mrs Smithson said as she nodded her head.

'We didn't go for lavish, but then again, we thought you wouldn't want to be thought of as . . . cheap. It's only a shame you weren't well enough to see it for yourself.'

'The doctors thought it would be better if I . . .'

'Of course,' the man said. 'And I gave you a special deal, because of our connection. We're so glad to learn you're feeling better now, and that everything has been settled. It's inevitable that, with a six-month delay in payment, the interest did add up somewhat.'

'I didn't really think about interest . . .'

The man pressed his palms together. 'Understandable in the circumstances. Try not to give it any more thought.'

'And there was nothing left in the bank account?'

He shook his head. 'We don't regulate how our residents spend their own money. It's important for them to maintain a sense of freedom.'

'I'm sure she appreciated it,' Mrs Smithson said, rubbing

at her eye. 'The freedom. Being her own boss, right to the end.'

He cleared his throat. 'Right, well, I've put the receipt in this bag along with a couple of possessions that got missed. Mrs Charley, who moved into the room, found them under the dressing table.' He bent down over the far side of the chair – he was carrying quite a pair of love handles – and then stood up with a blue plastic bag in his hand. He presented it to Mrs Smithson.

She stood up and took it. It looked heavy. 'Well, thanks again,' she said.

I pulled my head back, jumped up, and made for the main doors. The change in temperature hit me as I walked through, past the palm trees and green pineapples. It had dropped to freezing on the promenade, and there was nowhere to hide.

I started towards the Royal, hoping to get into the reception and avoid being seen.

'Hello.'

I turned round. Mrs Smithson was standing on the pavement outside the Paradise, the carrier bag in her left hand. 'Not much of a spy, are you, miss?'

'Not the best,' I said. 'Sorry.'

'And you're definitely not a reporter.'

'No. Just an interested party.'

'Fair enough.' She walked up to me and tilted her head along the promenade. 'Are you going this way?'

I shrugged, and we fell into a slow, steady pace past the Royal. I stole glances at Mrs Smithson whenever I could without being too obvious. Her attention was fixed on her feet. She looked exhausted. There was a looseness to her features, as if she lacked the energy to hold them up any more.

I searched for something to say that might lead to answers without being too invasive. 'I'm glad you're feeling better now, Mrs Smithson.'

'I was just under the weather,' she said. 'That's all. The doctors thought it best I didn't do anything too demanding for a little while.'

'Like go to a funeral?' I ventured.

If she realized that I'd been listening to her conversation in the Paradise she didn't show it. 'I would have liked to go.'

'Of course,' I said, aware of how similar I sounded to Mr Potato Head. It seemed there was a tone of voice one used with the bereaved.

She shifted her carrier bag from her left hand to her right. I could see the handles stretching. 'I didn't see her often as it was. It was an effort to find the time.'

I tried to keep my voice soft as I leaped on her mistake. 'But you said you didn't talk to her at all.'

She scowled at me. 'When?'

'Ten minutes ago. In your back garden.'

'But that was Crystal. I was talking about my Crystal then.' Her pace increased, and I matched it. We were already passing the bandstand; time was running out. 'I hadn't talked to Crystal for years. Not since she came out of prison. I told you that. She used to come down to visit her gran once a month, and she always stayed in one of the hotels, never with me.'

'So it wasn't Crystal you were talking about in the Paradise?'

'Why would Crystal be staying in a retirement home?'

It clicked. Crystal had been visiting her grandmother, Mrs Smithson's mother, in the Paradise. That was the reason for her presence in Allcombe. And the grandmother and granddaughter had both died recently.

We were at the corner, between the Slaughter and the chip shop. 'Right, I'm going off this way,' Mrs Smithson said, pointing to her cottage.

'Could I ask one more question?'

She hesitated, and looked around her. 'I have to get going.' She swapped the carrier bag from her right hand to her left, and the handles gave way. The contents spilt on to the ground before my feet.

I kneeled and gathered them up, stacking them in a pile. There was a crocheted red scarf (home-made, I guessed from the dropped stitches); a cheap photo-frame containing a black and white photo of Crystal clipped from a newspaper; a bottle of cheap perfume three-quarters empty; and a hardback book.

I turned the book in my hands as I placed it on top of the pile. The title was *Words for the Faithful*.

'Thank you,' Mrs Smithson said. I handed back the possessions. The skin on her fingertips was cold and papery.

'Who died first?' I asked her, my instinct telling me this was my last chance. 'Was it your daughter? How close together were the deaths?'

She looked over her shoulder again, back along the promenade. 'A week apart, it was. Mum, then Crystal. Now Henry. I can't talk about this.'

She walked away before I could think of a way to stop

her, and she didn't move slowly. Hunched over, head bent, she looked like she was trying to escape. From me, perhaps. Maybe someone else.

'Who's Henry?' I called after her. She didn't turn round.

Fifteen

The café was on the first floor of the shiny department store, halfway along the high street. I had to walk past three make-up assistants with blue eyes and orange faces before I reached the escalator. There was a group of children riding up it, running down the adjacent stairs and riding it all over again. It was obviously the high point of excitement in Allcombe.

I took the stairs, opting to dodge the kids rather than squeezing on to the escalator beside them. The café came into view. It was directly ahead of me, past the nightwear section, and I could see Lena sitting at one of the chrome tables arranged around a freestanding counter, which housed a puzzled-looking teenage lad with lank blond hair. He was repeatedly hitting the side of a large silver coffee machine.

Lena was watching for me. She frowned and moved her eyes slowly to her left, tilting her head. I followed the movement.

Mr Tunnell was sitting at the furthest table. He was facing slightly away from me; I could see his profile, and his right hand holding up the newspaper he was reading. His attention seemed wholly focused upon it.

I raised my eyebrows to Lena and walked to the counter.

'An espresso, please.'

'Coffee's off,' the boy said.

Any kind of liquid refreshment other than water was being denied to me, and it was not conducive to a pleasant mood. 'Can you enlighten me as to why Allcombe is full of surly teenage boys and mad old women?'

'Cos everyone else is able to bugger off,' he said. 'Tea or sparkling water?'

'Tea.'

'Cinnamon Danish?'

I nodded and paid the money. The tea looked anaemic but the crockery was clean. White with a gold rim. It reminded me of my own, chosen and added to the wedding list nine years ago. I'd broken one teacup and put it away in the cabinet, where it had been since. The design no longer appealed to me.

'How did it go?' Lena said as I sat down next to her. She looked like a two-dimensional representation of a suspicious person, hunched over her tea and stage-whispering. I was sure Mr Tunnell could hear us, so I spoke for his benefit first.

'Dodgy skirting board,' I said, staring straight at him. He didn't look up, but something about the angle of his head suggested he was listening.

'What?' Lena said.

I leaned closer. 'Her mother died.'

'Mrs Smithson died?'

'Mrs Smithson's mother died,' I clarified. 'A week before Crystal did.'

'Died of what?'

I shrugged. 'Nobody's treating it as suspicious.'

'That doesn't mean much around here,' Lena said, tapping her fingernails on the lip of her cup.

'She was old.'

'Meaning what? She's not important?' Her voice got louder. Mr Tunnell rustled his paper.

'Don't be so thick. I'm just saying she might have died from natural causes, that's all.' I took a mouthful of my tea. It tasted of tap water. 'Did you find anything?'

She muttered something.

'What?'

'I couldn't get in, okay? I looked for a spare key but there wasn't one, and I looked for an open window but they were all shut. So I had a good look through the windows and around the garden, but didn't see a lot.'

She gave me a shrug. Maybe she was beginning to realize how little natural talent she had for the detective game.

'Mrs Smithson mentioned a third death,' I said. 'Her mother, Crystal, and someone called Henry. I think the key to this whole thing might be Henry. We should concentrate on that.'

'You think so, do you?' She smiled into her cup.

'All right, what is it?'

'I already know who Henry is.' She paused.

'Spill.'

'He died very recently. She buried him in her garden.'

I stared at her. After an embarrassing amount of time, I realized what she meant. 'Henry was a pet?'

'A ginger tabby cat. That was the hole she was filling in when we saw her. She finished it off with a photo of him, a little wooden cross and his collar. It's quite sad, really.'

'Sounds vomitous.'

Lena tutted. 'That woman has been through a lot.'

'Yeah. I can just picture her, kneeling in the dirt, saying a little prayer over his stiff ginger corpse.'

A prayer. The word triggered something in my mind.

'Do you want another cup of tea?' Lena asked me.

'Shush!' I thought hard.

'I'll get us both one,' Lena said. She slid back her chair and walked to the counter. I watched her order. And then I placed it. The book – *Words for the Faithful* – it had cropped up in two places. I'd gone through my whole life up to yesterday and not seen it once. I didn't believe in coincidence.

That meant Tunnell was involved.

I got up, crossed the lino, and sat down opposite him. 'Hello,' I said.

He folded his newspaper and put it down beside his empty glass. 'Hello. Been out fixing wardrobes?'

'Of course! That's my job.'

He gave me that look; the look he had given me last night that said he didn't believe me but was prepared to indulge me.

'I'm Pru. Pleased to meet you.'

He shook my hand. 'Mike.' He had a strong grip.

'Having fun in Allcombe?' I asked.

He let go of my hand and spread both of his own, palms up. 'What's not to like about it?'

'Perhaps it would be easier if you made a list of what's to like . . .' I ventured a smile, '. . . otherwise we'll be here all day.'

'Would that be so bad?'

'I . . .' I couldn't flirt back. I couldn't remember what flirting was. 'I don't know.'

'Oh.' He sat back, his mouth straight. 'Okay.'

I looked over at Lena. She was watching us, her attention fixed, her lips drawn together into a pinch. I wrinkled my nose at her. 'So what are you doing in Allcombe?' I tried to soften the question. 'If it's not too personal to ask?'

'Taking the air.'

'I suppose a place like this could yield results for one's health, if one believed in such things.' I swallowed. 'If one believed faithfully.'

He didn't blink. 'Well, this has been a pleasant meeting, but I'm sure you have wood to be working on.'

'Have dinner with me tonight.'

He pursed his lips. Then he said, 'Eight o'clock?'

'I'll meet you in the lobby of the Royal,' I said. He nodded, pushed back his chair, and disappeared down the stairs with a display of manly striding.

Lena slid into his seat. 'Taken a bit of a fancy to him, have you?' she said, crossing her arms and legs.

'That's rich, coming from you. And no, I haven't just chatted a bloke up for my own benefit. I think he's involved.'

'Our Mr Tunnell?'

'He agreed to go on a date with me far too easily. He must

have an ulterior motive. I thought you said this was an internet café? I need to do a search.'

Lena nodded her head at the counter, and I looked past to the one computer against the far wall, where the screensaver was flashing never-ending multicoloured triangles at me. It wasn't a modern piece of technology, and I could hear the hard drive chugging as I booked fifteen minutes with the teenage lad and conjured up Google.

'Damn.' The details I wanted wouldn't come to mind. I pinned my hopes on Lena, who stood behind me, leaning on my shoulders. 'The book on the bedside drawer in Mr Tunnell's room – *Words for the Faithful*. Can you remember the author?'

'I can't even remember the book. Are you going to explain any of this?'

'Ssh.' I tapped in 'book', 'words' and 'faithful'. 516,000 results. With the kind of hope born from not really understanding the internet, I scanned the first ten results. All of them were for American religious sites and two dealt specifically with Armageddon. I had no clue how to get the information I wanted.

I turned to Lena. 'Can you do me a favour for tonight? Can you do me up?'

'Can I what?'

'You know: hair, make-up. I'll need to get something new to wear.'

'You're going out with Mr Tunnell.' She glared down at me.

'There's a good reason, I promise.' I switched over to Yahoo and logged into my email account, on the off-chance that someone cared enough to contact me. 'I need to get into his room, to get a look at that book again.'

'I see. All for the sake of the investigation.'

'You don't get to have an attitude about this,' I told her. There was no way I was going to admit that excitement was creeping up my spine and turning my mind to mush. I wanted to be the glamorous spy. I wanted to think there was the possibility of illicit, motive-driven sex. Sex – something that had become late-night programmes on Channel 4 and daydreams encased in cheap novels – could be tied to other things again. It could be the bedfellow of mystery, romance, a tall dark stranger.

If sex could happen to Lena, it could happen to me.

My inbox flashed at me. I clicked the mouse button.

'Flipping heck,' I said.

Sixteen

To: greenprudence@yahoo.co.uk
From: SGreen548@bas.mod.uk
Subject: I Still Love You

Darling Moo

I know I haven't spoken to you for a while. I've got no excuse, but I hope you'll understand that it's this place, this hellhole, that makes me keep my distance. I would hate to make you feel even the smallest part of the depression I feel: the constant attacks, the flying into danger at night and the unbearable heat of the day . . . I can't imagine that there is a place away from here, and that you are in that place, waiting for me.

I picture you, my darling, in our house, in our bed, and I hope that you picture me there with you. Try to remember the way it once was. I love you. And I'm going to keep sending these mails in the hope that you still love me too.

Meeve

Seventeen

Mike Tunnell, like my husband, had good timing.

He walked down the stairs with the grace of a dancer, and made the lobby at eight o'clock precisely, wearing a sharp suit and a raised eyebrow.

The plan was to get into his room, and with that end in mind I'd made the kind of superhuman effort women usually reserve for wedding days. Lena had attacked my eyebrows with her tweezers and my legs with her razor, and I'd squeezed myself into a dress made with a younger, thinner woman in mind. High heels gave my calves a gentle curve and brought me up to Mike's shoulder as we walked up the promenade, past the pub and the fish-and-chip shop, to Allcombe's high street. Halfway along, buried between a gift shop and a chemist, was a pizza restaurant. It had the decor of a Kentucky Fried Chicken outlet, but at least it was empty, and the inevitable male teenage waiter was keen to leave us alone.

I ordered a four-cheese pizza with garlic bread. Mike ordered the same, and asked for a jug of water. It seemed alcohol was not on the cards tonight.

'I have a confession to make,' I said in a low voice.

'What's that?'

'I'm not a carpenter.'

Mike ran his thumb and forefinger over his moustache. That was the third time since leaving the hotel. I wondered if it was a nervous habit or if he did it when he was feeling sure of himself. 'I know. Phil told me you're staying in the hotel. He said you were in my room because you wanted to see the spot where some child star hung herself?'

The pause told me that he knew exactly who had died there. I filed that piece of deduction away and changed the subject. 'Don't mention Phil to me. He's a Devon wide-boy who thinks his smile makes up for his personality.'

Mike raised an eyebrow. 'I don't think that's an opinion your friend shares.'

'News does travel fast.'

'Let's say Phil likes to brag.'

It didn't surprise me. I crossed my legs and made sure my hair hadn't escaped from the pins Lena had forced into my scalp. 'Lena's not firing on all cylinders at the moment. She can't see that the last thing she needs right now is a boyfriend.'

'How about you?'

'What?'

'Do you need a boyfriend?'

'I – I've got a husband,' I stuttered.

'That doesn't mean there isn't a boyfriend, or at least the desire for one.' He was smiling, his eyes on my fingers as I tapped them first against the wine glass and then on my bare collarbone. Then his gaze moved down to my breasts.

I finally understood why women dress up and wear make-up. It's putting on a disguise. More than that – it's becoming someone else. Sitting at that table, feeling Mike's eyes on me, I could have been anybody other than Pru Green: Pru, approaching thirty-four with an attitude problem and an obsession with suicides. And that meant anything I did tonight would not be quite real. Make-up and tight clothes were the next best things to alcohol.

I leaned over the table. 'Was that an offer?'

Mike shifted in his seat and fiddled with his paper napkin. The pizzas arrived, ready-sliced and saturated in orange grease. He didn't speak until the waiter had walked away. 'Are you looking for an offer?' he said.

'Are you?'

'I asked you first.'

This wasn't working. Maybe he was shy and needed more conversation. I tried a different tack.

'So you wanted to talk about the benefits of Allcombe – for the faithful.'

'That depends on whether you're the faithful type,' he shot back.

'Haven't we already discussed that?'

'I don't recall you giving me an answer,' he said, his face reddening.

'Do you want me to do all the flipping work here?' This was like having a conversation with Steve. 'Can't you be funny, or charming, or any of the other things single men are meant to be to married women they want to have meaning-less sex with?'

'So you do want to have meaningless—'

I threw him a warning look. 'You want it all on a plate, don't you?'

'The first time I saw you . . .' he said, very slowly, not looking at me, '. . . I thought there was a connection. Between us.'

It was a horrible cliché, but it was all I was going to get in the way of romance this evening. I pictured myself as Lauren Bacall in *To Have and Have Not*. 'Did ya, handsome?'

'Garlic bread,' the waiter said. He put the plate on the table, rolled his eyes, and wandered off.

'You saw me standing in your wardrobe . . .' I persevered, determined to get into his room if not his underwear, '. . . and thought what? Exactly?'

'That you were beautiful and . . . that you had a lot of personality and . . .'

It was too painful to listen to any more. I put up one hand. 'You don't actually want to have meaningless sex with me, do you?'

'Ummm . . .'

'And you're not going to make a grab for me later and kiss me into submission, are you?'

'Maybe . . .'

'Shall we eat the pizza and go?'

His chest slumped and his fingers smoothed his moustache. 'Yes please.'

After that, it was a pleasant night. The pizza was hot, if not tasty, and the garlic bread didn't make my breath smell, even if it didn't actually taste of garlic. We talked about neutral topics – God, death, politics – and Mike turned out to be good company.

As we walked up the stairs to the first-floor landing, I decided to make one more play for information about the book.

'Thanks for a lovely evening,' I said. 'Got anything good to read I could borrow? Something of a religious bent, maybe?'

He cocked his head towards me. 'That might be the most unexpected choice of reading matter I've ever encountered.'

'Well, it just occurred to me that I've got a long night ahead without anything else to do, since you're not interested.'

'I never said I wasn't—'

'Look, I haven't got the patience for all that again,' I told him. 'Let's not go round in circles. Do you want to talk to me about books or not?'

We reached the door to my room. The narrow corridor forced us together, and he shifted his feet as if impatient to be gone. 'I'm not really a reader,' he said.

I stared at him until he met my eyes. I couldn't see whether he was telling the truth or not. Only one thing came across loud and clear, in the way he held his head and kept his jaw clenched: he didn't want to be this close to me. Either he had just realized that I wasn't only ugly on the outside, or else he had never wanted to take me out in the first place. I couldn't understand it. But I didn't want to think about it any more, and I didn't want to see discomfort in his handsome face for a moment longer.

'Right, well, bye then,' I said.

He didn't hesitate. 'Yes, goodnight, and thank you for a lovely evening.'

As he turned and took the stairs to the next landing two at a time, I realized a part of me was relieved. I wasn't sure that I was quite ready to cheat on my husband.

· And there was Steve's email to think about. He had talked of love. He had used pet names that hadn't been dusted off for fifteen years.

He had gone mad in the desert.

There was only one thing for it. I would have to check my email account again the next day. Steve had said he would write every day. If there was nothing in my inbox tomorrow then today's email had been a moment of weirdness on his part that could be forgiven. That would be easier on both of us.

Then I could concentrate on unravelling the murder or assisted suicide, and ending Lena's relationship with Phil, and finding out why there were two copies of that book floating around in one small seaside town.

I knocked on the bedroom door.

It opened a crack. Phil's eye stared out at me. I caught a glimpse of his naked pigeon chest. 'What is it?' he said.

'What do you mean, what is it? This is my room.'

'Lena's asleep. She's very tired.'

'I'm sure she is. So am I.'

'Just . . . take a key from under the reception desk and find somewhere else to sleep tonight, all right?'

'Let me talk to her,' I said, standing my ground.

'Look . . .' He rubbed the one eye I could see. 'You can

talk to her tomorrow about your stupid little plot to get Mike to let you look at his book.'

'Since when do you get a say in what we do?' I leaned on the door and he pushed back.

'Since you're the worst detective ever. Chasing a fucking book.'

'What do you know about it?'

'Lena's got some news for you. She'll tell you tomorrow.'

The door closed.

I gave it the V-sign and stared at it for a while. It didn't reopen.

Eighteen

Yvonne Fairly couldn't live without her husband. Does that mean she was really truly in love with him?

I've never felt anything like that. For me it's about what men can do for me. Yes, I love David, but that doesn't mean I'll die without him. It just means that I'll be sad for a while and do a few stupid things. Love has always made me do stupid things. I thought I'd buried that side of my personality when I got married, but it turns out I'm as prone to ridiculousness as ever.

Am I repeating myself? Making the same mistakes? Blaring out the same things in the hope that, at some point, somebody will tune into my radio station and sing along? Which reminds me of the ridiculous radio broadcasts you get during RAF tattoos and display weekends. Attendance is practically compulsory if you want your husband to have a shot at promotion (one must have the right sort of wife, don't you know – a joiner and a taker-parter) and they always have their own radio stations set up specially for the occasion, playing songs that cannot be construed as anything but light entertainment. It's as if the RAF would go to any length to persuade people that they're a perfectly jolly organization with no connection to that horrible business of war. The planes are crowd-pleasers only, joy rides for the kiddies and spotters; and the uniforms are just so they all look jolly nice: no loss of identity here.

It's possible for a person to be one of those radio broad-casts. You can transmit *Take That and Party* every minute of every day of your life, and you'll be guaranteed listeners because plenty of people want to pretend that they only have a happy side, that all songs are written in celebration and all planes are used for going on holiday.

But my radio station plays Leonard Cohen. It plays Nick Drake and Radiohead. Maybe that's why nobody wants to tune in to me – at least, not for longer than five minutes on a wet Sunday morning. I just want to talk about these things: what's so wrong with that?

Pru wouldn't have a radio station. She never listens to music. Not in all the time that I've known her has she once put on a CD. I don't even know if she owns a stereo.

Early on in our relationship, when we had just discovered the other existed and were enamoured of one another's iso-lationism, we agreed to go out with the other wives in a kind of 'girls' night out' attempt at socializing. Swindon after office hours is not a welcoming place. We went to a cocktail bar in the Old Town, acting on the rumour that it was the closest thing to sophistication among the tower blocks and concrete roundabouts, and we stood in a close huddle, eight of us, being elbowed by the pushy throng of pierced and adorned teenagers, all lathered in fake tan and mid-range perfume.

The music was deafening, a thick heavy beat that made my stomach shudder, and the songs were always the same, running into each other, the only differences a squeal here, a groan there. There was no attempt at conversation. We stared at youth, and realized how far we had come from it with our houses and husbands, pets and kids, leather sofas and walnut veneer dining tables. These things remove you from your enjoyment of life, don't you think? They make you believe that you have to invest in living, rather than treat it as the best freebie you'll ever get.

Anyway, seven rounds of gin later, and the sweaty teenagers surrounding us had reached a stage of abandonment. They dropped the act of coolness and looked for some enthusiasm, finding it in the DJ who obligingly led the charge with a change of beat. I recognized the song immediately. 'The Grease Megamix', beyond loud, and wonderfully camp. Everybody postured in time to the opening bars of 'Greased Lightning', and every word was known by the room. Who was it who said that we're born knowing the lyrics to all the Beatles' tunes? Maybe it applies to show tunes too. Even the hard-cases with shaved heads and tattoos of snakes wrapped around their necks sang along. The prearranged groups of our arrival were forgotten. We smiled. As a team, we smiled.

Pru stood in the middle of that team and rolled her eyes.

I so wanted her to be one of us. 'It's *Grease*,' I said. I

stepped close to her ear. '"Grease Megamix".' Or something like that.

'What?' she shouted.

'Olivia Newton John,' I shouted. I loved Olivia Newton John when I was younger. I even bought her horrible post-*Grease* albums, such was my devotion. Like many women of my age, I wanted to be her; well, her post-transformation, with clothes so tight you have to be sewn into them and a cigarette expertly balanced on a glossy red pout. She's the reason I started smoking; her, and because I heard it kept you thin. Being thin has always been important to me. Put it down to my previous line of work – an extra pound would have been seen, believe me, and probably poked by a paying customer with meat on his mind.

Just to keep you up to date, Diary, from the age of sixteen to nineteen, I was a human plate. I lay naked on a diamond-encrusted tabletop in a private club in Kyoto, and had a selection of delicatessen products placed on my body for rich businessmen and celebrities to spear with their forks. During the wildest nights, when champagne flowed freely from the silver fountain surrounded by red velvet cushions, I could have oysters on my breasts, blowfish on my stomach, and shark meat between my thighs. It turned out to be a good way to get rich, but no way to get happy.

Anyway, to return to the point: what difference does it make that Prudence Green didn't join in with the 'Grease Megamix'?

Pru's a closed book. Or should I say she's like that terrible unauthorized biography of Crystal Tynee. She looks like an overweight, unhappy housewife, a girl waiting to be loved;

and all the time she's something else, something more. Pru's not hoping that some day she'll join in with the 'Grease Megamix'. She doesn't even know how to sing it.

But she wasn't always like this. I've seen photographs of her at university, and I know that when she first met Steve, she was trying – really trying – to get over whatever awful thing it was that happened to her. And when I first met her, she wasn't as bad as she is now. She laughed occasionally. I remember, for one of the coffee mornings, perhaps our second or third meeting, she baked flapjacks. They weren't bad.

I think sadness is a road that you commit to, a road that never goes anywhere. It stretches onwards into the night, and if you decided to turn round you would see dawn on the horizon behind you, but you don't dare look over your shoulder for fear of seeing something in your past, something that you imagine pursues you. Maybe it does, maybe it doesn't – but Pru will never know. Because she never turns round.

All it would take is a decision. Why won't she turn round? And why, for the first time in my life, do I care about mysteries like this? All I know is that I want to get to the bottom of one thing. Is there a reason for Crystal's death? For Pru's problems? For my loneliness?

I'm going to try to solve a mystery. Any mystery. Maybe if I do, I'll learn something about myself in the process.

Nineteen

'At least it's not going to melt,' I said as I glared at my vanilla ice-cream. My hand was white around the cone, and my bottom had gone numb on the hard iron bench. The chocolate flake poking out of the yellow confection didn't move a millimetre when I tugged it. 'What kind of an ice-cream salesman goes out in the middle of winter?'

'An insane one,' Lena said. I swivelled on the bench and looked over my shoulder at the van. The teenager standing at the window was wearing a white t-shirt and a tiny conical hat that appeared to be made of cardboard. He gave me a wave.

I waved back. 'He looks like your type,' I said to Lena. 'You've known him for less than thirty seconds, he seems convinced he's a catch, and he's not old enough to buy his own half of cider. Oh, and he's probably gay as well.'

'I don't understand why you feel you have to be so mean to me.'

'Defence mechanism,' I muttered, dumping my ice-cream

in the bin next to the bench and sticking my hands in the pockets of my coat. 'Had it since I was seventeen.'

'Yeah, well, I've had my breasts since I was eleven, but I don't keep thrusting them in everyone's face.'

'No. Just Phil's.'

Lena leaned over me and dumped her own untouched ice-cream. 'You really turn my stomach sometimes.'

I looked out over the sea. The shapes of the scudding clouds were reflected on the surface of the water. The dark patches they created looked like great shoals of fish. My breakfast sat in my stomach, and the sense of possibility I always felt on a Saturday morning, a leftover from early childhood, I suppose, had kicked in.

Today was a day to get things done.

'Look,' Lena was saying, 'while you were out with Mr Tunnell last night, I asked Phil if maybe he could get me back into the room for the book.' She rubbed her lips together, her eyes on me.

'So you didn't think I could get in his room, then?'

Her reply was as delicate as a snowflake. 'I thought . . . if you did get in the room, the book wouldn't be your first priority.'

I felt a rush of heat from my stomach to my cheeks. I swallowed it back down with a slice of cold air. I didn't want to hate Lena.

'And?' I said.

'Phil told me all three books were in his possession now anyway. Mr Tunnell had passed them on to him on his first night in the hotel.'

'You're sure Phil's talking about the right books?'

She nodded and reached into her bag. 'He gave me the Smythe one.' She pulled it out and handed it to me. *Words for the Faithful.* I ran my thumb along the thick cream pages.

'Did he say why?'

'Apparently it never belonged to Mr Tunnell.' A lone car crawled along the promenade. It was an unusual enough event to make us both turn and watch its progress. The green Vauxhall was piled up with teenage boys, and Jimi Hendrix blared out of the open windows and sunroof. It turned the corner at a crawl. I ignored the hopeful wave of the ice-cream seller and returned to the problem at hand. 'It had been left there by a previous guest, and never tidied up,' said Lena. 'Phil says the book is a red herring. He says it doesn't mean anything.'

'Phil says, Phil says . . .'

'Okay, so tell me what you're thinking.'

'I'm thinking . . .' I couldn't keep quiet any longer. 'I think Phil's lying. I think he can't be trusted. I think . . . he might be sleeping with you to throw us off the scent.'

She stared at me.

'I'm just throwing out ideas here,' I said.

She looked away from me and shook her head.

'I might be wrong,' I said.

'Well, I think Mr Tunnell is more suspicious than Phil,' Lena retorted.

I pursed my lips. 'You said yourself the book didn't belong to him.'

'So he can't have lied to Phil about that? Only Phil can be the liar?'

'I don't think Mike Tunnell has got anything to do with this,' I said, hoping I sounded authoritative.

'What you mean is, he wants nothing to do with you.'

I slammed *Words for the Faithful* shut. 'Nice, Lena. So Phil's teaching you how to screw other people as well as get screwed.'

She leaned towards me, and gave me the kind of glare usually reserved for naughty children. 'Oh, shut up, Pru. Go for a walk. Go somewhere else. Just go away.'

'Go where?'

'Get lost, before I lose my temper.'

She'd never talked to me like that before – as if I was smaller than her; a responsibility that she wanted to shrug off.

'Up yours,' I said. I got up and walked away.

Twenty

After four rings on the doorbell, Mrs Smithson opened the door. Her face registered the kind of surprise I was feeling at finding myself there.

'Can I come in?' I said.

'I don't want to talk to you,' she said. She glanced over my shoulder into the street, and then opened the door wide enough to let me into the hall.

The smell of cooked fish was pervasive. I took a step back so she could close the door and felt a jab into my lower back; I turned and steadied a small plate that was suspended from the wall on a white plastic rack. Painted on it was a robin, nestled in a heart-shaped holly bush. It was one plate of maybe twenty, all of them decorated with garden birds, surrounded by green, one round, black eye and a sharp beak central to each design.

'They come with a certificate. I've got one more to get,' she said, pointing to the one remaining empty spot on the wall, level with my eyes, 'and then I've got to start paying for them.'

'Nice,' I said. 'I don't want to talk about your daughter or anything like that. I was just passing and . . . I heard that your cat died. I'm sorry.'

She nodded. 'Thank you.'

There was a silence. For fear of being ejected I said what was really on my mind. 'Actually, just since I'm here, I wonder if I could ask you if you were the one who sold your daughter's suicide note on the internet.'

She squinted at me. 'What would make you think a thing like that?'

'Because I'm the one who bought it.'

'Right,' she said. 'Right. I don't want it back.'

'I wasn't offering.'

A spasm of pain crossed her face. A moment later, her expression was neutral. I had to admire her control. 'Fancy a cup of tea, then, miss?'

I followed her into the kitchen. The smell of fish intensified. A small sink was piled high with blue bowls and plates in a haphazard fashion, and topped by a frying pan with a greasy black handle and an oily sheen of water floating inside it.

'I'm getting round to that,' she said, and moved the frying pan on to the counter next to the sink so she could fit the kettle under the tap.

Above the sink was a sash window with a view over her back garden. It had been turned into a hazy pointillist picture by the net curtain strung across the lower half, held in place by a dirty white cord secured by two tacks.

I could see the black cross at the bottom of the garden, but it was too far for me to be able to make out any of the details Lena had described. Next to it, a knobbly, moss-covered tree pushed its longest branches out across the length of the window. Beyond that, the sea was calm and grey.

'Lovely view,' I said.

'I haven't got any biscuits,' she said.

'That's okay.' It was okay. I wasn't there for biscuits. I was there because of a deep urge that I didn't want to examine. I had a feeling selfishness came into it somewhere, and loneliness. I watched her stretch to retrieve two mismatched cups from an overhead cupboard. She dropped a teabag from a jar next to the kettle, which was beginning to make a soft sighing noise.

'So, what do you want? You want to have a look at the bereaved woman, desperate enough to sell on such a thing, do you?'

'No. No. I just . . . I don't know. Wanted to let you know that I have it. I take good care of it.'

She didn't reply.

'Thought it would be kind to let you know,' I added. 'People should be kind to each other. If they can be. Help each other out.'

'You've had a bit of a disagreement with your friend, then, have you?' she said, darting her eyes to mine as she poured two splashes of milk.

'Is it that obvious?'

'She's not here, is she?' Mrs Smithson clicked off the kettle and sloshed water into the cups and on the counter. She worried her lip with her teeth. 'And you've got that look.'

'Oh yes?' I said, accepting the cup. Apparently I didn't get the option of sugar.

'Crystal used to get that look when she had an argument at school. She was always a difficult one, didn't take kindly to people who fell out with her.' She took a sip from her own cup and mumbled, 'Probably why she never got on with me very well.'

'I'm like that,' I said. 'I can be like that. Difficult.'

'Oh yes, she was difficult. And selfish. And tight-lipped. You had to force things out of her.'

'I don't talk to people. Haven't done for years.'

'Why? What happened?'

'Nothing,' I said. I drained the cup and rinsed it under the tap, my gaze on the view. The black cross was a cross-hair in the centre of my vision. 'How old was your cat?'

'Henry. He was four.'

I tutted. 'That's not old.'

She shrugged, and turned to stare at me, her eyes searching mine. Then she nodded, as if making a decision.

'I hope he put up a fight. Gave 'em a few scratches. He used to hate having his collar on. There's no way they would have got that rope around his neck easily.'

It took a moment to understand what she was telling me. I felt a wash of revulsion at the thought. 'Where did you find him?' I asked.

She came up behind me and touched my left shoulder. I resisted the instinct to slap her hand away.

Her index finger pointed at the tree. 'There,' she whispered.

It was so close to the house. 'And you didn't hear anything?'

Mrs Smithson drew back her hand and stepped away

from me. I turned and saw her shrug. She was slightly bent over from the waist, rather like a hedgehog on the point of curling itself into a protective ball.

'When did it happen?'

'Sunday. Sunday night. Late.' One of her hands gripped the other. I could see white marks on her knuckles where the nails dug in. 'I heard it. I was in bed. I couldn't go downstairs. Even when I heard Henry choking. He was just choking and choking, and I was going to do something. Call the police, go out there. But then I heard them laugh. They were laughing. I think they wanted me to try to save him so that they could . . .'

'So they could what?'

Mrs Smithson's eyes cleared. She gave me a weak smile. 'What's your name?'

'Prudence. Pru.'

'I've lived in this town all my life, Pru. Everybody knows me, and I know better than to answer the questions you keep trying to ask me. Now, you take my advice and forget about the note. It's none of your business anyhow. Come along now, out, I've got washing up to do.' She made a shooing gesture with her hands, flapping them at the wrists.

'You're scared,' I said as I backed into the hall, 'and that's understandable, I mean, something is going on, and it's not pleasant, and your cat died, and I think you sold that note because you needed the money badly, and maybe your cat died as a threat to pay up . . . but I really want to help you . . . and I think you want me to help you . . .'

'Reading that, are you?' she interrupted.

I was still holding *Words for the Faithful.*

'One of Mum's most precious books, that.'

'I know,' I said. 'I saw it in the bag. The one that man gave you in the Paradise.'

'It's a good read.'

She pushed past me and opened the front door.

'Is that an obscure attempt to point me in the right direction?'

She gave me a patient stare. 'Pru. You're probably a lovely lady, but it seems to me you know bugger all about real life.'

'That's not true!' I said as she ushered me out of her house and shut the door on me.

Mrs Smithson didn't know me. I consoled myself with that thought, but still, her comment hurt. I wondered what she would have made of Lena. If she thought I was naive, she'd find Lena was a Disney Princess.

I opened the book at random and read from the top of the left page. The print was small and hard on the eyes.

A Prayer for Equality

It should be remembered that all living things are worthy of respect, from the beetle to the bank manager. God is to be praised for all creation, not just those elements of his invention that please humanity. We love the robin, but do we love the tic that burrows amongst its feathers? How, then, can we imagine that we are able to make decisions wisely and fairly for the Earth and all that lives upon it?

In the same line of reasoning, we love the strong young man who embodies our spirit of adventure, but do we love the woman who has given up her desire for achievement so that her children may live and grow in her care? Until we do, we are not fair judges of our society, and so our society cannot be judged to be fair.

It all seemed a bit Buddhist for the 1900s. The sacred quality of motherhood was a concept that had always annoyed me. I wondered if, in the author's eyes, my childlessness would have been a factor in judging me worthy of respect.

I closed the book and looked up.

Across the road, leaning against a battered green Vauxhall, were three teenage lads. They stared at me.

I heard a rattling behind me. It took me a moment to place the noise. Mrs Smithson had just put the safety chain on her door. That noise was followed by another – the scrape of the key turning in the lock.

The teenagers couldn't have heard those sounds from their distance, but smiles spread across their faces. Maybe they could see something in my face, something like panic, because that was what I was starting to feel.

My legs wouldn't take me away, and I couldn't have outrun them anyway. They certainly didn't need their Vauxhall to catch me. Sprinting had never been my strong point.

I moved my free hand behind my back and tapped my fingertips against the wood of the door.

'Got a light?'

The shortest lad peeled off from the trio. His friends followed him, keeping a step behind. They stopped a few feet away, standing in the road.

'Pardon?' I said.

'Got a light?'

'Ummm . . . no.'

'S'lucky I have, then, innit?' The small lad reached into the pocket of his denim jacket and produced a plastic green lighter, cylindrical, with a metal top that fitted into the palm of his hand. He flicked it with his thumb, and a fat orange flame leapt up.

He moved his thumb and the flame snapped off.

There was silence.

I couldn't turn my back on them, and I didn't dare push through them to walk away. The small one took another step forward. He had light blond hair and a fat, pale face, with dimples inset into his wobbling cheeks.

I recognized him. The last time I had seen him was in the Slaughter. He had been in the spotlight, his mouth forming the words to a Led Zeppelin track. The red-haired one with angry raised skin on his face and neck had been playing the drums, and the one with arms like a gorilla was the lead guitarist.

I looked at the big guitarist again. His T-shirt, emblazoned with streaks of lightning which formed the word 'WASP', was cut off at shoulders and neck to expose his formidable muscles to the cold. His throat was as wide as Lena's thigh, I would guess, and his Adam's apple was obvious. Running from that proud lump, over his chin to finish just below his left cheekbone, was a set of three parallel marks, bright red against his winter-white skin.

He smiled and jerked his head to the side, almost as if to give me a better view, and I realized that the marks were scratches.

The small one was close to me now; I could see the brown

roots of his dyed hair. I moved backwards and felt the shock of the door handle against my back.

'Dead Vegetation,' I said.

He inclined his head.

'I know who you are,' I said. 'You're that band. Dead Vegetation.'

'So you know who we are. Have a fucking medal.'

He flicked the lighter again, and the flame spurted up from his clenched fist. He moved it towards me, so that it was maybe five inches away, level with my chest. I felt the heat on the front of my chin.

'Just carry on doing what you're doing. Keep hanging around this house, and around the Paradise, 'cos then I'll give you a light. Do you understand?'

'Oh,' I said. 'Right.'

He removed his thumb from the metal part of the lighter and the flame slunk away once more. The other two lads, standing behind him, shuffled their feet and looked around the street.

'Right, then,' he said in a friendly tone. 'See ya.'

The others made a gap for him as he walked away. Then they followed him back to the Vauxhall, taking up their positions once more, lounging against it like extras from a school production of *West Side Story*. Not one of them looked at me.

The worst part was that they weren't even going to run away from the scene of their crime. They had me scared, and they knew it.

I stepped away from Mrs Smithson's house and started a brisk, self-conscious walk back up the promenade. I wanted to prove them wrong about me. I wanted to walk up to the car with a smirk and break off one of the wing mirrors; I wanted to sashay back up to Mrs Smithson's door and knock out a cheery tune upon it.

I wasn't brave enough to do either. But I could do the next best thing.

My guess was that Lena would still be sitting on the promenade. We could find Allcombe police station together.

Twenty-one

The policewoman had a straight line for a mouth and her mousy hair was pulled back into a bun that bore streaks of silver. But there was something reassuring, even maternal, about the lines around her eyes and the folds of skin on her neck. I guessed she was in her early fifties. Her gaze upon me felt compassionate.

'Are you sure you don't need medical assistance?' she said. She had a soft local accent. It was the first time it hadn't grated on me.

I shook my head. 'I told you, I'm fine.'

'Try to relax, now, lovey, okay? It's all over now. Nobody will hurt you here.'

I believed her. Ostensibly we were sitting in an office within the confines of Allcombe police station, but it looked nothing like the set of a TV cop show. Instead it reminded me of Lena's front room. I had been guided to a squashy floral sofa next to a big window with a view out to sea. Lena was ensconced in a matching armchair. The feminine touch had definitely been brought to the surroundings; I got the feeling this had been the policewoman's home from home for a few years.

She was sitting behind a small pine desk: an unobtrusive computer screen, a keyboard and a mouse on her right; a silver vase holding dried flowers, a yellow desk tidy and a pad of A4 paper on her left. The wall behind her head bore a framed collage of photographs, showing her on holiday, getting married, smiling through the years. I took her advice and made an effort to relax.

'It's such a relief to be here,' I said. 'What's your name?'

'Sergeant Roper. Maureen.'

'Good name,' murmured Lena. She shifted in her seat. 'I just mean that it's got a ring of dependability about it, that's all. Sorry. Police stations make me nervous, and I say silly things when I'm nervous.'

I rolled my eyes at her. 'What have you got to be nervous about? Nobody assaulted you!'

'Nobody assaulted you either, Pru. Are you bleeding? No. Have you got bruises? No. Has anything been wounded but your belief that you should be in control of every situation? No.'

'It was bad,' I retorted. 'It was really scary. You had to be there. Besides, there's more things to report than that. There's the cat and the retirement home and Phil . . .'

'What about Phil?'

'You don't think Phil's suspicious?'

'Look,' said Maureen. 'It's easy to let emotions run high after an event like this, but try to stay focused on what happened, okay?'

'Yes, Maureen,' I said. She was right. We'd been getting off track. 'What do I need to do?'

'Well, how about I fetch you a cup of tea and you have a think about making a statement? Consider what you want to say?'

'Yes, okay, Maureen, that would be great.'

She gave us both a warm smile on the way out of the office. The calm feeling she had engendered in me left with her.

Lena gave me a hard stare. 'What actually happened at the house, Pru? Did anybody say any more than boo to you?'

'Listen, stick insect, you sat on your bum outside the Royal and felt hard done by while I went out and did some real detective work. I reckon Mrs Smithson sold Crystal's suicide note to raise money to pay off Potato Head. He was pressuring her to pay her mother's funeral costs, and he got Dead Vegetation to kill her cat as a warning. Then I came out of her house and found the Three Stooges waiting for me.'

Lena sat back in the armchair, sinking into the fluffy white cushions, and pursed her lips. 'Got any proof of the cat thing?'

'Mrs Smithson saw them do it.'

'Yes, but do you think she'll tell the police?'

I considered. I didn't get the feeling that even Sergeant Roper would be able to coax a statement from her. 'She's too scared. And who can blame her? Look what they did to Henry.'

'I don't suppose the police will be able to do anything, then,' Lena mused. 'Not about the cat, anyway.'

'Well, what about the money? Payments to Potato Head?

They must be able to trace it. And how come Crystal's grandmother was so broke when she died? Crystal came to see her every month. I don't think she would have let her go without a little something in her bank account.' It was too confusing and scary. 'Maybe we should write all this down . . . get it clear in our heads before Maureen comes back.'

'Although, what if Phil's right, and the police are involved too?' Lena said, her eyes wide with revelation. 'Covering up Crystal's murder?'

'I'd trust Maureen over Phil any day.'

'Well, isn't Maureen the bee's knees?'

I decided not to dignify that with a response. Instead I plucked a blue pen from the desk tidy, took a sheet of paper from her notepad, and started to write.

*I was standing outside Mrs Julie Smithson's house
(6 Long Row, Allcombe, by the pier) and I was
approached by three young men (known to make up
the local band Dead Vegetation) and threatened by
them. One said he would give me a light, and swore.
Then they returned to their car.*

It sounded pathetic. Padding was definitely required.

It was terrifying and I was

'What's another word for terrified?' I asked Lena.

'Do I look like a thesaurus?'

'You look like a stick figure in a Lowrie painting, but that's beside the point. Do you know one or not?'

She thought. 'Really scared?'

It was terrifying and I was really scared.

Also I have reason to believe that Dead Vegetation killed Henry, Mrs Julie Smithson's cat, in order to intimidate her into paying suspicious funeral expenses to the man who runs the Paradise retirement home on the seafront. Mrs Julie Smithson's mother died recently, as did her daughter, ex-child star Crystal Tynee (in possibly suspicious circumstances). I think maybe the man who runs the Paradise retirement home is a suspicious character who should be investigated further, and that Dead Vegetation work for him and follow his orders. Thank you.

I signed my name and passed it to Lena. 'What do you think?'

She read it through and handed it back to me. 'You've used the word "suspicious" too much. And it all sounds a bit . . . paranoid.'

'But it's the truth!'

She shrugged. 'I'm not sure that matters a whole lot around here.'

The door opened and Maureen sidled in. She had a small green tray balanced on her left hand, which she put down carefully on the desk. She gestured at the two china willow-pattern cups upon it. 'Here we are. Good strong tea. How are you feeling?'

'Good. I got it all down on paper.'

'Well, procedure is to talk it through, and then I'd type up a statement and you'd sign it. Never mind, this is a good start, I'll read it through now and we'll go from there.' I held it out across the desk and she took it from my fingers.

The silence in the room lengthened. I caught a few of

Lena's darting glances and then deliberately looked away – I refused to let her make me nervous. She coughed and shifted position, then crossed her long legs and her arms, twisting in her seat. The desire to tell her to shut up and keep still grew, but I resisted it.

Maureen laid the report back down on her desk and fixed me with a steady gaze.

'Right, well, I think I can help,' she said.

I smiled at Lena. 'That's brilliant.'

'First of all, I can tell you categorically that there was no sign of anything – um – suspicious in the death of Crystal Tynee. It was investigated thoroughly, and the Coroner's Office was satisfied that she took an overdose of sleeping pills.'

'So she didn't hang herself?' said Lena.

'No, no, certainly not. Who told you that?'

'Doesn't matter,' Lena said quickly.

I sighed. 'Right. Okay. Let's move on. What about Mr Potato Head?'

'Who?'

'Sorry, the man who runs the Paradise.'

'Ah, Mr Penhaligon. I can confirm that at least one member of Dead Vegetation does work for Mr Penhaligon.'

'I knew it!'

'Kyle Roper. My eldest son.'

I stared at her.

How could such a calm, pleasant woman have given birth to a cat-killing heavy-metal freak? Lena interrupted with her particular brand of useless response before I had the chance to ask.

'Wow,' she said.

Maureen pushed back her chair and pointed to the collage of photographs above her head. 'There we are in Disneyland last year. Does the one on the right look familiar?' I followed the angle of her finger to a snapshot showing a family of five wearing Mickey Mouse ears. Maureen was in the centre, her face beaming out a wide smile, and her husband wore a similarly goofy expression. Three children made up the ensemble, and a pink castle with an iconic set of turrets filled the background. The lad on the far right of the picture was taller than the others, with a muscular build and a sullen hunch to his shoulders. He wore his ears with attitude. The only things missing were the three long scratches across his face and neck.

My instinct told me to get up, walk out of the room, and run for my life, but something in Maureen's face stopped me. She didn't look like an outraged mother, or a bent cop. The corners of her thin mouth fell downwards, and her eyes held profound apology.

'Kyle started having issues last year,' she said. 'Shoplifting, joyriding, teenage-lad stuff. But I've seen enough to know it's a slippery slope. Still, he got the job at the Paradise and I thought maybe this is a turning point. I suppose what I'm trying to say is . . . is there any chance this is just a slip-up on his part? Hanging out with the wrong crowd?' She looked back up at her wall of pictures. 'I'm certain he's trying to be good. He's got a big heart. Young lads go through these phases, I'm sure you know . . .'

'No, I don't,' I said, feeling my faith in Maureen drain away.

'I'll bet he's not the one who threatened you, is he?'

'What difference does that make?' said Lena, leaning forward, her hands on her knees. The husky note in her voice took me by surprise. 'If a crime's been committed, a crime's been committed, hasn't it? Regardless of whose son it happens to be.'

'That's absolutely true, but technically speaking Kyle hasn't committed a crime, has he? He was just in the wrong place at the wrong time. Now, don't think that he won't be hearing from me about this—'

'And what about Potato Head . . . I mean, Penhaligon?' I interrupted. She didn't reply. I banged down my untouched tea on her desk. It slopped over the rim and formed a puddle. She stared at it, then at me. I got the feeling I had just lost her sympathy.

'Of course I'll investigate your claims. But I would ask you to let me deal with this in an informal capacity, okay? Mr Penhaligon is very well respected around here, and the deaths of elderly residents, well, that's a sensitive issue, isn't it? Sometimes there's a lot of guilt on the side of the family and they try to deal with their own feelings by blaming somebody else.'

'Are you talking about Mrs Smithson?'

'You know, Mrs Smithson's mother, Grace, was very old and confused at the end. Sometimes . . .' Maureen dropped her voice lower and gave me plenty of eye-contact, '. . . death can be a blessing.'

'Not to Grace, I'd bet.'

Lena stood up. 'Come on, Pru. Let's go.'

Maureen stood up too. 'It's a retirement home, Mrs

Green. People die all the time, and it has to be dealt with sensitively, but also as a business. Now, rest assured that I will look into your claims. And I can promise you that you will not be threatened by my son again.'

'And you can guarantee that, can you?'

She walked to her office door and opened it, revealing the empty white corridor of the police station. Lena set off at a fast pace and I followed her, jogging to keep up. I heard Maureen close her office door behind us.

Lena's walk was as graceful as ever. Only the raised line of her shoulders told me how angry she was. I put on a burst of speed to catch up with her, and touched her shoulder, feeling the knotted muscle there. We reached the end of the corridor. 'Which way is it?'

'Left.'

We burst through the doors into a light drizzle and the sight of an occasional passing car, rolling down the hill towards the high street.

'So what now?' Lena said. 'Now you've alienated the police and made us look like morons?'

I had to wipe that smug expression from her face. 'Follow me.'

'Where are we going?'

'To find evidence,' I said. I'd had enough of being doubted. It was time to prove my point. 'To the Paradise.'

Twenty-two

By the time we reached the Paradise, Lena was struggling hard against my grip on her arm.

'Let go!'

I dropped her arm and she clutched at the promenade railings, turning her back to me.

'Come on,' I said, not wanting to lose my momentum.

'You know, for once, Pru, you could actually talk to me instead of dragging me along.'

'Are you coming or not?'

She let go of the railings, swivelled, and looked past the ever-cheery ice-cream van boy to the green pineapples that decorated the posts outside the Paradise. 'But what are you actually going to do?'

I walked away and had the satisfaction of hearing her footsteps behind me. 'Pru!'

I didn't even pause at the gate. I walked up to the double doors and pushed through them, not caring if they caught Lena on the backswing.

There was nobody at the reception desk, but the doors on

my left were open and I could hear a mixture of voices floating through them.

The doors behind me banged.

'What's the plan, oh mighty one?' Lena said.

'We need to talk to a resident, pump someone for information. And we need to be subtle about it.'

'Right. Then let's get on with it.' She walked past me and stood next to the battered upright piano, her back to me. The voices stopped.

'Ethel?' Lena called.

There was no reply.

'Then how about . . . Doris?'

Nothing.

'Is there a Gladys in the house?'

'Um . . . yes?'

It was a small, weak voice. Lena's head jerked to the left. She moved out of my line of sight. The voices began again, in a low hum that built up to a normal volume. I got up the courage to enter the room.

It appeared that there were only old women in the Paradise. There were perhaps thirty of them, either alone or in pairs, sitting in worn armchairs, most with ragged paperbacks in their hands and immaculate collars on their cardigans. No one had combined to make a group. Everyone looked alone.

The only person under sixty years old in the room, apart from myself, was Lena. She was occupying the chair Mr Potato Head had sat in yesterday, and she was leaning forward, making wide hand-gestures as she talked to a small, orange-haired old lady, who was sitting where Mrs Smithson had sat.

I crossed the room to them, and stood next to Lena's chair, my hands clasped behind my back, my legs crossed at the ankles, feeling like a teenager eavesdropping on an adult conversation.

'. . . since you've been here so long, if you've seen anything unusual, at all?'

'Do you mean the bin bags?' The old woman tutted. 'It's terrible, those bin bags, but no one will do anything, not the authorities, or anything.'

'I was thinking more about the other residents, or the staff,' Lena steered in a soft voice.

'Oh, well . . . I don't know if I should say . . .' The old woman's eyes flicked to mine, and I attempted a smile.

'This is Pru. Pru, meet Gladys. It's okay, Gladys. You can tell us.'

Gladys sniffed. 'I've still got my wits, you know, and I know you're not meant to be here. You all think the minute you turn sixty your brains dry up and you go gaga, but I'm sharper than I've ever been. I didn't have a clue when I was your age. What are you two up to? Are you with the police?'

'No,' Lena said. 'We're not police.'

'We're RAF wives,' I added. I'm not quite sure why.

'And what was it you wanted to know? About the staff, is it? Well . . .'

We leaned closer.

'. . . Danny has a new ring. It's gold, with a St Christopher on it, and he wears it on his thumb. And Badger bought a motorbike. A big one.'

'Good for them,' I muttered. Lena threw me a look.

'Dezza came back from his holiday all tanned. He went to some island somewhere. I heard him say he had a hard job explaining it to his mum. He told her he was going to the Lake District with the school.'

'How old is Dezza?' Lena asked.

'Gosh, I wouldn't know for sure, dear,' Gladys said. She seemed to have taken a shine to Lena. Apparently the ageing process hadn't taught her that being thin, beautiful and polite didn't necessarily mean a person had a wonderful personality. 'About the same as the other orderlies. Sixteen, maybe?'

'Sixteen?' I said incredulously, but was ignored.

'Isn't that a bit young?' Lena asked.

'I wouldn't know. It must be difficult to get people to work here, don't you think? I wouldn't want to do it. Mopping up all sorts. And they're nice young men, as a rule, some of them, apart from the bin bag thing. I think Mr Penhaligon chooses them quite carefully. He calls them his boys.'

'Sounds like they get paid well for their troubles,' I said.

'Oh, they don't get paid,' Gladys said.

It might have been my imagination, but I could have sworn the volume of conversation in the room diminished. I looked over my shoulder. Nobody was paying any attention to us, but somehow the atmosphere had changed, as if less light was coming through the windows.

'Maybe this wasn't a brilliant idea,' I whispered to Lena.

'They don't get paid,' Gladys repeated. 'But they get a share of the cheques.'

'What do you mean?' Lena said in her prim voice.

'What do you call it when someone takes your cheque

book and makes you sign all the cheques? You know, so that they can cash them? Does that have a name?'

The question was directed at Lena, but she seemed speechless so I filled in. 'I don't know.'

'Oh. Well. So I'm sure it's worthwhile, working here, for those lads. And we're all old, we can't give them any trouble.'

'But,' Lena managed to say, 'but that's—'

'Terrible. I know,' Gladys finished for her. 'It's lovely that you believe me. My family don't believe me. They think I'm not all there, you know. What with the bin bags as well . . .'

A suspicion occurred to me then that I had to voice.

'The bin bags,' I said. 'What's in them?'

'Let's see . . . the last one was about six weeks ago, and that was Mrs Taylor. Before that, it was Nora . . . Nora Bear, she was a lovely old thing too . . . and before that, Mrs Smithson . . .'

'People?' I said, just to make sure. 'Dead people in the bin bags?'

'Well, I don't think they would have stayed in there if they were alive, dear,' Gladys said.

'Mrs Smithson . . . Crystal's grandmother . . .' Lena breathed.

'Did you know Crystal? Sweet girl. She came to visit, not like my lot. I keep telling them that my savings are being used up, but do they listen? You know,' Gladys smiled at Lena and leaned forward to pat her on the knee, 'you remind me of Crystal.'

'Really?'

'She used to ask lots of silly questions too.'

'Oh,' Lena said. Her shoulders slumped. That woman loved a compliment.

'Do I remind you of Crystal?' I asked.

Gladys looked me up and down. 'No,' she said. And then she did a strange thing. Her eyes moved upwards, so that her line of sight was over my head. I saw the light blue irises widen, and the straggly grey hairs of her eyebrows rise. It was the closest expression I had ever seen to terror.

'Can I help you?' a voice behind me said.

I recognized it. I had heard it only yesterday.

I straightened up and turned round.

He was smaller than me; I could look down on the crown of his bald head, which was a shiny pink. He was smiling, baring white teeth under flaking red lips, and lifting bushy brown eyebrows high on to the blank canvas of his forehead. I knew both Gladys and Maureen had mentioned his name, but it had been pushed out of my head by his appearance and replaced with a much more fitting title: Mr Potato Head.

Lena stood up and faced him. She shifted her weight from one foot to the other. 'We were wondering if you were employing any . . . chambermaids?' she said.

'We're not chambermaids,' I said. 'My friend is confused. We were visiting Gladys.'

'How lovely for Gladys,' Mr Potato Head said. There was nothing sinister about him: he seemed perfectly amiable. Besides, it's difficult to feel intimidated by someone under five foot four. 'She doesn't get many visitors. I think it's partly due to the medication she's on. It tends to make her a little imaginative at times.'

133

Lena breathed out. I swear I could feel her wanting to believe him.

I looked at Gladys. Her expression had not changed. I glanced around me, and saw the same wide eyes and trembling mouth on every other little old lady in the room.

'She seems perfectly lucid to me,' I said.

'Well, that's nice.' His eyes didn't move from mine. 'That's very nice for all of you. But I'm afraid you've probably tired her out. She's not used to chatting.'

'Maybe we should go,' Lena said. I heard her footsteps cross behind me, heading in the direction of the double doors, and then stop. My attention remained fixed on Mr Potato Head. The room was so quiet I could whisper. 'Bye, Gladys. I'll be back to see you again. Soon.'

Gladys was silent.

Potato Head didn't flicker. 'She'll look forward to that.' He took a step towards me. Up close, he had great skin. It was like the skin you see on those naked mole rats at the zoo – folded around the neck and ears to produce a nest of wrinkles, but delicious in its pinkness, the blood vessels visibly blooming under the surface. 'I'll get Kyle to show you out . . .' His big lips parted into a smile, baring blunt white teeth. He snapped his head away from me and looked towards the double doorway. I followed his gaze. Kyle Roper was standing there, his bulk strapped down into a clean buttoned smock, incongruous with his thick black boots and jeans with worn-through patches on the knees. The three long scratches were vivid red on his cheek.

Earlier, in the street, he had looked scary. In the confines of the retirement home, knowing he had free rein over these timid, tired geriatrics, he looked like a nightmare.

I couldn't move. Lena walked back to me and poked my upper arm. 'Come on.'

We walked forward. Kyle smirked at me as he stepped out of the way, just far enough to create a gap between us and the relative safety of the promenade. There was an awful moment, as I passed him, when I felt his breath on my throat and caught the edge of his scent – musky, hormonal, masked with strong aftershave, maybe Hugo Boss. Then we were out of the room and heading for the patch of grey light through the main door. Lena no longer had to pull me forward.

I didn't take a breath until we had passed the green pineapples on the gateposts.

Lena let my arm go. 'Before you say anything—'

'Get back to our room,' I said. 'We need to get back and lock the door.'

She stared at me. 'You don't seriously believe that old lady?'

'Her name is Gladys, and yes, I believe her.'

'But—'

'Come on!' I reached our hotel, and marched into the reception.

A man was standing by the desk with his back to us. He turned.

He wasn't a man: he was a teenager. He smiled. He made a movement with his thumb against his fist.

A spurt of flame leapt up from the lighter he held.

Twenty-three

'See you,' he said. The flame snapped off and he pocketed the lighter.

It didn't occur to me that he was talking to someone else until Phil stepped through the beaded curtain behind the desk and looked at all of us in turn.

'Yeah, all right,' Phil said.

The teenager gave a florid bow. 'Ladies,' he said. His small eyes roamed over Lena. I wondered if he had been discussing her better points with Phil when we came in.

I stepped to one side and heard Lena follow suit behind me. He walked past us and out of the hotel.

I strode up to the desk and put my hands on the counter. 'Do you know him?' I said to Phil.

He coughed once, and looked at his fingernails. 'Yeah.'

'He threatened me earlier.'

Lena came up to stand next to the stairs. 'There must be some mistake—'

'Yeah,' Phil said.

'He killed Mrs Smithson's cat.'

'Yeah.'

'What?' Lena said. I looked at her. Her attention was fixed on Phil. 'Why did he do that?'

I carried on speaking over the top of her, voicing my worst suspicions. 'He terrorizes old ladies for money on the orders of Mr Potato Head.'

Phil gazed at me steadily. 'Who the fucking hell is Mr Potato Head?' he said.

'You know.'

'And you should stay out of it, peanut.'

'Are you warning me off?' I couldn't handle murdering thugs like Kyle and the one with the lighter. I couldn't handle orchestrators of grand, evil plans like Mr Potato Head. But I was absolutely sure that I could handle jumped-up idiots with nothing but sex on their minds.

'I'm just saying, you should leave it alone now.'

Lena spoke before I had the chance. 'And why did you tell us those lies about Crystal? Saying it was murder?'

'I'm bloody amazed you fell for that line,' he said, sliding the black pen on the desk in and out of its holder.

'I can't believe that you . . .' Lena began, and fell into silence. She started again. 'Pru, please go upstairs.'

'No,' I said, mainly because of the way she said it. Actually, it wasn't a bad idea – it had been a day of unpleasant incidents, and although it was only the afternoon, going back to bed and hiding under the covers would have suited me well.

'Pru, please let me deal with this.'

'Yeah, Pru, piss off,' Phil said.

'Fine.' I turned and stomped up the stairs with plenty of

attitude. I decided to leave the bedroom door ajar, and hopped under the bedclothes, fully dressed. As I had hoped, the volume of the argument taking place downstairs meant I could hear every word.

'You're not the person I thought you were,' Lena said. What a cliché-ridden drama queen she could be at times. I felt sorry for her.

'Who did you think I was? A bit of fluff? Brad Pitt?' Phil said loudly.

'I'm well aware that you're neither of those things, Philip.'

'And you're not my mum. You're a corpse-chasing grockle who lies back and thinks of your homo husband while I give you one.'

There was a sharp intake of breath. Reality and romance had just clashed, and reality was winning. How predictable that Lena would react as if a baby seal was being clubbed to death in front of her.

There was a silence. Maybe she was crying.

I picked up *Words for the Faithful* and let the book fall open to a random page.

On the Weakness of Women

Many would have us believe that women are the weaker sex. Men talk of the demands of the working day, followed by the difficulties of disciplining unruly children. They feel that a good meal and a soft presence is all that a woman is capable of providing to a home. Marriage is often viewed as a natural state of domination, not unlike that of a pride of lions. Man is the King of his home just as a lion is King of the Jungle. He is the master of those who are less than him, and that includes the lioness. She has no say in how she lives. She must find a mate and abide by his will in order to survive.

'At least my husband treats me with respect,' Lena said.

'Yeah, he sounds like a fucking great guy.'

'Don't you talk about him like that!'

'Sooo sorry,' Phil said, in a drawn-out tone. I winced at the sarcasm. Young people always do sarcasm so well. 'She's getting upset. Somebody call out the fucking doctor. I can say whatever I wanna say. S'up to you if you believe it or not.'

'What does that mean?' Lena said. 'You mean – you've been lying to me?'

At first glance, traditional religious teaching seems to agree with this point of view. It states, in the marriage ceremony itself, that women must promise to 'obey' their new husbands. This suggests that marriage is a form of ownership, a contract that works most effectively when one person is responsible for all decisions. After all, men are assumed to have a better knowledge of the complexities and pitfalls of the outside world. How could a wife and mother ever hope to deal with the lies and tricks that are an inevitable part of the wider world?

'I never thought I'd say this to someone your age,' Phil said in a tired voice, 'but grow the fuck up!'

'Oh, so now I'm naive?'

'You and that frigid blob you share a room with, yeah.'

It didn't bother me: I'd heard worse. It was an unimaginative insult, though. And, annoyingly, Lena hardly pounced to defend me.

139

'Just because I trusted you, I'm the child? Giving your trust to someone – that's the most adult thing you can do, you moron! Only a teenage moron wouldn't know that!'

He laughed. 'It's like you come from the moon or something, mother. Oh no – wait – from an RAF base in Wiltshire, isn't that right? I can fucking well see it now . . . armed guards keeping the likes of me out, flower-arranging classes every day, cake for tea.'

'Good guess,' I murmured.

But isn't it about time that we accept how roles have changed? The job of mother is not an easy one. Women raise children by themselves, in some unfortunate instances. And who among us does not consider their own mother to be the linchpin, the real source of comfort and inspiration, in our own family?

'It's not real life, is it? No wonder you and your barking sidekick are off looking for adventure.' I heard footsteps on the stairs, quick and heavy, followed by a second set of footsteps. When Lena next spoke, I jumped: she was standing right outside the door to our room.

'It's a real life,' she said, biting out each word.

'Have I given you enough excitement? Enough of a break from your homo husband and fat friend? Or do you want more? I can always give you more, babe.'

In the Bible, did not Christ turn to women for help when he most needed it? Was it not a woman he spoke to first after his resurrection? He did not consider them to be too fragile to receive the most stirring messages ever passed down to us – why, then, should they be considered incapable of maintaining a partnership in a marriage, and of expressing reasonable thoughts and opinions?

It is time we realized that there is no longer a weaker sex. There is only a bond between men and women that is most fruitful when treated reverently and respectfully. Men are not Kings, and women are not the fripl creatures

I stopped reading. I looked away from the page for a moment to rest my eyes, and then read the last sentence again.

Men are not Kings, and women are not the fripl creatures we once held them to be. Treat your daughter, your wife, your mother with honour. If they are not offered fairness, they will surely find their own way to achieve it, for no creature is without the desire for revenge when it suffers prejudice or ill-treatment at the hands of another.

Fripl. Fripl creatures.

Twenty-four

It took Lena a long time to reply. When she spoke, her voice was dignified.

'I've had quite enough, thank you.'

'Not up for a farewell fuck, then?' Phil said. He sounded quite serious.

The door opened, and Lena slipped in through the gap. Then she closed and locked it.

We both listened to Phil's laughter, followed by his retreating footsteps. Lena moved away from the door and sat down on the edge of her bed.

'I can't believe I've been such an – idiot,' she said, giving a hiccup. She was the only person I knew who could manage to look beautiful while in despair. She was bending forward from her waist, forming a perfect curve as graceful as the neck of a swan, and had her hand pressed against her mouth.

'I can,' I said.

She shook her head. 'Please be kind, Pru. Just this once, I need you to be kind.'

'That's not my strong point.' I put down *Words for the*

Faithful and rolled on to my side so she couldn't see my face. 'Ummm . . . would it help if I called him a fartface?'

She shrugged.

'Or that you could do so much better?'

'Did you swallow a copy of *Cosmo*?' Lena said. 'That's not helping. Because I obviously can't do so much better. If I could, I wouldn't be here right now with you.'

'Well, thanks very much, string bean!'

She got off her bed and crossed to mine. I didn't look round. I felt her weight on the mattress beside me.

'I've been a twit, haven't I? A twit over a spotty teenager.'

'Yes, a bit of a twit,' I said in my best consoling voice.

Her face twisted and fresh tears erupted. 'If only the sex hadn't been so good!'

This was definitely new, and uncomfortable, territory. 'Yeah,' I said. 'Listen, about that book—'

'Not that I came, but I missed it, really missed it, the excitement, with a stranger, like he really wanted to – I don't know – shag me into submission.'

'Oh God,' I said.

'I know,' she said. 'To think I might never – might never have it again is just—' She bent her head and stretched out her hand to touch my hip.

I jumped off the bed and moved to the window. It was all too much. 'Lena,' I said, 'I think you're mistaking me for someone who gives a shit.'

I still couldn't look at her. Instead I focused on the view. The promenade had been washed to a dove grey by a flurry of rain I hadn't heard, and the fading afternoon sunlight was

143

hitting the drops of water that hung from the rails and lamp-posts, making them glisten. It was beautiful.

When she spoke, her voice was very soft. 'Will you tell me something, Pru?'

I didn't reply. I wanted to walk out of the room, but was scared to leave. I was so hungry. My stomach was rumbling: I was sure she could hear it.

'What happened to you when you were seventeen?'

'Nothing,' I said.

'I know something happened, and I know that's the reason why you clam up whenever we talk about stuff. Was it – some sort of abuse?'

'It was nothing,' I said, 'and it's none of your business.'

Behind me, the bed squeaked. I kept my eyes on the view even though I was desperate to know what was happening. When I felt her hand on my back, I froze. She was so close.

'You can trust me,' she said. 'I won't tell anyone.'

It was hard to breathe. The sunlight was fading: soon it would be dark. I was sweating, and was sure she could smell me, the dried sweat in my old clothes and the fresh drops squirming their way from under my arms. I felt so greasy, and so ugly. 'I don't want to . . . I can't . . .'

'Let it go, Pru. It's been so long. Let it go.'

She rubbed my back, and for a moment I was ready to turn to her, tell her everything.

The moment passed. The ridiculousness of it, of two women standing in a shabby hotel room and baring their sad little souls, punctured the bubble Lena had been trying to blow around us.

I pushed past her and walked into the bathroom.

144

After a splash of cold water on my face and a look in the mirror to check I was back in control of my expression, I spoke. 'Perhaps we should get you a dictionary so you can look up the meaning of the word "nothing"? You know that word? The concept that also defines what you have to show for five years of marriage?'

Lena's head appeared around the doorway. Her eyes were dry. The look she gave me wasn't friendly.

I cleared my throat. 'I've got some news about Crystal's suicide note. Let's go and get something to eat; fish and chips okay with you?'

She shook her head. 'Listen, Pru. I know that you've got problems, but this isn't healthy.'

'Oh.' I attempted a smile. 'Well, we can try and find a salad bar but I don't rate our chances.'

'Denial is not healthy. And I've had enough of unhealthy relationships.'

'You've been watching too much *Dr Phil*.'

'I want to know what happened to you. You need to get it out in the open, and I need to hear why you've been such a b— a blooming nightmare to get along with, so . . .' She smoothed her hair back from her face and put her hands on her hips. '. . . So we are going to find out the truth about that note, and about the Paradise, and then we are going home. And if you haven't told me the truth about yourself by then, I don't want to be your friend any more.'

'Ooooh,' I said. 'I'm really scared.' But she had already gone back to the bedroom. I listened to her movements for a while, quick and methodical rustlings. I guessed she was getting undressed.

'It's still early,' I ventured. 'We can go out and get something to eat, and talk about this thing I found in the book—'

'Goodnight,' she said.

So there was to be no dinner, and no conversation. And no more friendship, because there was no way to tell Lena – tell anyone – what had happened to me on my seventeenth birthday. There were no words for that.

I stared at my dry eyes in the mirror until daylight deserted me.

Twenty-five

The Diary of Lena Patten
12 December, 8.12 a.m.

Is life really just about what you can put inside you? Is there nothing more than the pleasure of a steak, a fag, a fuck? Because it occurs to me that nothing and nobody has ever managed to plug even one of my holes to my satisfaction.

Right now, it's eight in the morning and there's barely enough light to write by. Pru is emitting a low purr of a snore. It's the only gentle thing about her. I've been tasting sick in my mouth since I opened my eyes, reached for the diary and started to write. When I go to the bathroom and brush my teeth in an attempt to take the taste away and find some energy for the day ahead, I'll stare in the tiny flecked mirror over the sink and there'll be nothing on my face, no extra line, and no mark of experience. My forehead won't be branded with an 'A' for Adulteress or an 'I' for Idiot.

Does this come across as pitiful? Lovelorn? But it's neither of those things. I know I don't love Phil and I'm fairly sure that he never loved me (although you can fool yourself when a man gets that look in all three of his eyes, if you know what I mean), but God, how I wanted to be wanted. Turns out Phil thought I was desperate for him. I wasn't his Mrs Robinson; I was last year's blow-up doll – still serviceable in an emergency, but a bit on the saggy side and liable to whine.

Forgive me for my overblown imagery this morning, dear Diary. Blame it on this town, if you like. Pru swears she can't see the appeal of the place, but she must feel something when she stares at the battleship-grey sea and the dead white fronts of the buildings. There is a mystery here, and I don't just mean the mystery of Crystal Tynee, which may turn out to be nothing more than the product of the overactive imaginations of two women who aren't quite old and aren't quite young.

I'm referring to the mystery of Allcombe. Where does everyone go in the winter? Why do they return in the summer? What draws people away and brings them back? What kept Crystal here, clinging like a limpet to the Royal when the rest of the world had left on the autumn tide?

I'm a pretender: I always have been. I wanted to fool myself about my marriage, and about Phil. I don't see how I'm ever going to stop pretending. But if I'm going to pull the wool over my own eyes, why not play the role of glamorous sleuth for a while, the lady with heart and brains, stranded in a strange little seaside town full of dark deeds and dangerous devils?

What a tagline.

At least in Allcombe there is something beyond what you see. I grew up in Chelmsford, and that town has no mystery to it; only shopping opportunities. My parents made the most of the furniture stores. Throughout my childhood they decked out their detached abode in real leather sofas and matching pouffes. And they weren't alone – everyone in the town seemed to be obsessed with interior decoration. There was practically a street party when *Changing Rooms* hit BBC One.

I didn't get that gene. I was more anti-materialist than antimacassar. Needless to say, I rebelled, initially in small ways which quickly grew larger. I slashed the leather sofa and scrawled rude words on the pouffe as a finale. Then I walked out and stayed out. I've never been back.

Yes, of course there's more to it than my description. Naturally there's a whole dirty heap of information that I'm not sharing, and a catalogue of well-fingered snapshots that I'm refusing to relive in this little leather book.

Have you ever considered that you don't need to know everything about a person in order to love them? And it's not just people. Everything is better in small doses. I never wanted to feel full: smothered by a person, or a place, or an emotion. And, of course, I never wanted to eat to excess, either. That's why the anorexia.

A-ha! I hear you thinking, Diary, *Now we're getting somewhere!* But the anorexia is no big deal. Given my previous line of work, I think that's perfectly understandable. Funnily enough, it never actually affected me when I was working as a human plate. I used to eat as if I was starving back then; one of the perks of the job was the leftover sushi. But after I'd returned to the UK with enough savings for my

London apartment and a comfortable life, boredom kicked in and with it came the anorexia. It's been with me ever since.

It's funny how you cope with momentous events. I mean, everyone finds a way to cope, don't they? You live through the unhappy childhood, the terrible job, the festering and failing relationships, and it's only when things begin to go right that you have time to collapse.

I bet psychiatrists never see anyone during their horrific times. I'm guessing they always see these damaged people afterwards, don't they, with the label PTSD pinned on the back of their jumpers by some overworked GP?

All right, to get back to the point, I keep the anorexia in check. I mean, I will eat a light salad or even a full-fat yoghurt occasionally if I feel it's necessary. I don't want to think about this any more; I've got a very busy day lined up, what with having to make up with Pru, although God knows why that's my responsibility. I tried my best with her last night, I really did. I attempted to open up to her, to treat womanhood as a sorority rather than a rivalry, and she couldn't bitch-slap me back into my box fast enough. It's all very well, this apparent friendship that offers nothing other than someone to argue with when you feel tetchy, but I've come to realize over the last few days that I need more than that.

We can't go on as we are. Either she makes a leap of faith and trusts me, or . . . or what?

Twenty-six

Case 476: Mrs Prudence Elspeth Green
Transcript of conversation recorded Sunday,
12 December 2004, 10.03 a.m.
Location: Allcombe promenade

PATTEN: It's a misprint. The author probably meant it to
read frail. Women are frail.

GREEN: Yeah, that's what I thought.

PATTEN: So the copy of *Words for the Faithful* – the one
in Mr Tunnell's room – that must have belonged to
Crystal. Her grandmother had a copy and so did she.
It was left there when she died.

GREEN: And she wrote that word in her suicide note as
a message.

PATTEN: A code word that her grandmother's murderer
wouldn't be able to decipher.

GREEN: But we have.

PATTEN: I wouldn't get too puffed up with yourself just
yet, Sherlock. We've still got a long way to go. Why
that word? From that book?

GREEN: To point out that women really are a bit on the frail side?

PATTEN: I think it's more than that. We need to look into it further. Somehow.

GREEN: Wow. That sounded like the beginning of an idea, but it petered out into a vague, meaningless sentence.

PATTEN: Oh God.

GREEN: What?

PATTEN: It's the funeral today.

'Whose funeral?' I said.

Lena opened her handbag and rummaged inside. 'Whose funeral? Yvonne's funeral. Remember Yvonne? Lived on the same street as us? Committed suicide in her wedding dress? I should call.'

'Er . . . I don't think she'll answer.'

'Shut up, Pru,' Lena said, producing her dated, chunky mobile phone. She was pretending to be a confident person this morning. The illusion had been marred only by her refusal to enter the dining room for breakfast in case she saw Phil.

'Look, I don't think we should . . . oh look! The ice-cream van!' It was an attempted diversion, but an ice-cream did sound pretty good in my state of near-starvation. 'I'll buy you a cornet. With a flake.'

She waved one hand at me and with the other hand pressed buttons on her phone. I decided I didn't want to hear her conversation, and wandered over to the van.

The usual teenager stood behind the counter; it occurred to me that he was the friendliest young man I'd met in Allcombe, with bright blue eyes and a fetching mop of black hair. Maybe the 'thug' gene had skipped a generation with him. I ordered an extra-large cornet and gave him a warm smile when he handed it to me. He smiled back. I thought I saw something in that smile. I suppose I could see the appeal of younger men: all that enthusiasm, combined with gratitude for taking them under your wing. But after my wearing experience with Mike Tunnell I was far too jaded to consider taking a lover: I didn't have enough energy to paint my toenails, let alone dress up and play hide and seek with a Boy Scout.

I decided not to have a conversation with him and walked a little way down the promenade instead. Yesterday's rain shower had left the sky and sea looking sharp and bright, as if cleaned and polished. It actually made the place look attractive, in a dated way. Or maybe I was just getting used to it.

I licked up my ice-cream, ate the cone, and headed back to the bench. Lena had finished her phone call, and was sitting with her legs crossed, right over left, her fingernails drumming against her kneecap.

'You missed a smashing ice-cream,' I said. 'I'm going for a stick of rock and a kiss-me-quick hat next. One hell of a holiday, this.'

'I feel guilty,' Lena said.

'About missing the funeral?'

She shook her head. 'I've just been speaking to David.'

'Blimey.' I sat down next to her. 'The gay husband rears his perfectly coiffured head. That must have been an expensive call. How did you get through?'

'He's not in the desert. He's at home.'

Just the thought that he was in the country was unsettling. It felt as if the world had shrunk, and things that had seemed a safe distance away were creeping up behind, waiting to shock the hell out of me.

'Apparently there's a lot of forms to fill in and questions to be answered when someone's dependant checks out,' Lena said. 'And Derek asked for him to accompany him on the flight back.'

'You're having a laugh. He's not going to tell them the truth, is he?'

Lena made a small noise, maybe a sob, but her face was set and her eyes focused on the horizon. 'I don't know. He wants to sort things out.'

'Of course.'

'That's why he's on his way down.'

'What?'

'He's driving down now. He'll be here this afternoon.' There was smugness in her voice. It took me a moment to understand why.

'So you got him to forgo the funeral to meet up with you instead? That's got to be one in the eye for Yvonne's husband.'

'I haven't persuaded him to do anything of the sort. He volunteered.'

I could read her like a book. 'That must feel good.'

She leaned back against the bench, and a smile escaped her. 'It feels wonderful.'

'But you're forgetting something. Phil. You think he's

going to keep his mouth shut if he sees you with your other half?'

Lena winced. 'I suppose we'll have to go out of town. Maybe a pub in the country for lunch – that should be safe.'

'Great! I could do with a roast dinner.'

'I don't think . . . that is, Pru, I really thought . . .'

I was pushing my luck and knew it. Still, her response annoyed me. Yesterday she wanted to know all my dirty little secrets and today she wanted me to disappear in case I blabbed out one of hers. Talk about double standards. 'I get it – I'll disappear. You have fun, and I'll see you later, traitor.'

'You don't have to go right now . . .'

I stood up. 'Just before he arrives, right? Eff it. I'm going for a walk.'

To be honest, I was hoping she would call me back, maybe apologize, so I kept a slow pace and was well within earshot when she shouted after me.

'You'll have to find a new trick, Pru.'

I ignored her.

David, here in Allcombe. It was as if Mars had collided with Earth. To me, it felt like betrayal: the first real sin Lena had committed.

I reached the corner of the empty promenade and considered turning in the direction of Mrs Smithson's house, but the memory of those teenage lads was too fresh. Besides, she had asked me to leave her alone for a good reason – I knew what happened to ladies who disobeyed Mr Potato Head and his cronies.

Instead I turned right and glanced into the fish and chip shop.

Closed. Typical.

I sauntered past it, and then past the pub, which appeared to be closed too, but I suppose it was a little early. I knew this road led to the high street, with its boarded windows, shabby signs and one department store that was bound to be closed too. There was nothing tempting ahead of me, and I had at least six hours to kill. For the first time I wished myself back in Lyneham; at least the gin bottle and the other wives, however annoying, would have been close by. Anything was better than being alone.

Alone.

I stopped walking and listened. Wasn't that a footstep behind me? Before I could give in to fear, I turned round.

There was nobody there.

I'd never been in a town and not seen or heard one living thing before; surely there should at least have been distant traffic, or seagulls. The loudest thing I was aware of was my own breathing. There had to be some reason why the world was so quiet: maybe a malevolent presence scaring everything else away. I had been an idiot to leave Lena, knowing that people in this town wanted me silenced and probably had been waiting for just such an opportunity.

'Melodramatics,' I said under my breath.

It didn't shake the feeling.

'Come on, Prudence, come on, come on,' I whispered. The sound of my own voice was enough to start me walking once more. I took up a steady pace, straining to listen behind me but hearing nothing but the occasional echo of my own steps.

The sensation of being watched, of somehow being judged, intensified.

I broke into a trot. My breathing sounded loud in my ears, pushing out any chance of hearing an approach from behind me. I reached the high street, which was as empty as the promenade, and upped my trot into a jog. I passed shops with dark windows and locked doors.

'Please,' I said. I was running for the first time in years, and my breath was coming in loud gasps, leaving my lungs sore and my knees creaking. A pain was growing in my stomach; I was bending over and hurrying along like an old woman, and I knew what happened to old women in Allcombe.

Then I saw it – electric light spilling out from a wall of windows. I could see pine shelves strung with fairy lights, and a bright green carpet leading up to a large desk. Standing at a row of shelves was a middle-aged woman with glasses and scraped-back grey hair.

It was enough that she wasn't a teenager.

It took the last of my energy to make it to the door. I pushed against it, found it locked, pushed harder as if that would make a difference.

The woman looked up, shook her head at me.

'Open the door!' I shouted. I hammered on the door with my fists. The woman's delicate eyebrows shot up, then knitted together. She moved round the shelves and came to the door with amazing slowness.

I lunged inside, pushing her back against the wall, then wrenched the door from her grasp and slammed it shut again.

I turned the key and stood there, panting, my eyes fixed on the street.

'Are you all right?' the woman asked. I heard her take a few steps backwards.

'I—' I had no breath for a conversation. I kept my gaze on the high street. It was still empty.

'Do you need help? Shall I call someone?'

A noticeboard on my left caught my eye. One poster had been tacked up on it at a slight angle. Only the title was big enough for me to read from my position.

PUBLIC LIBRARY

An idea occurred to me. 'Yes,' I gasped. 'I want to join.'

'But – we're closed. I'm only doing a stock check. I shouldn't have opened the door.'

'It's an emergency,' I told her. 'A local history emergency. And I really need access to the internet and the expertise of a qualified professional.'

It was just the right thing to say.

Twenty-seven

To: greenprudence@yahoo.co.uk
From: SGreen548@bas.mod.uk
Subject: Life Is too Short

Moo

Today I found a camel spider in one of my boots. They teach us to shake out our clothing every morning, and this morning I did it without thinking, as usual. This thing the size of my hand fell out of my left boot and on to the tent floor. It didn't even run away. It just looked at me.

I think it was meant for me. It had my name on it.

Is that paranoid?

One of the lads smacked it with his water bottle. It took three hits to kill it, it was that big. And it never moved.

I feel like I've cheated death, Mooey, and that has to be for a reason. I think I know what that reason is. I have to come back and tell you to your face that you are the moon, the stars, the world to me. Life is too short for us to fight. Every day my feelings are growing stronger.

If you don't love me back, I'll die.

Meeve

Twenty-eight

'What's the matter?' the library woman said from behind me.

I shut down my mailbox and clicked back to the home page. 'Men,' I said.

'Got one that's giving you trouble?'

'Looks that way,' I muttered.

'Well, at least you've got one. Count yourself lucky.' I noticed her eyes on my wedding ring and sneaked a look at her own hands, clasped in front of her. Her fingers were ringless.

'Aren't there any older men in this town?' I asked her.

'Not any who want me,' she said, without a hint of embarrassment. I warmed to her. She shuffled back to her desk. 'I've put you on the system; I'll just laminate your card.'

I clicked on to Google. Once again, I typed in 'Words for the Faithful'. There had to be a way to narrow the search further, but I'd left the book in the room and the name of the author escaped me. It just wasn't in my head any more. I pictured the book: the plain red cover, the gold leaf writing on the spine, the cream pages . . . nope. It wouldn't materialize.

'Flipper the flipping dolphin.'

'Problem?' the library woman said, reappearing over my shoulder and looking at the screen. I guessed she didn't get a lot in the way of clientele.

'I'm just trying to think of—'

'The author? Reverend John Smythe.'

I swivelled in the chair and looked up at her. 'Blimey.' It seemed librarians had decided to fight the rise of the internet by becoming omniscient.

'We have a copy, if you're looking for it . . .'

'Actually, I already have one.' How many copies of this weird little book could there reasonably be in this weird little town? 'I was looking for information about the author.'

'You're not from round here, are you?' She walked to the pine shelves opposite the computer terminal and stood under a sign that read 'Local History'. 'Don't bother with the internet. I've got what you need here.' Without even seeming to look, she pulled out a book and handed it to me.

ALLCOMBE HISTORY – SHAME AND SCANDAL.

'Wow,' I said. 'So he was the town's bad boy for a while?'

'It's a well-known story around here,' she said, crossing her arms under her sagging chest as if to bolster it.

'What happened? An affair?'

She smiled. 'I won't ruin the ending for you.'

'Is it all right if I stay here and read it?'

'Of course. It'll be nice to have the company. Cup of coffee?'

'Great. Milk and two sugars.'

She wandered back to her desk and through the doorway

behind it. I heard the soft click of a switch and then the building huff of the kettle, which didn't sound too healthy.

I swapped to a more comfortable chair with arms, out of sight from the window, and opened the book to the contents page.

1. *The Fishing Wars*
2. *Richard III and the Innkeeper's Daughters*
3. *Houses of Ill Repute*
4. *Bad Traders*
5. *The Witch Burnings*
6. *Civil War Shenanigans*
7. *Robbery on the Highway*
8. *Victorian Tourist Traps*
9. *The Smythe Affair – Not So Reverend*
10. *Drugs at the Folk Festival*

The whole book sounded fairly entertaining, but I flicked forward to Chapter 9 and started to read.

Words for the Faithful, the third book to be published in the trilogy entitled 'New Thoughts For a New Age: Religion and Life', had been eagerly awaited by the West Country for over five years. The previous two volumes had been instant successes amongst the religious community and, to a lesser extent, in philosophical circles, leading to intense speculation as to the identity of the reverend who so closely guarded his privacy and refused to appear in public.

'Coffee, hope it's okay, I don't have any sugar, but you

know it's bad for you, don't you?' The library woman held out a fluted white cup with pink roses around the rim.

'That's fine, thanks,' I said, taking it and putting it on the nearest table. The lack of sugar made it practically undrinkable to me. 'Can I ask you something?'

A smile pinched up her cheeks and put some colour into her face. 'That's why I'm here.'

'Why are Allcombe people all so tight-lipped?'

'About what?'

She sounded suspicious. I put down the book and took a sip of boiling coffee, trying not to grimace. 'Well, I suppose I mean about events. Nobody will just give me a straight answer.'

She removed lint from the sleeve of her cardigan. 'Maybe you're not asking the right questions.'

That was far too smug for my liking. 'Oh, please.'

'What I mean is – no event is simple, is it? When you start looking into it. Complicated. Not down to one thing happening, and maybe not to be summed up.'

'So you don't think . . .' I coughed. The library woman wasn't to know it, but this conversation was just about to enter extremely personal territory for me. I couldn't forget the look on Lena's face as she had thrown down her ultimatum last night. '. . . you don't think that getting to the bottom of one mystery means that you'll no longer be interested? I mean, if you find out what makes a person tick, that you won't want to know them any more?'

The library woman gave me a stare that reminded me of the ones my mother used to bestow whilst telling me off. 'I should tell him how you really feel, if I were you.'

'Sorry?'

'He might understand, lovey. And if he doesn't want you because of something in your past, well, he wasn't Mr Right, was he?'

I drained the coffee, ignoring the bitter taste in my mouth, and handed her the cup. 'I think I'll get on with my book now.' It took a good minute of pretending to read before she sighed and walked away.

I let out a long breath and slumped down in the chair, There were still hours to kill before Lena would return from lunch and I would find out what she planned to do next. Until then, I had only one distraction.

I flipped forward a few pages, scanning for mention of the Reverend Smythe.

. . . impossible to discover whether it was a deliberate error, and the resultant ado might well have been avoided completely if the publishing company had been prepared to accept it as a misprint. However, instead of admitting culpability, Howard & Howard released the following statement:

'All of our publications are meticulously checked before going to print, and Howard & Howard would like to make it clear that any such error, particularly when located in a potentially blasphemous context, would have been identified and corrected long before the publication was made available for purchase.

'In the light of this, Howard & Howard would like to confirm that a thorough investigation into the editing process pertaining to *Words for the Faithful* has been concluded, and the word "fripl" was found in the original handwritten text as presented to us by the Reverend Smythe. This was duly queried by the proofreader allocated to the manuscript, who was informed by the author via letter that the word "fripl" was correct and was not to be changed.

'Any further concerns regarding the apparent use of a "nonsense" word in a serious religious text should therefore be addressed directly to the author, who should be expected to defend himself from any resultant criticism.'

So it seemed the 'fripl' incident had been the start of a witch-hunt. People around here certainly took their religion seriously. Or maybe there just hadn't been enough to moan about back then.

I felt a pang of sympathy for Reverend Smythe. It wasn't clear whether he really had wanted a made-up word in his masterwork, but he had certainly been stitched up because of it.

Maybe that was the point. Perhaps Crystal Tynee had written that word on her note as a sign that she had been framed; possibly it was intended as a clue to the identity of her grandmother's murderer, or even referred to an older event, such as her conviction for manslaughter.

Clues within clues. The library woman was right. Discovering the truth about one event led to myriad new questions, and brought forth new mysteries to be solved. Was I ever going to find answers?

I crossed my legs, propped the book open on my thighs, and picked up reading where I had left off.

Twenty-nine

The afternoon dragged on. I've always been a slow reader, the kind of reader who wants to drag meaning out of every single word, and so I was only a quarter of the way through by the time the sun began to set and the library woman began tapping the glass on the face of her wristwatch.

I waited until she had locked up and then walked along with her, grateful of the company and feeling fortunate that she was heading in my direction. Her platitudes about the importance of honesty in relationships were a small price to pay for the safety of travelling in a pair.

'So, you're in for a big surprise at the end of the chapter,' she said, when her words of wisdom on the subject of men had been met by continued and implacable silence for long enough for her to get the message.

'What's that?'

'I won't ruin it for you.'

'Then why mention it?' I tucked the book further under my arm and quickened my pace. We turned on to the promenade and walked a while in silence. The multicoloured glow of the reindeers and the beckoning of the blue porch light of the Royal were reassuring in their familiarity. 'Can I ask you a question? Do you know the man who runs the Paradise retirement home? I hear he's well respected in the local community.'

'You mean Mr Penhaligon?'

'Penhaligon, Penhaligon . . .' I repeated, determined to make it stick this time. 'Is he a nice chap? Does he do a lot of good work for charity? Pleasant to children and animals, that sort of thing?'

'Well, he's not a member of the library,' she said, as if that was akin to suffering from halitosis, 'but he's certainly very active in the town. And so he should be, considering the fact his family has lived here for generations.'

'Really?' I said, without much interest. Ancient history wasn't my thing.

'He inherited the Paradise. It was very run down when he got it – his father hadn't taken care of it – but he came back from Bristol and did it up, used local builders, and opened it up as the retirement home.'

'What was he doing in Bristol?'

'Solicitor, I think. Something like that. Something professional.' She looked out to sea. 'He studied at Oxford. Or was it Cambridge? A good university. He did tell me once, at a Rotary Club meeting.' There was a dreamy quality to her voice.

'You fancy him!' I said. 'Why on earth would you fancy him? He's got a face like a scrubbed vegetable.'

'Charisma is hard to come by in Allcombe,' she confided. 'Besides, he'd never look at an old lady like me.'

'I've seen older,' I said, trying to be helpful.

'Yes, well, he's married. With children. Lines have to be drawn somewhere.'

'Good for you.'

'Although it's his third or fourth marriage, I think, so he's obviously open to persuasion.'

'Aren't they all?' I sighed. I considered warning her against getting too enamoured of a possible criminal, but I just couldn't think of a way to say it without sounding either jealous or paranoid.

Besides, we had reached the Royal. Parked outside was a car I recognized – a small white MGF with a black hard-top. The windscreen was smeared with dust and dead insects, and behind that lurked the outline of a broad-shouldered man.

'Right, well, thanks for everything,' I said to the library woman. 'Hope you find a husband worthy of you.'

She gave me a conspiratorial smile. 'And good luck with your problem. Just be yourself. And enjoy the book.'

'Yeah, will do,' I said. I had decided not to return it even before I signed for a card, and had given a false address on my application. I've always been a bit of a rebel.

I stopped by the MGF and waited for the library lady's skinny legs to propel her beyond earshot before I tapped on the passenger window.

David Patten opened his eyes and stared at me. For a moment I thought he didn't recognize me. Then he got out of the car and moved round the bonnet to stand in front of me, his hands on his hips, looking like an officer in his regulation off-duty polo shirt and chinos. Even in the glow of the street-lights I could tell he had an amazing tan.

'Looks like the desert agrees with you,' I said.

He took it as an insult, and I can't pretend it wasn't intended to be. 'Same old Prudence,' he said. 'Lovely to see you.' It's an old officer trick to be superciliously polite whilst actually being deeply sarcastic.

'Where's Lena?' I asked him.

'Up in her room. Just freshening up. She thought I could take the opportunity to enjoy the sea air.'

'How thoughtful of her.' A thought occurred to me. 'If you're going to spend any time in Allcombe, watch out for vicious-looking teenagers.'

He smirked, and even that looked charming on his handsome face. 'Ah yes, the evil teenage thugs. Lena told me all about it.'

'And did you tell her all about your adventures?'

'I hope you won't mind if I point out that that's a private concern.'

'Just you, her, and all of RAF Lyneham. Not forgetting Yvonne Fairly. It obviously concerned her.'

David maintained his smirk well in the face of my provocation. 'Interested in everyone else's business, Prudence. Such a shame you're not taking care of your own.'

I had to bite. 'What's that supposed to mean?'

'Heard from Steve lately, have you?'

'Actually, I have. Some emails.'

'Really? Emails from the desert? That's surprising, considering . . .'

Lena's voice came from behind us. 'Considering that you two haven't been getting along so well.' She brushed past me and stood next to David. She looked tired, but not upset.

I had been expecting the marks of tears, runny mascara and so on, but her eyes were dry and wide.

'Yeah, well, I don't really care,' I said, more for David's benefit than Lena's. There was something going on – something Lena didn't want me to know. I could tell by the way she buttoned her coat and patted her hair, as if they were welcome distractions from looking me in the eye. 'How was lunch?'

'I'll tell you later,' she said, turning to face David. She muttered something to him and he nodded. Then he held out his hand and she took it, in what looked like an unconscious gesture on both their parts.

'I'm going indoors,' I said, but they were already walking away. I watched them for a while. They had always looked like a fabulous couple. She was only a little shorter than him, and both of them had wonderful posture. Together, they looked like a commercial for a holiday destination, even amidst the dreariness of Allcombe.

The warmth of the Royal's reception area was welcome. I looked around for Phil, but the desk was tidy and the curtain of beads to the back room was still. I enjoyed the silence for a moment, reluctant to head up to the room because I knew, once I reached it, it would be too tempting to stare out of the window and watch them together, taking their walk as married couples do.

'Pru?'

I looked up. Mike Tunnell was leaning over the banister from the first floor. His face was serious. 'I just wanted to say I'm sorry if I scared you earlier.'

'Right,' I said, unwilling to admit it. I walked up the

stairs, into the shadows of the first-floor landing, and stopped outside my door, aware of his presence behind me. 'Why were you following me, anyway? Are you in league with the criminal element in this town?'

'Criminal?' The surprise in his voice couldn't have been faked. I leaned against my door and faced him.

'Either you're a really good liar or you don't have a clue what I'm on about. I'd still like to know why you followed me.'

He looked at his shoes and fiddled with the hair at the nape of his neck, one finger against the wash of stubble that spread over his chin. It looked soft to the touch. 'I'm not sure I'm ready to tell you that yet.'

'Oh.'

His hand moved to his shirt collar. He was dressed in the suit he had worn to the pizza restaurant, but now it was crumpled and that suited him better, I thought; it made him look more rugged.

'Are you . . .' I started, but couldn't phrase my thought.

'Am I interested in you? Is that why I followed you?'

I didn't answer. His voice was relaxed, as if this was a scene he had rehearsed many times and therefore knew his lines perfectly. He didn't need me to fill in the gaps to give him his cues at all. 'We've been through this before. Talking about it doesn't seem to do us any good. Maybe we should try actions instead.'

It was so smooth, so easy to let him take charge, and such a relief to turn off my brain and concentrate only on the feeling of his hands moving around my waist and pulling me in. His cheek touched mine, and his stubble wasn't soft, as I had imagined, but tough as a wire brush against my skin. It was a delicious contrast to the tickle of his moustache and the wetness of his lips against my cheekbone.

'Do you want this?' he said. He kissed my earlobe. 'Tell me what you want.'

'I'm not very good at talking about this kind of thing,' I heard myself say in a ridiculously little voice.

'No?' I felt his mouth break into a smile against my neck. One of his hands moved down my back, approached the cleft of my buttocks, and tiptoed away from them. 'Shall I stop, Pru?'

I think it was the way he said my name that made up my mind for me. I told him the truth. 'No. Don't stop.'

I felt his smile widen. Then it was gone. He pulled back from me and adjusted his tie. His lips glistened in the shadows; he took out a handkerchief from his trouser pocket and blotted them.

'That was all I needed to know,' he said.

I opened my mouth and shut it again. The way he looked at me reminded me of Madeleine Kish, a girl I'd been at school with, who had asked me to play doctors with her and examine her between her legs. His gaze contained, just as hers had all those years ago, a challenge and an intimacy, as if this were a private ritual I was taking part in, whether I liked it or not.

'Up yours,' I said. The secret dare in Mike's eyes vanished and was replaced by something else, something I interpreted as guilt.

I opened my bedroom door, walked in, and slammed it shut behind me.

Mike didn't knock on the door. And Lena didn't come back that night. The white MG remained parked on the promenade until 7.13 a.m., at which time David slunk into it, his hair sticking up and the collar of his shirt turned up, and drove quietly away.

There was no noise from the room upstairs: I guessed Mike was still asleep. I took the opportunity to leave the hotel.

I didn't want to see her.

Thirty

I couldn't drop off last night. David slept, somehow, in that tiny single bed with a crocheted blanket that was slowly unravelling itself. And he dreamed: his eyelids fluttered and his legs twitched, as if he was running. That's an old dream of his – sprinting through bright grainfields in spring, feet skimming the emerging ears of wheat. He told me once that he felt he was running towards a clear horizon in that dream, which surprised me. I had always assumed he was running away from something.

Last night was a mistake, obviously. I think we knew we were going to make it as soon as we saw each other. As he parked the car on the promenade I watched from the window of the hotel, and had the perfect view of his face through the windscreen: the concentration on the manoeuvres, the care that went into the task at hand, and something else. Something I hadn't seen in him before.

I saw fear.

I've stood close by as David boarded planes for war zones. Upon his return I've heard him tell stories of emergency landings and rocket attacks, and never once did I see anything in his eyes other than the conviction that he was untouchable, like a blasé trapeze artist with the knowledge of a safety net below. That was what made him so attractive. But as he climbed out of the MG and stared, unblinking, at the tired façades of the hotels along the promenade, he looked as if he had just realized there was no safety net this time.

It was probably a revelation caused by Yvonne Fairly's death. That's the kind of event where your own mortality comes into focus; a wake-up call for people who have never considered death as undeniable. That's all of us, I suppose. But a part of me hoped that his newly found fear was prompted by the thought of facing me. I wanted to believe he was dreading hurting me, and that was enough to send me out to him with the determination to try to salvage our marriage.

Oh yes, I want the marriage back: the respect, the contentment, the platonic love that serves a higher purpose. I don't care about the sex now. Sex, however great it is, never has been and never will be my primary motivation.

Now I think about it, every time I've fucked someone I've destroyed something precious, whether it's the feeling of peace that had existed between us, or, plainly and simply, my self-respect. Sex is, at its core, such a destructive act, isn't it?

Which, given that my motivation was to rescue my marriage, makes it surprising that I ended up in bed with David.

The circumstances were all against me, in my defence.

David was determined to be as attractive as possible, and we always were stunningly good together when we wanted to be. We greeted each other with an unfakeable warmth, and as we left for the restaurant, he opened his car door for me and even bothered to cast an appreciative glance at my legs. During the drive I complimented him on his tan, as if he'd been on an extended holiday, and before we'd even reached the restaurant we'd come to a silent understanding about how superficial we were going to be.

The awfulness of the meal made our pact easy to keep. We laughed through the prawn cocktail starter and he pulled silly faces with each mouthful of roast beef in gravy. I picked at the chicken, and I could tell he was relieved that he had an excuse not to mention the eating disorder.

He only mentioned Yvonne Fairly once. 'I was sorry to miss the funeral, but you're more important to me; you do understand that, don't you?'

I nodded as if I did. 'Was there going to be a wake?'

'Of course. Nobody passes up an excuse for a party in this air force.'

'In Yvonne's lounge?' I asked. He nodded. I could see it as clearly as if I had attended: the walnut dining table; the wives in black trouser suits, their shiny court shoes grinding cake crumbs into the carpets; and the kids, sitting cross-legged in front of the television, watching something multicoloured at a respectfully low volume.

David took my hand over the table. 'It's so painful, seeing Derek this way. He's . . . Well, he's . . .'

'Destroyed?' I offered.

David plumped for, 'Very upset.'

'What about the baby? Where will she go?'

'Nobody's quite sure yet. Yvonne's parents aren't keen. They're just about to retire.'

'What does Derek want to do?' I said. I was amazed I could say his name so calmly, that this conversation was even possible.

'I don't know,' he said. He let go of my hand and I realized that I'd stumbled upon a bone of contention between the happy couple. Maybe their future wasn't quite as assured as David had led me to believe.

So I filled in the gaps with stories of Allcombe: Pru's snoring, the teenage boys in the Bosworth Slaughter, our attempts to play detectives. I made myself sound like an idiot just to make him laugh.

After coffee we drove the car to the cliffs and walked along, holding hands, staring at the sea. Other couples sneaked glances at us; we must have looked like a tourist board advertisement. We talked about superficial things in an intense manner, heads close together, voices weighted with the pretence of meaning. This was an act I found it easy to keep up, and so, apparently, did David: by the time we'd returned to the promenade and parked the car once more, the sun was long gone.

I got out of the passenger seat and ran up to the room to go for a wee. When I came back down, Pru was talking to David, and she took some getting rid of.

After she'd taken offence and flounced off to the room, David touched my back between my shoulder blades. 'I should get going.'

'When do you have to be back?' This kind of knowledge – the next call of duty – is always ingrained in the RAF officer.

'Transport plane leaves at 16.45 tomorrow. I was only given enough time for the funeral. Derek's staying longer.'

'So you have tonight,' I said with a confidence I did not feel. 'Help me find somewhere to stay for the night.'

'You're not going to stay at the Royal? With Prudence?'

'There'll be plenty of time for Pru in the morning,' I said, and he smiled. There's no love lost between David and Pru. We set off along the promenade, looking for a hotel with a lit porch or a welcoming aspect.

'How is Pru?' he said.

'Manic. Don't even get me started.'

'I don't know why you put up with it.'

I didn't know either, so I said, 'She's trying not to think about her and Steve at the moment.'

'That's understandable.'

'You know about the emails, then.' It wasn't really a question. Everybody in the RAF knows everybody else's business. I was told about the plan three weeks ago during one of the coffee mornings. Tracey Sharp whispered it to me, the other wives giggling, Pru out of earshot in the downstairs loo. I know I should tell her. But what you know and what you do are two different things, particularly if you don't fancy being on the receiving end of Pru's temper. 'It's cruel. Can't you stop it?'

As usual, he rallied to the role of hero. 'You're right. It is cruel. I'll do something about it. I would have earlier, but I've had a lot on my mind.'

I laid a hand on his elbow as we walked along, side by

side. 'Of course.' And I actually felt sympathetic. But you can't turn off love. Once it begins, it doesn't end. It's a stream that flows on, carving itself a path, no matter where it might lead or what it might destroy along the way. I read that in a greeting card once.

Can you be rational about love, dear Diary?

We'd reached the end of the promenade without seeing one welcoming light. The Bosworth Slaughter was yards away, and past that, the pier, looking like a long-abandoned bridge to nowhere.

'We could go for a drink,' David said, but it occurred to me that Phil might be lurking inside the pub, so I shook my head. A strong light, up ahead, caught my attention. It was coming from the front window of one of the fishermen's cottages, and it flickered, as if an object was moving in front of it at regular intervals. Call me morbid, but my first thought was that something large had to be swinging from the light fixture to create such an effect.

'That's Mrs Smithson's cottage,' I said aloud.

'Who?'

And then I started forward at such a pace that David was left behind. He caught up with me as I slowed to a jog.

The flickering began to make sense. The breaks in the light were caused by a figure pacing back and forth in front of the window. The silhouette of Mrs Smithson was easily recognizable: the frizzy hair, the bowed head, the bulky woollen cardigan. I couldn't see her expression, but something in the sharpness of her movements spoke of distress. I walked up to the door and knocked twice.

David came to stand beside me, and his silence told me

he felt out of his depth. I was displaying behaviour he had never seen before: running in the street, knocking on strange doors, taking the lead and leaving him behind.

The tarnished metal letterbox snapped open.

'Who is it?' Mrs Smithson called.

'I don't know if you remember me, but I'm—'

'Who's he?' she shouted over me. I bent down and met her eyes through the letterbox.

'It's my husband, Mrs Smithson. We've come to check if you're all right.'

There was a silence. The letterbox snapped shut, and the grating sound of a stiff bolt being drawn back was followed by the click of a key in a lock. The door swung open. Perhaps it was the dim light of the hallway, or the way she squinted up at David, but my first thought was that she looked older.

'I'm fine,' she said to David. She didn't even look at me. 'Thanks for asking.'

'I just had a bad feeling,' I said. 'But if you're sure you're fine . . .'

'Come in,' she said to David, and stepped to one side so that he could enter, which he did before I could decline the offer. She touched his back and steered him past the array of decorative plates fixed to the wall, through an open doorway to the left. I followed and found myself in her living room. David had already sat down on the sofa. I sat next to him, my thigh touching his.

The suite was old but well kept, with high sloping backs and angular arms that suggested the seventies. A mismatch of colour made the room feel smaller than it was; I suspected that if the spider plants in their pink macramé pot holders were removed it would feel like an empty room. A sideboard behind the one armchair held an incongruously new cordless telephone, and the tall, thin display case behind the sofa was crammed with dusty glasses, champagne flutes and tankards, and a large silver-framed photograph of a chubby baby in a white knitted cap whom I took to be Crystal. There were no photos of her as an adult.

'It's a cold night,' David said, as an apparent opening bid for small talk.

'Well, lovely to have a man in the house,' Mrs Smithson replied. She perched on the edge of her armchair, her hands in her lap, and gave a coquettish smile.

'Missing someone to keep you warm?' David said. He never could resist a flirtation.

Mrs Smithson gave a breathless little laugh. I gave a deliberately audible sigh, which got her attention. She stared at me, as if just realizing I was there. 'Where's your friend?' she said. 'The large one?'

'She's not here,' I said.

'She's asking for trouble around here. You too.' She turned her attention back to David. 'You look after them both. Those lads, they won't mess with you. They're afraid of a real man. Cats and women, that's all they're good for. I wish I had one of you meself. I feel better already, with you in the house. Cup of tea?'

'Yes please,' David said, and off she went after a victorious smile in my direction.

Did I feel resentful? Of course. But it's true to say those feelings didn't leap into life at that moment just because

David flirted with a cat-bereaved OAP with family issues. I was used to keeping my hostility buried when it came to my husband. So although I wasn't expecting to spend the evening in her company, the tea was surprisingly palatable, and when that was followed by a light meal of toast and jam, and marmite for the more adventurous, that was easy to stomach as well.

She wanted to talk to a man, that much was obvious from the outset. I got the feeling she would have told David her life story in order to get him to stay, but he didn't know what needed asking and I couldn't get a moment alone with him to tell him. Eventually it was only by coincidence that the conversation swung round to an interesting direction. Mrs Smithson was moaning about television.

'Nothing on,' she said. 'I don't know why I bother paying the licence fee. It's all policemen and flies on walls.'

'I loathe all that,' David said.

'It was much better when my daughter was on.'

I felt the muscles in my shoulders tense. In order to look uninterested, I shifted position on the sofa and pretended to inspect the display case.

'Oh really? Your daughter was on television?' David said.

Mrs Smithson puffed up in pleasure. 'Oh, all the time when she was little. A born entertainer, that one. Not now. She's gone on.' She swallowed, and bared her teeth for a moment. 'Gone on before, like. To heaven. But maybe not. Jesus doesn't like those that do it themselves, does he? Take their own lives. Still, I've got to hope for something.'

'How very sad,' David said. 'I'm so sorry for your loss.

But I'm sure you're right, and you'll see her again in heaven some day. Jesus loves everyone, doesn't he?'

'Do you really think so?'

'Of course. I'm sure of it.' I wondered if he felt guilty, giving hope to a desperate stranger in order to keep the conversation flowing. 'Jesus would never turn away someone in need, even if they had ended their own life.'

'And she was in need,' Mrs Smithson said. She leaned forward, her trembling hands pouched in the thick material of her skirt, between her knees. 'She'd had a terrible time, such a terrible time. I couldn't help her, you know. And I did try, I really did try.'

'I'm sure you did,' David soothed. 'And I'm sure she knew it, too.' He even touched one of her hands for a moment. She twitched in response and jerked her chin upwards in recognition of his maleness.

'Oh, she knew it. She told me that. But knowing a thing is not the same as acting on a thing, is it?' That was the most interesting thing she had said so far, maybe in years, but she didn't pause to give me time to consider it. She plunged her hands into the frayed pockets of her cardigan to produce a yellowed envelope that had been folded in half so often that it stayed pressed flat. 'Look at this. She wrote me this when she first went inside.'

'Inside . . . to prison?' David said. I nudged him with my knee.

Mrs Smithson nodded emphatically, and pressed the letter into his hands with the delicate precision of one handing over an heirloom for evaluation by an antiques expert. 'You can read it,' she said. 'I want you to see what a beautiful writer she was.'

David read the letter with his body angled away from me but it was easy to read over his shoulder.

Dear Mum

I don't want to see you for a while. Don't make a special effort to come here, please. Just imagine that I'm round the corner instead, fetching an ice-cream or playing hopscotch on the pier, just like a little girl again. Keep that picture of me in mind and don't even think about changing it until we're together.

I don't want to talk about what it's like in here. Instead I want to tell you about what it was like for me outside, back when everything went wrong the first time. I've never managed to tell anyone about it before, not even Tony, although I wanted to. When you two split up and he became my business manager, I wanted to very much. But he's dead, and I need someone, and that someone has to be you, Mum. That's still your job, isn't it?

So here goes.

When Dad left, I blamed you. There's nothing unusual in that, I suppose, but in my case I was right to blame you, and you knew it. You'd met one Tony Gamberetti at the Ten Items or Less queue in Tesco's, and you'd decided you had to have him. I didn't feel angry with him in the least for your weakness. I liked him straight away, and was glad when he moved in the day after Dad moved out. At least I didn't have to spend any time alone with you.

I always assumed you stopped Dad from having any further contact with me. Is that true? Or did he really just walk away for good that day? I don't suppose it matters now. Actually, I think I'd prefer not to know. Don't ever tell me.

Still, Tony was better than a dad. He always had time for me. He drove me to all my singing lessons and talent shows, do you remember? He said he'd never get tired of hearing me sing or watching me dance, and that made me feel so desirable. Not as a daughter, I'll admit. I loved to flirt with him, and I knew he'd flirt back. There always was a spark there. Even a twelve-year-old girl knows what attraction is.

So there, I've written it down. I wanted Tony straight away, even though he belonged to you, and I did what I could to drive a wedge between you. I'm sorry. For my part in what happened next, I am sorry.

Anyway, when things took off for me showbiz-wise a couple of years later Tony and I spent more and more time on the road, touring and performing and memorizing the locations of motels that did a decent English breakfast. Your relationship with Tony hadn't been going well for a while – how could it have been? – but it was still a surprise when you ended it by phone one night. He knocked on my hotel room door at midnight and told me. He wasn't at all upset, Mum. I can see now what a bastard he was to you. He didn't cry a single tear, not in front of me, anyway. But he did tell me it was time to put our relationship on a more professional footing.

I followed him back to his room and he brought out a clear plastic folder from his suitcase. It was a contract. God knows how long he'd been waiting for the right moment to produce it. I didn't read it and I could tell that pleased him. Straight after I had signed my life away, we kissed for the first time.

So he never cheated on you, technically speaking. At least not with me. Does that make you feel any better?

On the following night I sang 'The Candyman' at Princess Margaret's birthday party. I decided during the second verse that I would never see you again. And I think I would have kept to that decision if things had gone differently. So maybe everything did work out for the best, after all.

As for the actual event, the night when everything went wrong, well, really it's very commonplace. Much less exciting than everyone would have you believe.

My eighteenth birthday had come and gone without a single card. There wasn't even one from Tony, and it was obvious to both of us that my career, and our relationship, had shrunk to inconsequentiality. It wasn't necessary for either of us to point those facts out, but he did anyway. He said it loudly in the damp kitchen of the self-catering apartment we had use of during my two-week stint in the Bella Vista Holiday Complex at Margate. It was 7.45 a.m. and I'd annoyed him by slicing the bread unevenly – a common fault of mine.

I don't think I minded the sentiment much. It was more the fact that he was shouting it directly into my left ear, adding to the headache I'd woken up with. We had words: I told him not to raise his voice and he told me I was a talentless whore. So far so boring.

I was still holding the bread knife, and when he pushed me against the counter it slipped back in my hand and clipped my knuckle. I sucked the blood away and examined the pink edges of the tiny wound. Tony said he was leaving and I said good. The subject turned to money. I told him I'd start again with the money I'd made over the years, and that's when he revealed there was no money left, at least, no money that belonged to me.

I had nothing. Worse than that, I'd lost more than I'd ever made. I'd lost my family. I'd lost my mum.

After I stabbed him in the arm and the stomach, he didn't really think he was going to die. He was shocked, and expressed surprise that it didn't hurt more. I recall he was quite angry when I told him I wasn't going to call an ambulance, but he was never afraid, not even at the end. He never stopped swearing at me. His final words were a comment

*along the lines of how he'd always had to fantasize
to get it up with me.*

*Okay, so that's not an excuse, but hopefully it
gives you some idea of why I didn't speak to you for
all those years, and why you were the first person I
called after I was arrested. It's amazing how some
information, such as your mum's home telephone
number, can never be erased from your memory.*

*So, I'll see you soon, Mum. Let's leave it at that.
See you soon, and then we'll make up for lost time,
okay? No man, no mistake, is worth any more time
spent apart. You see, I know that you've always
loved me, but for some reason that love meant less
than a man's love. I can't explain. I can only finish
by writing that I love you too, Mum, and I hope
that means more to you than whatever you once felt
for the man I took away from you. I love you,
Mum.*

    Crystal

I managed to get through each page twice before David
collected it up, refolded the envelope along its creases and
handed it back, with an impressive show of care.

'What a lovely letter,' he said.

Mrs Smithson stuck it back in her pocket. 'Yes, it's meant
a lot to me, after everything that's happened, you know. Specially because we never did get to make up. She turned up on
the doorstep fresh from prison and I got such a shock. I didn't
know what to say apart from, "What brings you here, miss?"
We had a real blue and she left. Never spoke to her again.

Mum said she wanted to get back on television, but something serious, documentaries, that sort of thing, journalism, crime . . . Caught a glimpse of her in the high street, sometimes, or on the prom. Only ever from a distance. Last time was about a month before . . .'

'The suicide?' I said. David and Mrs Smithson looked at me as if I had just entered the room. 'Did that come as a surprise to you?'

She shrugged. 'She was never a very happy soul,' she said to David, as if he had asked the question. 'I s'pose it wasn't a shock, no.'

I needed to know. Let them think of me as insensitive. 'Did you think there was anything . . . unusual . . . about it? How she did it, I mean?'

For the first time she looked at me. 'Don't you be believing all the rumours you get told around here, miss. Some bad things happen in Allcombe, it's true. But life goes on here too. My family has been here for centuries, and I'll be here until I die. I think Crystal wanted to die here, too. Underneath it all, she understood the importance of place. We belong here, us Smithsons. Dead or alive, this is where we belong, and anyone who tells us otherwise is in for a fight.'

I took advantage of the following silence. 'It's late, David, and we still have to find a place to stay tonight.'

'I've got a bed made up in the spare room,' Mrs Smithson volunteered.

'That's very kind of you, but we really couldn't impose . . .'

'I'd sleep better if you were here,' she said, and the hope

in her voice told me that she had been dreading a long night alone.

David agreed without consulting me, but I can't say I minded. There was a sense of rightness about watching over that old lady; she had been through so much, carrying that letter about for months, hoping that someone like my husband would come along so that she could say – *I loved my daughter and she loved me. Here's the proof that we were once a family.*

So we stayed in the spare room, and we gave her peace of mind for one night.

We also fucked for hours.

I wanted to reclaim him as mine. The letter – the loneliness of Crystal that came through the writing as clearly as the ink had marked the page – affected me, and affected him as well, I think. So we used each other to feel loved for a little while. We made love as if we were an old married couple: with the lights off, the dusty mattress creaking, no words, no kisses, just soft, slow movements and the comfort of a gently reached climax.

I'd recommend that kind of sex. People are so quick to throw the familiar away. The grass is always greener, that's the cliché, isn't it? Well, last night I got a glimpse of how it could have been if David had noticed that our grass was as green as the Emerald City.

But he's thrown me away. And that realization has brought me to the knowledge that this really is the end of our marriage. Unless a miracle happens, we will no longer be a family.

In the morning we left the house before Mrs Smithson had

surfaced. The sun was barely up by the time David hopped into his MG and drove himself away without a word. For the first time since I've known him, he looked guilty.

And now I'm back in the hotel room at the Royal. I'll have a shower and change my clothes, put on something that makes me feel good. Pru is not here. She hasn't left a note. I'll have to go looking for her, so that she can begin her interrogation. None of it will seem real until I've denied it ever happened.

Thirty-one

Case 476: Mrs Prudence Elspeth Green
Transcript of conversation recorded Monday,
13 December 2004, 8.53 a.m.
Location: Mingles department store – internet café

PATTEN: I've been looking for you everywhere.

GREEN: Starting in your husband's trousers?

PATTEN: If it's going to be that kind of conversation, let me drink my tea first.

GREEN: Overtired, are we?

PATTEN: Yes, actually. I've been up talking all night.

GREEN: I'll bet you have.

PATTEN: Deciding on the future. Trying to plan my life, unlike some people.

GREEN: Are you telling me David gave you some sort of choice about what happens next? How did he put that? 'So, Lena, do you want us to stay married? You could sleep on the sofa or in our bed with my butch widowed lover.'

PATTEN: I don't think I'm going to discuss this with you.

GREEN: Are you getting a divorce?

PATTEN: I'm not discussing it.

GREEN: Do you think you'll move off the base?

PATTEN: Do you think you'll ever tell me what happened
to you when you were younger?

GREEN: Tell you what. You drink your tea and I'll read
the paper.

'You? Interested in what happens outside your little world all of a sudden?' Lena said. Her mouth was turned down at the corners; I couldn't tell if it was from annoyance at me or the bland taste of the tea. The expression was at odds with the low-necked pink jumper and snow-white jeans she wore.

'It's the local rag. Someone left it outside our room.' I smoothed it out on the plastic tabletop and read the headline of the *Allcombe Post*:

BIN DAY MOVED TO TUESDAY

'Maybe that's it.'

'What?' Lena inclined her head to read over my shoulder. 'Someone in Allcombe is desperate to let you know the timetable for rubbish collection?'

'Don't you remember what Gladys said?'

Lena's lips parted and her gaze wandered up to the ceiling.

'Do you even remember her?' I said. 'That woman you were so desperate to help? Or have events in your own life overtaken all other considerations?'

'Of course I remember her. Why what she said relates to bin day is beyond me.'

I took a quick look around the restaurant. It was empty.

Even the acne-ridden teenager who usually skulked behind the counter had vanished. I could see his jaunty candy-striped hat poking up from the far side of the shop – the ladies' underwear section. 'You know what she said about the residents being . . . you know . . . bumped off . . .'

'And smuggled out in bin bags,' Lena finished. So your theory is that one of the residents has been murdered in the past week and the body will be sitting somewhere in a black plastic sack because the council isn't going to collect it until tomorrow, and someone wants us to know this so that we'll go over and investigate and find the evidence we need in order to prosecute the owner of the Paradise.'

'Look,' I said. 'If you have any better ideas . . .'

'If we're going back into the Paradise again, it's to look for some real evidence, not turn out bin bags on the strength of one mad woman's fevered imagination. If you even begin to think it through you'll realize that they wouldn't be putting obituaries in the paper for old ladies who've been taken to the town dump by uncharacteristically helpful dustmen, because there wouldn't be any bodies, for a start, would there? We'd be looking for Crystal's missing grandmother, not wondering how her funeral expenses were paid.'

'So the bin bag thing is stupid, then,' I said.

'Yes. Besides, I'm wearing a nice outfit and I don't intend to get it dirty.'

A brainwave occurred to me. 'How about accounts?'

'What?'

'If P . . . Penhaligon is ripping people off, surely it would show somewhere in the accounts? Dodgy payments? Used chequebooks, something like that? We could get into his office and try to pin him down that way. Like Al Capone.'

Lena sniffed. 'Sounds marginally better than turning out bin bags.'

'Are you prepared to do anything that doesn't involve chasing your gay husband around to satisfy your own selfish urges?'

'He has a name, as you well know. David.'

'Yes. David "Arse Bandit" Patten.'

Lena slammed her hand down on the table. The empty teacup skittered in its saucer and clattered down to rest on its handle. The noise reverberated through the café. When it dissipated there was only silence left; a scary silence. One that told me I had succeeded in pushing Lena's buttons. I felt equal amounts of triumph and fear.

She righted the teacup and held it steady in the saucer by her fingertips, as if it were delicate porcelain rather than a 99p special. 'I think that maybe it's time to just—'

'FUCKING WHORE!'

It came from the other side of the store. It was a male voice, abrasive and shrill, shocking in its volume. Lena's head snapped up. I followed her gaze to the outdoor clothing department.

There was nobody to be seen.

I tracked my gaze left, over to ladies' underwear. The counter assistant's head was visible over a row of black satin basques. His expression was comical with surprise.

'FUCKING CHEAP SLAG!'

'Who's there?' I called. I stood up and my plastic chair shrieked backwards over the linoleum.

'Leave it, Pru,' Lena muttered.

'I will not!' I said, ashamed that it was the most venomous thing I'd managed to say so far.

'Honestly, its fine, I don't care . . .' There was something smug in the way she was sitting there, shrugging her shoulders and blushing as if she was the wronged woman in all this.

'What makes you think that comment was addressed at you?' I said.

She stared at me.

'I'm just saying . . .' I backtracked.

'Spill.'

'I'm just saying it might be something to do with Mike Tunnell, that's all.'

'Mike Tunnell?' The surprise in her voice was galling.

'Look, it was just one snog, no biggie,' I said. I folded up the newspaper and handed it to her. She took it without glancing at it. I felt an immense satisfaction to be the one with a sexual conquest for once – I wasn't about to ruin that feeling by telling her the truth.

'FUCKING JUMPED-UP TART!'

'Did that sound like Mr Tunnell to you?' Lena said.

She was right. I didn't seriously think that it was Mike Tunnell. Still, it was time to put an end to the abuse, even if it wasn't aimed at me. 'Ninety-nine!' I called out. 'One hundred!'

'What?' said Lena.

'COMING, READY OR NOT!' I charged through the chairs and headed for the outdoor clothing section. I reached the first section of cagoules and rattled the rail. A tall, slim figure darted out from behind one of the mirrored pillars and made a dash for the escalator.

It was Phil. I would have known that greasy blond hair and beanpole body anywhere.

'You . . . a-hole!' I called after him. He turned, mid-flight, and presented me with the finger. Then he tripped on the foot of a hat display and sprawled on to the floor.

I walked up to him, wondering what I was going to say upon arrival. Luckily, he decided to prop himself up on one elbow and recline on the carpet in a male centrefold position, and this gave me the ammunition I needed.

'You look like a prize twit.'

'Fuck off, you fat old bag,' he said. He climbed to his feet. His black T-shirt was dotted with beige fuzz from the carpet, and the pale blue waistband of his boxer shorts was visible over the lip of his expensive brand of jeans. 'You're gonna get yours.'

'Was that comment directed at me?' I asked in my best scary voice.

He snorted. 'Don't make me fucking laugh.'

I knew he had dangerous friends, but there was no way I was going to back down to the oversexed runt on his own. 'I'll make you laugh, you sorry little excuse for a—'

'That's enough,' Lena said from behind me. I turned and faced her. She was pale and poised, her right hand clenched, the local paper rolled up into a tube in her left. 'Please, Pru, I can handle it.'

I shrugged and stepped back. She walked up to Phil until there was less than a metre between them. In her pink and white outfit, with her hair pulled back into a severe bun, she looked like a prim teacher about to scold an unruly pupil.

'Philip,' she said, in a voice as cold as a tray of ice cubes.

'What?' he said. The squeak was back in his throat.

She didn't take her eyes from him. Her left hand came up over her head. For a moment she resembled the Statue of Liberty. Then she smacked the local paper down hard on the top of Phil's head.

He cringed. When she stepped away from him, he looked so utterly chastised, so like a boy on the wrong side of his mother, that I couldn't help but laugh.

A deep shade of red shot through his cheeks and joined all his spots together in a mottled flush. He snatched the paper from Lena and held it in front of her nose. She didn't flinch, to her credit. 'If you're not careful you're going to end up on page thirty-four,' he said. Then he hooked one finger into the V of her jumper and pulled the material to make a tent, into which he rammed the newspaper.

I kept silent. There were times to get involved, and this didn't strike me as one of them. Instead I watched as they eyeballed each other, looking absolutely nothing like lovers. Eventually Phil walked away. He moved through outerwear with a pronounced limp. He must have twisted his ankle when he fell over the carousel; it seemed there was some justice in the world. I watched him travel down the escalator until the top of his greasy head disappeared from view.

Lena pulled the newspaper from her cleavage, unrolled it, and leafed through the pages with quick flicks of her fingers, her head scanning backwards and forwards as if she was watching a tennis match on fast forward.

'So what's on page thirty-four, then?' I asked.

She pursed her lips. 'Obituaries.'

'Mmmm. A five-syllable word. No wonder he couldn't manage to just say it.'

She drew in a large breath and locked her eyes on mine. 'What is it?'

'That's why you were left the paper. Someone wanted you to look at the obituaries.'

'Who did? Phil? Mrs Smithson?'

She shrugged and handed me the paper. I scanned the messily organized obits; it looked like a fairly boring list of local dead people. None of the names meant anything to me. 'Am I meant to be seeing something significant?'

She leaned over me and tapped a fingernail against a four-line announcement:

> Gladys Little, born 5 March 1924, died in her
> sleep 11 December 2004. Will be missed by
> loving daughter and friends at the Paradise.

'Murder at the Paradise,' I breathed. 'It has to be . . .'

'Not just that,' Lena said. 'Look again. Look at the name.'

Gladys.

The little old lady who had helped us that day when we first set foot in the Paradise was dead.

Thirty-two

'Okay, so we enter the establishment, we locate Mr Pen-haligon's office and look for any accounts or records, if we find anything relevant we contact the authorities.'

'Or, to put it more directly,' I said, 'we sneak in, we have a gander at his inner sanctum, we run like stink.'

'Just trying to use the correct terminology,' Lena said, rather huffily, I thought. Perhaps it was nerves. Standing outside the Paradise at 11.30 on a freezing Monday morning with the intention of putting yourself in a highly dangerous situation was not my idea of a relaxing time.

'Are we going in the front door?' Lena said.

We stared at it from the railings along the promenade, the sea wind whipping across our backs. It was open. The lobby desk and the grand staircase were just visible in the grey daylight.

'We could make a bolt for it,' I suggested. 'In the front, through the main room. The office must be in the back, mustn't it?'

'I suppose so.'

'What if we see Mr Potato Head?'

'Penhaligon,' Lena corrected. 'Mr Penhaligon. I don't know. Run the other way?'

It wasn't much of a plan but it was all we had. 'Okay.'

Lena took a deep breath and tucked her hair behind her ears. 'Right then.'

'Is that what you do when you're getting ready to run? You rearrange your hair?'

'Shut up and give me your hand.'

She pulled at my sleeve until I unclenched my fist enough for her to slip her own, much smaller, hand inside. Her skin was colder than mine, and very dry. I felt her nails, long and brittle, press into my palm.

It was impossible to deny the urge to squeeze in response.

'Shall I count to three?' I said.

'No.' She sprang forward as if from starting blocks, and dragged me along with her, our elbows banging against each other until we fell into step.

We reached the main room, both out of breath, and were once more surrounded by the clusters of threadbare armchairs and the pungent smell of old lady. It was empty, and Lena dragged me onwards, through the door at the back of the room.

A long corridor with no natural light to break the gloom awaited us. The carpet was a faded plum colour, and dusty framed prints of seascapes punctuated the yellowing walls. We passed perhaps ten of them, and then Lena jerked me into a sharp right turn. We found ourselves in a strip-lit kitchen, permeated with the smell of old fat. Ten deep-fat fryers sat on a long greasy counter on our right. Beyond that were two huge black ovens and a row of off-white refrigerators with squat grey feet fixed to the tacky lino.

We ran to the door at the back of the room and found ourselves in a small utility area with high brick walls. A selection of filthy mops and buckets skulked in the far corner.

'Wrong turn,' I said. 'Go back.'

We turned round, and he was standing in the kitchen.

'Hello, ladies,' Mr Penhaligon said.

I would have run if there was any way to be sure that Lena would follow. But Lena and I had not communicated for any such eventuality. There were no hand signals I could make that she would understand, and nothing I could do to be sure she would follow my lead.

So I turned round and locked eyes with Mr Penhaligon. His real name came easily to mind; he didn't look like a children's toy to me any more. 'Hello,' I said.

He took five steps forward to draw level with the counters, and clicked his heels together. 'Were you planning on mopping up?'

'Let's just say something stinks around here.'

He opened the nearest drawer and took out a wooden-handled butcher's knife. The sharp edge was dotted with rust, or maybe it was dried-on food. 'Mmm,' he said. 'This needs sharpening. Seen too much use. Does anyone know the law regarding defending oneself from trespassers?'

'We weren't trespassers,' Lena said behind me. 'We're hygiene inspectors.'

She really was the most atrocious liar.

'I don't want to pressure you, but I think the best course of action would be for you both to come with me,' Mr Penhaligon said. He gestured with the knife, moving the tip in an arc towards the door we had come through.

Lena moved first. As she passed me she grasped the hem of my jumper, and pulled me along behind her, keeping me so close that my breasts were pressed against her back and her hand was squashed against my abdomen. I could feel her breathing, fast and shallow, and smell her sweat.

I didn't dare to look at Penhaligon as we passed him. Instead I concentrated on the knife. He held it with a floppy wrist, as if it were a frying pan and he was about to toss a pancake.

For some reason I remembered a time a couple of years ago, when I'd gone into the attic to find a photograph of my mother to remind myself of her pale drawn face and slumped shoulders. I'd tiptoed across the exposed joists, torch in hand, then realized that the constant humming was not coming from the hot water tank, but from the massive wasps' nest directly over my head. As I'd made my way back and lowered myself down the ladder, I'd watched that nest as I watched Penhaligon's rusty knife.

We walked past him and I heard him fall into step behind us. I could picture the knife, inches from the small of my back. And then a strange thing happened. I separated, in my head, into two people. One was calmly weighing up escape options. The other was a ball of fear, rolled up tighter than a hedgehog in a bonfire.

'Are you going to phone the police?' Lena said.

'Left here,' said Penhaligon, directing us further down a darkening corridor, away from the relative safety of the main room. The corridor swung to the right. The carpet ended in a tangle of loose cords and revealed the unpolished floor-boards underneath. I heard footsteps overhead, slow and dragging, but there seemed no point in calling out to some old biddy who would lock herself in her room at the first sign of trouble. Besides, what would I shout? I couldn't think of any short phrase that might do the situation justice.

'Did you kill Gladys?' Lena said.

Penhaligon said nothing.

'Where are you taking us?' Lena said. I wished she'd shut up.

'People are looking for us,' she said. 'People know we're here.'

'Stop,' Penhaligon said. We came to a halt in front of a small panelled door that had been painted carelessly in the same dingy yellow colour as the wall. The paint had splashed on to the tarnished brass handle and the large bolt. 'Open the door.'

Lena hesitated, then reached out a hand and tried the bolt. It didn't move. She put both hands to it and tugged it, an inch at a time, until it released the door. Then she turned the knob and put her shoulder to the door. It shuddered as it moved backwards across the floor to reveal the darkness behind it.

'Where are we?' she said. Her voice was a hostage to her fear; she could hardly squeak out her words.

For the first time Penhaligon answered one of her questions. I could hear the smile behind his words.

'It's the basement,' he said.

And then I felt the point of the knife, like the sting of a wasp between my shoulders, urging me forward into the black.

Thirty-three

Lena pushed back against me and the knife sank deeper into my skin. I hissed in pain.

'Move,' said Penhaligon. 'Down the steps.' He sounded on the verge of laughter.

I would have turned, wrestled with him, done all the things the self-defence books tell you to do, but no thought came to mind but staying with Lena. We had to be together. Together, everything would somehow work out all right.

Lena let go of my jumper and stretched her arms out to touch the nearest wall. She ran her hands along it as she edged past the door. 'What steps? It's too dark.'

The knife twisted in my back and I jumped forward so I was pressed against Lena. 'Go!' I said, and she must have heard the panic in my voice because she started to walk into the dark, her hands flapping like birds' wings, her feet taking short jerky steps, all her grace robbed by fear. I saw her right foot shoot forward and her hip followed; she let out a loud gasp, and then she was gone from sight. There was the clatter of her body hitting the stairs, each thud solid and sickening.

Silence took hold once more.

'Lena?' I called.

Nothing.

I think my heart stopped beating.

I was alone, really alone, and all I wanted was for Lena's voice to rise up from that basement.

'Lena?'

So that was real terror. To call, and for nobody to answer.

'Your turn,' said Penhaligon. I felt the point of the knife move down my spine, scoring a line of fire into my skin.

I did the only thing I could. I got down on my hands and knees and, accompanied by the sound of Penhaligon's laughter, I crawled forward until I could feel the edge of the top stone step. I lowered myself into the basement, one stair at a time.

'Maybe this will teach you a lesson,' he called. For a moment he sounded like a schoolteacher.

His laughter gave way to the sound of the scraping of the door against the floor as he pulled it shut. I heard the squeak and the thud of the bolt being drawn. Then his footsteps receded.

I made it to the bottom of the stairs and lost myself in the darkness.

Thirty-four

I don't know how long I'd been crying for before I realized something was tugging at my leg.

I lashed out with my foot and scuttled backwards until I could feel brick wall against my back. Maybe I'd watched too many horror films, but my first thought was that Gladys had come back to life and was pawing at me to get my attention.

'Ow,' said Lena, and I was drenched in utter happiness. Then I remembered that I was trapped in a basement with death awaiting me at the hands of a knife-wielding maniac, and the moment of rapture passed.

'What're you bloody playing at?' I said. 'You scared me stupid.'

'I'm fine, thanks for your concern.'

'Really?'

'My elbow hurts a bit,' she said. 'I bashed it. And I'm freezing.'

It was icy cold in the basement, but at least I had layers of fat to insulate me. I was sure she would be shivering already.

'Can you see anything?' she said.

Everything was black. 'It'll take a while for our eyes to adjust.'

'Depends on how dark it is, doesn't it? Is there a limit of darkness?'

'I don't know.' I thought about it for a minute. 'Lena?'

'Yes?'

'I've just realized we know toss all about anything.'

'You're right,' she said. She didn't sound angry; more depressed, if anything.

'We don't know anything about Crystal, or this place, or why we've been locked up.'

'I don't think it's to prepare us for roles in *Prisoner Cell Block H*, Pru.'

Although I couldn't see anything, my nose was working fine. There was a strange, earthy smell emanating from somewhere nearby. It was a smell I was certain I had come across recently, only days ago. I tried to ignore it and focus on my train of thought.

'But what have we actually found out?' I said. 'What do we know?'

Lena sighed. 'All right, let's start from the top and work through this thing.'

'Right: Penhaligon's scared.'

She snorted.

'He wouldn't have locked us up if he wasn't scared,' I continued. 'That means he thinks we know something. So something dodgy must be going on here. Maybe murder. Maybe not.'

'Fair enough.' I heard a tremor in her voice. The cold was

beginning to take hold of her. 'But everyone in the town seems to think it's murder. And the residents are all convinced.'

'And Crystal's gran was a resident,' I said, 'so she must have known about it too. So why didn't she tell Crystal?'

'Maybe she did.' I heard Lena take a big swallow. 'Oh wait. Wait. Maybe Crystal told her.'

'What?'

'Mrs Smithson said that Crystal was hoping to get into investigative journalism. If she suspected the Paradise – and why wouldn't she, coming from this town? – she might have decided to look into it. It would be a great scoop.'

'When did Mrs Smithson say that? About investigative journalism?'

Her intake of breath told me there was a secret there she didn't want to share. 'Look, can we not get sidetracked? The point is, if she wanted to get some evidence, the best way of doing it would be a plant, wouldn't it? On the inside?'

'The gran?'

'The gran,' Lena confirmed. 'Looking for clues. Feeding information back during Crystal's weekly visits.'

'Right,' I said, filing away Lena's secretive attitude for later probing if we got out of here. 'That could be it.'

'So if Penhaligon discovered this, he could well have decided to . . . nip it in the bud. By getting rid of both people involved. Kill the grandmother, kill Crystal.'

'Maybe,' I said. 'Or maybe he does the gran, and Crystal kills herself after anyway. Solves his problem.'

'Maybe,' she echoed. 'I suppose – I don't know . . .' I could hear her concentration ebbing away. The cold was intense, and I was becoming aware of a gnawing sensation in my fingers and the tips of my ears, as if the icy air had tiny teeth.

'So we're no further ahead,' I said. 'We know nothing for sure. Nothing.'

'I can't feel my face,' Lena mumbled. I swept the ground with my hand until I found her leg, as cold as the concrete. I pulled at her calf until she moved closer to me, and slid my arms around her waist.

'Good idea,' she said. 'Keep warm. Fripl.'

'Fripl?'

'Fripl. It's still the key. Why did Crystal mention it? If it *was* Crystal who wrote that suicide note?'

I put my chin on her shoulder. 'Don't know,' I whispered. In the absolute dark, with her body so close, it was easy to believe that we were one person. 'Listen, Lena, I . . .'

'I know,' she said.

'And I'm sorry.'

'I know that too. You don't have to—'

'But I want to say it.'

'We're okay,' she said. 'We're okay.'

'Yes.' I couldn't tell if my eyes were open or closed. All I could feel was the soft, slow rhythm of her breathing. I wanted to crawl inside her and hibernate.

'Is this the end?' she whispered.

I tried to picture it. The end. It wouldn't come. Surely a person knows when they're about to die. They think of last words, or write letters to loved ones. I was getting no inspiration. 'I don't think so.'

'If this is the end, will you tell me something?'

I kissed her shoulder through her thin pink jumper. She always looked so good in that jumper. 'What?'

'What happened to you when you were seventeen, Pru?'

I thought about answering her question. I wondered where to begin, how to make myself go back there in my mind and relive the worst moment of my life, worse even than this moment. As I turned it this way and that way, I felt new warmth spread from my stomach and force its way along my veins to the ends of my fingers and toes. It was anger.

I pushed her away and forced my stiff legs to unbend so that I could stand up. 'We're getting out of here,' I said. 'This isn't our time.'

'How do you—'

'Shut up, get off your bony bottom and help me.' I swept the air with my hands and took tiny steps in what I guessed was the direction of the stairs.

'What's got up your nose?' Lena said. There was a new energy in her voice that gave me hope.

'Maybe our last moments together, and you want me to relive some awful event from my past. Well, up yours! You know, in some ways, you're the most selfish bitch I ever met.'

'Right,' she said. 'That'll teach me to be nice to you, you cow.' I heard her scuffle about on the floor.

'What are you doing?'

'Ignoring your bloody stupid rules and having a bloody cigarette.'

'You see? How much more selfish can you get? Not only am I trapped in a small space, now I've got to breathe in your smoke.' A thought occurred to me. 'You've still got your handbag on you? So you've got your mobile?'

'The battery's run down. I forgot to bring the charger.'

'Well, why have a bloody phone if you're not going to keep it bloody well charged?'

'Well, why don't you have your own phone instead of relying on me, you Luddite?'

'Like I need one more piece of equipment to tell me nobody's trying to get in touch with me.' I took a deep breath, then heard the dry rasp of a zip being pulled. 'Hang on. If you've got cigarettes in your handbag, you've got a lighter.'

The scuffling noise stopped. 'I forgot,' she said. 'I have got a lighter.'

I took a huge breath, feeling my lungs swell and my mind clear of panic. 'It didn't occur to you that a naked flame might throw a little light on things?'

'Okay, okay.' I heard her fumble with her handbag. 'I've got it.'

'Well, light it, Watson.'

'Right.'

I know why she paused. It was like a moment in one of those horror films. The fear of seeing what was hidden, of thinking an escape had been found and instead finding the face of a mad axe-murderer, was palpable. We had to dispel the dark, but with it we'd dispel our uncertainty.

She flicked the lighter.

An orange flame sprang up. It trembled in time with Lena's white, shivering hand. At first there was only the glare of light. Then my eyes began to adjust, and the blackness of the basement shrank back to reveal a large room, its four high brick walls shiny with damp. There was an uneven stone staircase, and at the top of that were the thick wood panels of the locked door.

The world shifted back into perspective. The cold didn't seem so disabling, and the dark didn't feel so hostile. We were both frightened, that was all, but we were alive.

Lena uncurled and stood up slowly, one hand wrapped around the other, the lighter held high like a beacon. Her eyes had a liquid look and her forehead seemed huge. The rest of her face was lost to the shadows.

'You okay?' I said.

She nodded. 'What should we do now?'

'Walk around. Look in all the corners for something we can use to break down the door, or turn into a weapon, anything. Come on.' I grabbed her jumper and pulled her towards me. She put one hand as far around my waist as she could reach and held the lighter in front of us with the other. Together we shuffled to the wall nearest the stairs and began the process of searching, one step at a time, anti-clockwise around the basement.

'Do you think Penhaligon's a loony?' Lena said.

'I don't think he's lining up for a Mr Normal award. He's probably a psychopath.'

'A psychopath or a sociopath?'

'What's the diff?' I said. 'When did you come over all Jungian?'

She cleared her throat. 'I've been doing some reading about that sort of thing.' I could tell we'd reached another area that she didn't want to discuss.

'Reading about psychos? Real-life crime stuff? Ed Gein, Jeffery Dahmer? Heads in fridges, human-skin lampshades?'

The flame snapped off. The darkness was total. I heard Lena's fingers on the lighter, once, twice. On the third try it sputtered back to life. 'Stop it, Pru. No, I've been reading about psychiatry. I'm thinking about taking a course, retraining as something, maybe as a counsellor. I've always been interested in what people think.'

We hit a corner and turned to the left. 'So that's why you've been trying to psychoanalyse me recently. All this "look into your past" claptrap.'

'That's not it,' she snapped. 'Is it me or is that funny smell coming from over here?'

We were approaching the third corner of the basement, and had found our first object on the floor. The flame from the lighter was dimmer – running out of gas, I assumed – so it was difficult to make out exactly what we were looking at. The light was being reflected at strange angles from its shiny, broken surface.

'What is that?' I said.

'Not sure.'

We shuffled a little closer. The smell of dead leaves intensified. I placed where I had come across it before.

It was the smell of death.

And that's when I realized what we had found.

'A bin bag,' I said, my voice wavering like the flame of the lighter. 'That's a bin bag.'

Thirty-five

There was a thump, followed by another. Then another.

The sounds became rhythmic, like the banging of a heart-beat against a ribcage. They reverberated through the basement.

'It's coming from the bin bag,' Lena whispered, high and fast. I shook my head. They were footsteps, overhead, moving to the door, and then they were replaced by the grating noise of a bolt being drawn back.

'Oh God,' Lena said. 'Oh my God.'

The lighter gave up and we were left in utter darkness once more.

The door scraped against the stone floor as it opened, inches at a time. Lena's hand tightened around my waist; I covered it with both of mine. 'I love you,' I said.

She didn't move. 'I love you too.'

The door, half open, stopped moving. The dim light of the corridor above spilled on to us. Illuminated against it, standing in the doorway, was the silhouette of a tall man. From his outline I could tell he was more muscled and stood straighter than Penhaligon.

He didn't speak.

'Come to do your job, have you?' I called. I was amazed by the strength of my voice.

'Pru,' he said. He coughed. And then I placed the voice.

'Mike?' I said. 'Mike Tunnell?'

Thirty-six

'Thank God,' Lena whispered. Trust her to find religion.

'We've got to get out of here,' Mike Tunnell said.

'You're not working for Penhaligon?'

'Don't be stupid, Pru,' Lena said. She tugged at my hands, and when I didn't respond, she pinched the skin on my knuckles. 'Come on, let's go, let's go.'

'Quick,' Mike called.

'But I don't understand—'

'Later!'

'I just need to look in this bin bag,' I said.

'No, Pru,' said Lena.

'I just have to . . .' I slipped my sweaty palms from Lena's grasp and touched the yellow tie at the top of the bag. It was tightly knotted; it would be easier to rip the liner.

'No!' She was desperate, but she didn't move. I had to admire her commitment to me. Maybe she did love me after all. 'Please, Pru, I can't take any more. Let's go; I just want to go, okay?'

'Just let me . . .' I slid my hands from the tie to the side of the bag and squeezed. The shock of solid material through the thin plastic layer struck me; the contents of the bag were heavy, doughy. The picture I got in my head was of a grey, dimpled thigh, patterned with broken veins and yellow-green bruises. I moved my hand downwards and squeezed something bony and circular; my mind informed me it was a kneecap.

'Please,' Lena said. 'Please!' She'd never asked me for anything in that tone of voice before. I felt sure she was about to drop to the floor and beg. But still she hadn't left without me. To her, we were together, no matter what. It was us against the world.

And because I couldn't bear to stretch her love for me any further, for fear of destroying it at the moment of discovery, I took my hands away from the bin bag and led her up the stairs and out of the basement.

Thirty-seven

We sat in the room in which Crystal Tynee's body had been found, side by side on Mike Tunnell's bed, looking at the curling corner of damp wallpaper next to the large oak wardrobe.

'Excuse me for pointing this out,' I said, 'but this wouldn't seem to be the safest place to hide out under the circumstances.'

Lena squeezed my hand, hard. She was staring at the meadow-print cover of the duvet as if it were a Magic Eye picture. The room smelled of strong aftershave, Old Spice or Kouros, maybe. An ironed blue shirt on a metal hanger was on the back of the wardrobe door.

Mike crouched and retrieved a black holdall from the bottom of the wardrobe, his jeans showing the strain of containing his muscular thighs and buttocks. As he unzipped it, I saw a mess of tiny cassettes and a sheaf of A4 paper with typescript upon it. He reached up, took the shirt from the hanger, and threw it into the holdall.

He straightened up and ran his hands through his hair.

Then he crossed to the bay window and looked out over the promenade, scanning from right to left. Apart from the expertly bunched jeans, he was wearing a checked shirt, the cuffs rolled back, and thick-soled boots. He was obviously one of those men who didn't feel the cold.

'It can't be helped,' he said. 'I couldn't leave my notes behind. And we should have a few minutes before they realize you've gone.'

Next to me, Lena was visibly shivering, her leather jacket offering no protection from fear. I pulled the duvet over our shoulders. Lena held one corner and I held the other. She shuddered and then let out a sigh that disintegrated into a cascade of soft sobs. From the corner of my eye I saw tears trickle down her face and cling to her chin. It wasn't long before she started to hiccup.

'I'm never – going – to get – over this,' she said.

'Oh you will,' I said. 'Think of home. Think of coffee-and-walnut sponge.' But that thought led only to memories of Yvonne Fairly, large and limp in her wedding dress, and the reason we had run away in the first place.

'I don't understand anything,' Lena said. I squeezed her shoulder through the duvet. Mike Tunnell finally turned round and looked us over with eyes narrowed to slits.

'Right, listen up,' he said. 'This town isn't safe for you. You need to go to your room and pack your bags. Right now.'

I stared at him.

'Come on,' he said.

It was the tone of his voice that got to me. 'Look, just because you saved us, doesn't give you the right to boss us about,' I said.

'I would have thought you'd realize that getting out of Allcombe was a priority.'

'It's not up to you, so I don't really care what you think.'

His cheeks puffed and his lips pinched into a line. Men always do anger so well. Sometimes I think it's the only emotion they're any good at.

'I'm not going anywhere until you tell me how you knew we were in that basement,' I said.

He smoothed his moustache. 'Is that really important?'

'Crucial, I would have said.'

He pointed at Lena, who paled amidst the meadow-print; more accurately, he pointed at her feet. I followed the line of his finger to find her crocodile handbag on the receiving end. The strap was tangled in one of her high heels. She drew up her feet carefully.

'At the bottom,' he said.

Lena swung her body round so she was lying flat on the bed, her legs behind me, and reached over to squint into it. 'What am I looking for? This?' She produced a dotted black disc that resembled the mouthpiece of an old-fashioned telephone. 'What's it for?'

Mike Tunnell bared his teeth in a forced smile. 'It's a listening device.'

'You've been bugging us?' Lena dropped the disc on the floor as if it were a spider.

'Well, I am a private detective,' he said.

I didn't feel violated or vengeful, or any of the things that flashed through my mind as possible emotions to express. I felt pleased. It was bizarre, but my first reaction was that we must have been right about Crystal's murder and the goings-on at the Paradise, for here was a private dick, stalking us, treating us as a danger at the behest of some shady character.

'Penhaligon. It has to be Penhaligon. He hired you, am I on the right lines? And you realized he's the bad guy in all this, right? So what do you know about the Tynee case?' The idea of pooling knowledge was intoxicating. I wanted to be a real solver of mysteries; a person that had some answers.

Mike coughed and folded his arms over his chest. 'Nothing.'

I stood up. 'What?'

'I don't know anything about Crystal Tynee. She was never my assignment. You were my assignment. Case 476. I planted the bug two weeks before you decided to come to Allcombe. I heard what you were planning to do, and drove down the night before you got here.'

'Before we . . .'

'Just you,' he corrected. 'But you're difficult to bug, not having a handbag and so on.'

'Just me?' I said. It didn't make any sense. As if Lena sensed that she had just been demoted in the importance of things, she let out a long sigh, turned over, and pulled the duvet over her head.

'The job was to tail you,' Mike said. He looked tired too. His shoulders had fallen and his stance was softer than usual. Maybe his pity for me, visible in his wet-eyed gaze, was a weakness. 'Record your conversations. Report back on everything you do.'

'I don't get it.' I scratched my cheek; I could feel the heat of my blood rushing under my skin, making my nerves prickle. 'Who would be interested in me?'

'Your husband.'

I stepped close to him and searched those hangdog eyes for a sign of a lie. 'That can't be right,' I told him, even when I didn't find one. 'It must have been somebody else, somebody pretending to be Steve. He's not even in the country. He hasn't been for months.'

'It was him,' Mike said with smug conviction. 'He wanted to see if you were having an affair. Or thinking about having an affair. Or even just open to the possibility. He gave me a photograph of you, from your wedding day. You had a red rose bouquet and he was wearing a silver waistcoat. He told me every detail of your personality. Believe me, he couldn't have made it up. It was Steve Green, your husband.'

It took a huge effort to find my voice. 'Where? Where was he when you met him?'

I heard a rustling behind me. Lena sat up to show her solemn, tear-stained face to the room. Her long hair hung in straggly tangles, and her mascara had clumped in the corners of her eyes.

'Shrewsbury,' she said. 'They met in Shrewsbury.'

Thirty-eight

Lena glanced at Mike Tunnell. 'Am I right?'

'Telford, actually. I'm based in Telford, but you're right, he's living in Shawbury, just outside Shrewsbury.'

I shook my head. 'He's in the desert.'

'No, he's not.' Lena scraped her hair back from her face. 'Maybe you'd better sit down again, Pru.'

'Just tell me why he's not in the desert with everybody else's husband.'

'He was, to start with. About three months ago he got posted back to the UK. To RAF Shawbury. Changing from Charlie-130s to helicopters.' She held up her hands, palms facing me. 'I'm only telling you what Tracey Sharp told me. The Housing Officer was informed that you'd decided to stay in Lyneham, and keep the house. Steve moved into the Mess at Shawbury. I don't know why.'

I looked around the room, at the hulk of a wardrobe and the limp, dusty curtains. There was nothing from which I could draw comfort, and least of all the pitying expressions on Lena's and Mike's faces.

I couldn't blame Steve. We were a terrible couple, always had been. Even at the beginning, when we took romantic holidays together: Paris, Rome, Vienna, ate from each other's forks and made up pet nicknames, it felt like a disguise we were wearing rather than an attempt to be naked and comfortable in another human being's presence. We'd been Moo and Meeve for a year at best, and, personally, I'd found it a relief to drop the silly affectations for grunts and farts in bed.

And I'd been so horrible to him. Telling him to piss off, take a posting, have an affair: anything to leave me in peace. I had thought myself separate from him. But it seemed that the act of being a couple had become second nature to me. Why else would I feel as if my security blanket had just been snatched away from my grubby little fingers?

A thought occurred to me. 'But the emails . . . they came through the MOD Basra account. They had to come from the desert.'

Lena dropped her eyes to her fingers, tracing an endless pattern on the duvet. 'I asked David about that. Darren Sharp was sending them from out there, so that you wouldn't get suspicious, you know, if you saw a normal email address.'

'I thought the tone was wrong,' I said. 'Too loving.' Steve must have asked him to send them. I knew Flight Lieutenant Sharp, mostly through the tales told by his bulldog-faced wife of their happy marriage, his sensitive side, how he was a man who could be trusted. Steve must have congratulated himself on enlisting the help of someone who could keep a secret. My husband was an RAF man through and through, but he still hadn't learned that every secret gets found out in the end.

I had no doubt that if David knew and Lena knew, so did every other smug cow on the base.

But wasn't it exactly what I deserved?

'Why didn't you tell me?' I asked Lena.

She had the grace to look ashamed. 'I didn't know how to.'

'What a lame excuse. What a lame, pathetic, utterly fucking ridiculous excuse, you excuse for a friend.'

She swung her legs over the edge of the bed and jumped to her feet. The room seemed so small with the three of us standing in it, arms crossed, making up the sharp points of a triangle. 'Our agreement was that you wouldn't swear. And you can blooming well talk,' she said. 'You knew about David and his affair, and you never said anything. You didn't know I was already in the picture. You're a hypocrite, Pru. You always have been.'

'It's not the same.' But it was an obvious lie, and Lena's expression told me that she knew it. It seemed I was a terrible liar too.

'Tell you what,' she said, putting her handbag strap over her shoulder with delicate effrontery, 'give me the car keys. I'll go downstairs and load up our stuff. You can come and apologize to me when you're ready, and then I'll apologize to you. Then we'll be equal again, and we can decide what to do next. Okay?'

'Fine.'

I took the keys from the pocket of my jeans and threw them on the floor. Then I faced the window and Mike Tunnell. His face had taken on a pink glow, as if he had found the sight of two women swearing at each other rather ener-

226

gizing. He combed his moustache with his fingers and smiled at me.

I waited for Lena's footsteps on the carpet and the quiet click of the closing door before I spoke.

'So . . . it was your job to see if I was having an affair?'

'Or open to having an affair.'

It began to make sense. 'With you, for instance?'

At least he had the decency to admit it. 'I wasn't keen, but your husband was adamant that he needed to know.'

'You weren't keen? Very flattering. You're not making things better here.' Then I wondered what, exactly, would ever make things better again. There was one last hope. 'Have you told him, then? About . . . us?'

Mike sucked his bottom lip and nodded. 'But there really wasn't that much to report.'

'How kind of you to say so.' My fear had been replaced with a weary panic. Everything had changed and I was too tired and too surprised to begin to adapt. The only rational thought I possessed was about my stomach. It had to be lunchtime. I could have eaten a hundred bacon-and-egg rolls, followed by fifty Danish pastries. There was no bottom to my hunger. I would have given anything to know the location of an all-you-can-eat Chinese buffet, but my guess was Allcombe wasn't sophisticated enough to possess one.

I hated Allcombe for not containing anything but weirdness and death. I hated the town at that moment like it was a person; the person responsible for all this. I wanted to punch its face.

My stomach rumbled, and the sound brought me back to

the dark little hotel room. The December light was barely making it through the window.

I needed to get out.

It must have shown on my face. 'Go home,' Mike Tunnell said. 'Go back to your house and forget all this. You've upset the wrong people here, but they won't care if you make your-self scarce. Trust me.'

'Don't you even want to know what's happening here?' I asked him, and he shook his head.

'The world is full of shit, Prudence Green. That's the first thing you learn as a PI. It's only worth investigating the thing you're being paid to look at, or you'll never sleep, eat or rest again.'

On that basis, it was clear that Lena and I would never make good detectives, and I found that in the course of that morning I had lost the will to even try. Who knew what malice lay behind the grubby, ageing façade of Allcombe? I could spend the rest of my life snooping around and discover a secret behind every salt-wind scarred door, every darkened, rattling sash window. Every bed and breakfast. Every retire-ment home.

The world was full of secrets, that was what it boiled down to. Even Lena had kept information from me.

I had to get out of Allcombe. It was impossible to think any more.

'You and Lena keep safe,' Mike Tunnell said, and I heard something in his voice that I should have noticed from the outset. He was not immune to Lena's charms. If he'd had a choice, he might well have pursued her, asked her out for greasy pizza and pumped her for information about me. Each second spent with me, on the other hand, had undoubtedly been clocked up on a time sheet. I really had become that undesirable.

'The number,' I said.

'I'm sorry?'

'Steve's telephone number.' We clashed eyes and my expression had to be saying what my mouth couldn't. I needed this.

He wilted. A blue ballpoint and a scruffy A4 ring-bound pad sat on the bedside table. He snatched them up, scribbled something and ripped the top leaf from its binding with quiet anger, then offered it to me without moving. When I stepped close to him to take it, he jerked away and stepped back to the window. The paper fell to the floor. I bent down in front of him to retrieve it.

'You didn't get that from me,' he said, and turned his back to me.

I straightened up and folded the paper once, twice, pinching the seams until they were as sharp as blades. 'Do you know what the worst thing is?' I said to the curls of hair hanging over the collar of his shirt: curls that had once seemed so luxurious to me. 'I would have taken you to bed. I still would, even after all this. But that doesn't mean I want to lose my bastard husband.'

'I shouldn't worry about it,' he said. 'You don't let any of it show.'

He was right. Of course, he was right. I never let it show: happiness, anger, fear, pain, desire, love. All kept under the surface of the cynical fat woman. But even the obese and the jaded can have moments of transparency, however rare, and one of those moments was upon me.

I came up behind him, stretched up on the tips of my toes, and kissed one of the curls that lay on his neck, just against the curve of his jawline.

'Was that enough of a show?' I said.

I felt the bunching of his muscles, like a dog that has just realized it is in a dangerous situation, but I stayed close for a second more, knowing that he hated it, just so I could breathe him in and file a memory of him away for the future: the attractive man whom I had kissed. Then I stepped back and accepted the fact that I would never imagine myself to be desired by someone like him again.

I had a casual goodbye on my lips, ready to go, good enough for the movies. But I never did get to say goodbye.

'Pru!'

The cry cut through the room. It was as loud as the whistle of a train, and the shoddy window panes rattled with its impact.

Before it had finished I was out of Mike Tunnell's bedroom and pounding down the stairs to the reception.

Thirty-nine

When I hit the bottom step, my breathing was the loudest sound in the room.

I grabbed the banister for support and tried to slow the movement of my chest. Lena was close by, in the centre of the reception. She held an armful of our possessions – books, clothes, hairbrushes and toothbrushes, and stood upright, serene, giving no sign that she had called.

She was facing the desk, behind which stood Phil, his elbows digging into the wood, his faded black T-shirt hanging from his coat-hanger figure.

Next to him were three other boys I recognized. It was a squeeze, but somehow they still all managed to lounge, their expressions amused, their languid mannerisms speaking of boredom.

The largest one, the policewoman's son with the muscles and the three long scratch marks across his face – Kyle, that was his name – was batting at the bead curtain like a bored tomcat. The red-haired beanpole with acne was sitting on the desk, legs dangling, revealing thick-soled black boots bearing scuff marks and combat trousers with surgically precise rips along the thighs, held together at regular intervals with fat, yellow-headed safety pins.

The small blond one was, of course, playing with his cylindrical green lighter.

It was strange how, only minutes ago, a small flame had been the source of such hope. Now it turned my stomach. The flicks and snaps of his fingers were mesmerizing. It took some effort to bring my attention back to Phil's pale face.

He was out of his league; one look at his eyes, scuttling backwards and forwards between the members of the gang, told me that. I guessed he had acted on his earlier humiliation by calling in Dead Vegetation.

I decided to try dealing with him alone. The others scared me rigid.

'Hey, Phil,' I said.

He didn't respond. His eyes flickered to Lena, and then away again.

'Where the thin tart goes, the thick bitch follows,' the small one said. The others sniggered dutifully, even Phil.

I cleared my throat and waited for the laughter to die down. 'We'll be off,' I said breezily to Phil, as if nobody else was in the room. 'Checking out today. Put the bill on my credit card. Come on, Lena.'

'A fucking stupid fat bitch,' said the small one. Nobody laughed. The humour had left his voice. In its place was thick disgust. 'Throw her a bone like an obituary column, and she laps it up without asking why. The only surprise is how she managed to escape.'

'We're going,' I enunciated to nobody in particular.

I let go of the banister and took a step across the floor, towards Lena. She didn't move. She wasn't looking at me. Even though there was nobody between us and the open door behind, her hunched shoulders and watchful eyes looked like those of a long-term prisoner. Escape didn't even seem to be a possibility.

'Lena?' I said, as loudly as I dared. Maybe she wanted to be caught, raped, dismembered, burned, whatever those thugs had in mind, and really, nothing could be ruled out. I wondered if she felt punishment was due for having cheated on her husband, particularly with such a lowlife. I wanted to take back every time I'd mocked her. Maybe then she might have had the confidence to move.

She licked her lips. The four lads watched that tiny pink flicker.

'I'm sorry,' she said. I guessed it was aimed at Phil. It sounded heartfelt, even if she had no reason to apologize. He shrugged his shoulders and scratched his forehead.

'So you fucking should be, cunt,' the small one said. I'd never heard that word said in that way before. He wasn't doing a favour for Phil any more. He hated us, maybe hated all women, and this was his moment to do something about it.

'Phil?' Lena said.

Phil bent his head and stared at the grain of the desk. 'Shut up, you cow,' he muttered.

'We're gonna do it,' Kyle said. His voice was as deep as the rumble of an oncoming train. He nodded to himself, gathering pace, as if listening to an internal drum, beating faster and faster.

'Do what?' I said. 'You'd better be careful or I'll tell your mother.'

The small one spoke softly. 'We're gonna do you, and then the Smithson cow. That's what we're gonna do.' He snapped the lighter into life once more and jerked his head towards us, in a movement that could have meant *come on*.

Kyle let the beaded curtain trickle through his fingers and drop. The red-haired one on the desk shifted his weight forward. His solid black boots hit the floor with a thud.

Still Lena didn't move.

So neither did I.

Kyle stepped forward.

'Stop.'

The command, given in a deep male voice, came from above us. I didn't need to look up to know Mike Tunnell stood on the landing, leaning over the banister, but I turned my face up to him anyway and let the relief of his presence wash over me.

He held the attention of the others too, as he walked down the stairs, taking his time. His eyes scanned the room. I moved to Lena's side so that he could stand on the bottom step, framed by the posts like a scene from a film.

'Is there a problem?' he said.

Nobody spoke.

He turned his steady gaze on me. 'Weren't you just going?'

I grabbed the back of Lena's jacket and gave it a yank. 'Right now.'

Kyle spoke under his breath.

'What was that, boy?' said Mike.

After a moment the small one cleared his throat in an elegant fashion. 'He said they're not going anywhere.'

'Is that right?'

I pulled so hard at Lena's jacket that I felt the leather stretch. She took an involuntary step backwards, and that seemed to be enough to break her stillness. Another back-step followed, then another. We reached the front door that way, without turning round to check our trajectory.

I felt the welcome chill of the December wind, saw the quality of the light change from the yellow stain of electricity to the stabbing grey of clouded daylight. The doormat was under my shoes.

'Don't you fucking dare,' said the small one.

I looked at Mike Tunnell. He gave a hint of a smile, no more than a quirk of the lips that, I imagined, only I could read.

One more step backwards, and we were outside.

Then I let go of Lena, turned to face the slapping, boisterous sea, and walked away.

I heard Lena's footsteps behind me, hurrying to keep up, but I kept my pace down the promenade until I reached the car. Only then did I stop, suck up a deep, long breath of knife-sharp air and dare to look behind me.

The Royal was quiet, as quiet as any other house in the row, with empty windows and a dark mouth for a doorway. The only other person on the promenade was Lena. She still held our possessions, cradled in rigid arms, fingers splayed wide, the nails as perfect as ever. It was hard, as I watched her hair whipping around her face and the sway of her body, not to believe that this whole experience was behind her.

'Open the door,' I shouted over the noise of the waves, when she was only a few feet away and still moving quickly.

She deactivated the central locking system, then opened the nearest door and dumped our possessions on the back seat. She straightened, slammed the door, and didn't look at me as she moved to the front passenger door and slid into position, her knees together, her hands linked on her lap.

I got into the car and started the engine with a comforting, familiar turn of the wrist. I realized that life consisted of such little actions, actions that could account for second after second if I let them. Perhaps I could live on automatic pilot, without having to pay attention to my life again. I pulled my seat belt across me, put the car in gear, indicated, checked my mirror and pulled away. My hands on the steering wheel were a source of comfort. I found myself watching them rather than the road.

'Will he be okay?' Lena said, next to me.

I noticed her knuckles, white in her lap. It seemed incredible that I could speak at all, but there was my voice in response, with a banal comment that was not worth vocalizing. 'I think so.'

'Were they going to kill us?'

'I don't know.' Anything had been possible in that hotel reception. The looks on the faces of the boys had been proof of that.

'Are they following us?'

'I don't know, okay? Maybe Mike will be able to . . . maybe they won't . . .'

I pulled the car over and left the engine running as I launched myself out. I made it to the iron railings separating the promenade from the beach before I was sick. My breakfast, sweet and chunky in my throat, hit the grey shale ten feet below with a splash that the sound of the sea did not entirely blot out. The seagulls called overhead, as if in appreciation of the meal I had just provided them with. I leaned against the top bar, my forehead on the freezing metal, and opened my mouth wide in the hope that the cold wind against my tongue would remove the taste for me.

A light touch on my lower back brought me back to life.

'I'm sorry,' I said.

'Shut up, Pru.'

Lena didn't mean it harshly, I could tell. It was as if she was the adult and I was the child, naughty at times, but always to be forgiven at the end of a long day. That was our relationship. But this time I didn't want us to brush the harsh words aside and start afresh tomorrow as if nothing had been said. I wanted things to change, for our time in Allcombe to mean something.

'Listen,' she said, before I could tell her what I was thinking. 'Just listen, okay? Stay here and wait for me. I won't be long. Stay here and if anyone comes just lock the doors, stay in the car and wait.'

'No. Why? Let's go home.'

Her hand slipped from my back. I straightened up and turned to face her; she had already taken a few steps away from me. We were on the corner of the promenade, between the Slaughter and the fish-and-chip shop. Lena was looking down to the pier and the small cottages opposite the rusty signs that offered fishing trips up the coast.

I knew what she was thinking. 'Leave it,' I said.

'I can't.'

She shrank into the distance, until she was little bigger than a figure on a television screen. It made it easy to watch as a dispassionate observer as she knocked on Mrs Smithson's door.

I wanted there to be no answer. What, exactly, were we going to do with Mrs Smithson once we'd found her? Take her with us, back to Lyneham? How, exactly, did Lena imagine she was going to take care of an independent loner who had left middle age behind? But it wasn't only that – I wanted Lena to myself. I wanted to talk as we had never talked before, and I couldn't do that with Mrs Smithson taking up space in my car.

The door to the cottage remained closed. Lena leaned over and peered through the letterbox. I turned back to my splat of sick and the beating rhythm of the sea. I couldn't bring myself to look in the direction of the Royal or the Paradise.

'He'll be fine,' I said under my breath. 'He'll be fine. He'll be fine.' But my mind insisted on presenting me with the image of Mike Tunnell's corpse, smouldering, dismembered, or maybe even bundled up in a black bin bag with a yellow tie handle. I began to understand why Buddhists chant. As I repeated the words it was easier to believe in them and take comfort from them. He was fine. Everyone was fine.

'Ridiculous,' I said. 'Ridiculous. Ridiculous.' I rolled the word around my mouth. In a moment Lena would return and we would drive back to Lyneham. Life would be frozen there, as normal; there would be Mess gin to drink, and sponge to snack on. In the mornings we would gather with the other wives of 24 Squadron and pretend not to know each other's intimate secrets while the children watched CBeebies. In the evenings we would moan about life in the RAF, and secretly feel relieved that we didn't have to live in the real world.

And there was Christmas to look forward to, of course; I had almost forgotten. I would put up my bright green folding tree and my mishmash of decorations. I'd untangle the lights and try to get them working again, give up, and buy a pack of 300 multicoloured tune-playing flashers from Homebase instead. Christmas would be my comfort blanket. I would actually try to enjoy it this year.

I'd invite Lena round for lunch. We could pull all the crackers between us.

She was trotting towards me, doing that funny jog she does when she's in a hurry. She waved her hands over her head when she saw she had my attention.

'Quick!' she shouted. 'Come on.'

'Where?'

'The cottage.' She arrived at the car. 'Mrs Smithson's locked herself in. She says she's not leaving.'

'Isn't that up to her?'

Lena leaned against the bonnet and shook her head so hard her hair wrapped itself around her throat. 'I told her she was in danger from those . . . and she said she was going to top herself anyway.'

Mrs Smithson had never seemed the suicidal type to me. 'She's being a drama queen.'

'She's calm. She's really calm, Pru. She says she's been collecting the pills for months. Sleeping tablets from the doctor.

She said they were called . . . Lorazepam. She shut the door and went to get a glass of water. She's really going to do it.'

'Lorazepam?' I said. 'Lorazepam?' It was a word I knew well.

And that was when I understood. I saw that I couldn't change a single thing that had happened to me throughout my entire life. There was a pattern here, something great at work, divinity dabbling in my life: call it God, call it fate, it was here and it was beyond my control. The only thing I could do was to get us both out of Allcombe as fast as possible.

'Good luck to her, then,' I said. 'Let's be off.'

The anxiety poured out of Lena in a rush of released breath. Her mouth stayed slightly open; each slow breath formed mist in the freezing air. She looked so beautiful, and so innocent. She had never come across the real face of suicide.

'Listen.' I came up to the car and put my hands over hers. 'You have to trust me on this. I know a bit more about suicide than you do. We can't stop her from doing this. If she thinks her life is over then she'll find a way to make it over. That's how it works. And even if you persuade her otherwise today, what then? Will you persuade her again every single day? You have to let her make her own decisions.'

'Get away from me,' Lena said.

I had to make her listen, for the sake of her own happiness. I tightened my hold on her hands.

'Get in the car,' I said.

'I'm not leaving her,' she said. 'You can piss off.' When she tried to pull free I held my grip. Her muscles were no match for mine. She tried to twist away and wrenched her elbow. Still I held on.

'You can't help her,' I told her.

'Fuck you! All this because you're scared. But Pru, I'm scared, she's scared.'

'I'm not scared any more.' It was true. 'I've had enough of being scared. Get in the car, Lena. I won't say it again.'

She put all her effort into trying to get free, and I felt anger surge through me and take control. I realized I was enjoying hurting her. It was like I held a moth in my cupped palms. It was no harder than that to keep her with me, keep her safe from herself, her fluttering, her confusion. She dug her nails into my arm and I felt no pain. She was so very weak when it came to dealing with real life and she didn't understand it.

I got her around the neck and brought her body up against mine, her legs bent under her, her back arched so that her head was level with mine. Her fingers scrabbled against my arm.

'Please,' she said. 'Please.'

I put one hand on her throat and squeezed, just for a moment, just to get her to be quiet so that she would listen to me.

Then I saw fear in her face and I let her go.

She found her balance quickly and took three steps back, in the direction of the Slaughter. Her fixed gaze, her tiny frown, her pinpoint pupils: she hadn't understood. She wanted to get away and was wondering how to do it. That wasn't what I had expected at all.

'I'm not sorry,' I said, because I got the feeling she wanted an apology and it seemed important to lay my cards on the table.

'Pru . . .' She coughed. Her hand went up to her neck and hovered there. 'Pru, wait for me, okay? I've got to help Mrs Smithson, but I'll be back and we can talk. Do you understand?'

'Of course. I understand.'

I waited until she was standing once more at Mrs Smithson's door, bending over the letterbox and staring through it without even wondering for a moment if the old woman deserved privacy.

I watched for a few seconds more. Then I got in the car and drove away.

Forty

The plan had been to go home, so it was a surprise to find myself driving straight past the M4 turn-off near Bristol.

It took five hours and forty-five minutes to get to Shrewsbury. I spent twenty minutes in a phone box situated in the lobby of a wearily wallpapered chain motel into which I had checked myself on impulse. It was past seven by the time I had dialled the number provided by Mike Tunnell and had a brief conversation with my husband.

Steve didn't seem surprised to find out I was less than ten miles away. But then, he was an officer in Her Majesty's Royal Air Force, and they are trained never to admit to being less than prepared. He even had the name of a restaurant where we could meet that evening on the tip of his tongue. After giving me clear directions, he said how much he was looking forward to seeing me and hung up before I could reply. The telephone didn't refund either of the pound coins I had fed into its metallic maw.

As I left the motel, the glass double doors reflected back a tired, ageing woman, with greasy hair and travel-dirtied clothes as crumpled as her face. Maybe we should have had kids, Steve and I. Then I could have had a reason for looking so awful. And aren't kids meant to bring a couple together? Or is that one of the lies we get told as a matter of course? I had always considered myself too screwed up to do a good job raising children, and too sensible not to recognize that fact. I would only load up the little versions of me with emotional baggage, all of it labelled to Crazyville.

But it occurred to me as I climbed into the car once more that I was just a coward. I was such a coward that I wasn't even going to think about Mike Tunnell, or Lena. Instead I was going to pretend that they were both safe, definitely out of Allcombe by now, and having fine old times. Lena was probably already back in Lyneham, ensconcing Mrs Smithson on one of her large cream leather armchairs next to the radiator, pouring her a large gin and soothing her with the knowledge that a fence and armed guards now lay between them and the outside world. If anyone could persuade Mrs Smithson to unlock the door and leave the pills to another time, it was Lena.

I drove to the restaurant, replaying Steve's dispassionate instructions in my mind, and found myself thinking of the way Lena had shinned the drainpipe to get into Yvonne Fairly's house – was that really only a week ago? She had swung one hand over the other and inched upwards, her thighs clenched tight, the muscles visible through her tight-stretched skirt. I remembered the grunts of effort that had escaped from her.

She was having a mid-life crisis. Her determination to rescue people, either in the 'superhero' sense of the word or by psychoanalysing them into a corner, was a symptom of finding out she wasn't enough for her husband. I would have put money on it. She had probably bundled poor Mrs Smithson into a taxi and badgered the old sod into playing word-association games and saying the first thing that came into her head when she heard the word 'suicide'.

There was no way she would still be in Allcombe.

I parked the car by a small stone wall that stood between the road and the fast-flowing Severn. The restaurant was an installation of glass, steel, and white lights. It was a slow Monday night: only three tables were taken, all by older couples who looked comfortable eating in silence, handling wine glasses as big as bowls and cutlery as shiny as newly minted coins. There was no sign of Steve.

I looked around for him but he wasn't in sight. Our possessions, Lena's and mine, taken from the hotel room, caught my eye; they lay in a pile on the back seat of the car. Amongst them was *Allcombe History: Shame and Scandal*, which I had liberated from the library. I leaned over my seat and plucked it from the heap. When I entered the restaurant with it under my arm I asked for a seat by the window.

I didn't get to open the book. My glass of Soave arrived at the table two minutes later, at the same time as my husband.

Forty-one

The tiramisu was excellent. In fact the tablecloth bore testament to my enjoyment of the meal: it was speckled with light brown drips and dark brown splodges. Opposite me, both Steve's plate and the surrounding tablecloth were spotless. He had placed his knife and fork together in a straight line on the plate; the only sign he had been there at all was the unfolded napkin beside it.

'I'll go then,' he had said after carefully putting down his cutlery and shaking out the napkin from his lap. 'If that's your last word on the subject?'

I must have agreed that it was, because he went, giving the young waitress two crisp twenty-pound notes and a wink on the way out. She had blushed. Well, he was attractive even though his waist had widened and his red-blond hair had thinned from his temples. The eyes had only been enhanced by the thin lines that radiated out from the corners. He was ageing in a textbook fashion. I think, early on in the meal, I had accused him of that – of always being the good-looking one in the marriage and enjoying that distinction.

He had been angry, I think: angry and determined not to show it. What else could those tight shoulders, the bunched muscles, mean? Since when had I lost the ability to read him? But I wasn't sure why he told me, 'You've changed, you know, with your weight, and your attitude, and everything, Pru, and you don't even remember that you were once a red-head who did yoga to work off the five-course meals in the Mess. And you never even liked gin back then, or junk food, and you never hated everyone so completely, you know? And you loved me. We were in love, remember?' He breathed out and smoothed the front of his jacket. 'I – you know what? I've waited a long time to say all that.'

It was disconcerting, to sit in an unfamiliar place, knowing everything was about to change, with all points of reference jumbled into a mess that could not be untangled, and remember so clearly, and with such nostalgia, how things had once been. Eighteen years old, traumatized by life, I had to dare myself to step out of my bedroom in order to make it to university. Yes, I had been in serious need of love, back before I developed a crust. And that was when we had met, during the first week of university, in a small, unfashionable tea shop. He saw me ordering slabs of hot white toast and ordered the same; we were united by our hatred of the bagels from the student union canteen.

Steve was right. That had really been me. I had really tried to forget my past and live. Funny how that desire to be different had gone. It was as if time had caught me and pulled me back into misery, erasing my willpower one month at a time.

My coffee was cold. I pushed the cup away and the edge

247

of the saucer caught on the corner of the stolen library book, splashing the cover. What was it Reverend Smythe had said about marriage? A marriage should not be a form of ownership. And I was just beginning to realize that a marriage could not be anarchy either. I had stopped trying to give my marriage any structure a long time ago, thinking it would keep rolling along without any input from me, and it had fallen apart.

'I felt sure there was another man,' he had said between mouthfuls of puttanesca.

Laughter had pressed against my throat.

'I couldn't come back, live with you, thinking there was another man, you know? So when I found out they were sending me home from the desert, I pulled a few strings to get posted out to RAF Shawbury. I thought it would be easier all round, but, but, it wasn't.' He took a mouthful of wine and then gave me the full wattage of his charm with a wistful smile. 'I had to know, you know, one way or the other, so I could decide whether we should start over or not; and Mike Tunnell, he seemed like the best option, nice chap. Took it seriously, you know . . .'

Mike Tunnell. Had I kissed Mike Tunnell only that afternoon?

'When I got Mike's report,' Steve had said, clearing the last mouthfuls of his meal in a dedicated fashion, 'he told me that there wasn't another man, and that you only, you know, caved in to him because of stressful circumstances. Is that true? What did you have to be so stressed out about?'

I considered explaining and decided I didn't want to spend another hour with Steve as he played his usual trick of not understanding how anything stressful could happen to a stay-at-home wife who never has to venture near a war zone or bomb civilians for a living.

The pleasant voice of the young waitress brought me back to my lonely table overlooking the oil-black Severn. 'Can I get you anything else?'

I looked around me. The place was empty. The waitress was probably hoping for an early night; a chance to get down the pub, maybe spot my delectable husband, pint in hand and smile on face, just for her.

'Another coffee,' I said.

'Espresso?'

'Cappuccino. Extra large.' I'd take my time over it, toy with my froth, dissolve coarse lumps of brown sugar in it slowly. 'And maybe another look at the dessert menu?'

I had let myself go, wasn't that Steve's point? I had let myself go, at pretty much the time he had let me go, in order to sod off on his RAF jollies. Training weeks. Exercises. Unaccompanied tours. Enforced social obligations. Battle of Britain dinners. Mess functions. Survival training. Diving. Climbing. Skiing. Golf. You couldn't tell me he didn't love each and every one of these activities. And who was I to complain? I had a house provided for me, and all the time in the world to perfect my coffee-and-walnut sponge.

The bitterness on my tongue was painful. I wished I was in a bad play, so that I could get up fast, push my chair over backwards, shout over its clatter on the floor, bang my hands against the expanse of shining window, scream at the passersby. But there was no audience. Everyone had already gone home.

The coffee arrived, and I waved away the dessert menu. For the first time in years I wasn't hungry. I felt light, empty. My hands were shaking like a frail old woman's.

Frail. Fripl. *Women are not the fripl creatures we once held them to be.* Wasn't that what the Reverend Smythe had said? Women are not frail. *For no creature is without the desire for revenge when it suffers prejudice or ill-treatment at the hands of another.*

'I'm sorry about the emails. But I know how sharp you are: you'd have picked up if they hadn't come from the MOD account. It did serve one purpose. The thought of Darren Sharp writing words like that to you made me realize I wanted to be the one to write them. I really did. Even after everything, I wanted to call you my Moo again.'

I had flinched at the word.

'So I've decided,' Steve had said as he slid one hand over mine and did not recoil from my sweatiness, even though it must have appalled him, 'that we should maybe give it another go? In all areas of life? I'll try to include you more, be around more, and you can lose the weight, you know, find your self-respect again, I'm sure of it, Pru. You could be like you were back in our student days. After you get fit we could try for kids if that would make you happy. Would that make you happy?'

So I told him.

I told him that happiness was something that it was beyond his ability to give to me. It could not be pinned down with three extra smiles a day. Fantastic sex wouldn't catch it. Producing children would not be sufficient bait. Happiness had not even popped its head above the parapet when somebody else had been writing to me using his name.

There wasn't going to be a happy ending.

'I'll go, then,' he had said. 'If that's your final word on the subject?'

My second scalding cappuccino arrived. I managed a few sips, feeling the tiny bubbles burst on my upper lip, while remembering that the real last words of our conversation were these: women will have their revenge. I had just revenged myself upon him for all the times he had not been there for me. Even though it was unfair on him, for he had always told me he wanted to join the RAF, I felt wronged and I had to punish him for it. It was the only time he had ever asked me for something, and my only chance to turn him down.

I couldn't wait to relay the whole conversation to Lena. She would appreciate the irony of it, and would understand if this had really all been about come-uppance. I wondered if she'd say I'd cut my nose off to spite my face: it was certainly a concept that kept running through my mind.

If I did get to tell her about this, what could I say to defend myself? How could I explain all the things that had happened to me, leading me to this moment, this decision?

And on that thought, as I burnt my lip on my coffee, the image of Crystal Tynee popped into my head. I saw Crystal in that mouldy, meadow-print-smothered hotel room, writing her note, just one word. FRIPL. Then I saw her taking her time, popping her pills, one after the other. Maybe they had even been Lorazepam.

With her suicide note, she had found a way to give the world a coded explanation. I just had to decipher it.

I put down the coffee and picked up the book I had liberated from Allcombe library. I had a chapter to finish before I could face the thin cold mattress of the motel bed.

Forty-two

. . . cartoons and editorials show how the public imagination was captured by the FRIPL incident. His identity became a matter of national interest. The *Herald*, a daily newspaper of the period, with a large readership, offered a sum of money for information about the disgraced Smythe, who was being used as a figurehead for the growing movement of Suffragism. The amount of money offered for this information rose each week over a three-month campaign until it reached the princely sum of £180, an amount that could not easily be dismissed, even by the tight-lipped inhabitants of Allcombe.

In the winter of 1903 the peace of the seaside town was shattered by a series of stunning revelations in the pages of the *Herald*. An informant had come forward and claimed the reward in exchange for the identity of Reverend Smythe, but it was a stranger story than anyone could have imagined.

Smythe was no young, progressive vicar with a passion for the rights of equality under the eyes of

God. In fact, the real name of the writer of *Words for the Faithful* was not Smythe at all, but Smithson: Avril Smithson, of Allcombe, a woman with little formal education and no teaching in theology or divinity.

At first the idea of such a woman being able to produce a book such as *Words for the Faithful* was treated with derision. The trade of the Smithson family was lacemaking, and she was not even considered to be adept at that. Being nineteen years of age and unmarried, she was held to be unattractive and unlikely to do well in life by those who knew her. When the allegations about her secret identity were made, it seemed that a cruel practical joke had been played on her by someone determined to pocket the reward money.

But the *Herald* persevered with its claims, and produced a series of revelations that stunned a nation of readers.

The informant it had coaxed into the light was a Mr Ernest Penhaligon, a twenty-seven-year-old businessman in the Allcombe tourist trade who was considered by the community to be personable and friendly. He owned four of the newly built terraced hotels in the town, and stocked them with local goods that could be purchased by visitors, including the Smithsons' lace. He had certainly met Avril Smithson during these dealings, and he claimed that a close friendship had developed from this acquaintance. She had agreed to meet him in secret at his main business premises and his home, the Paradise Hotel, and during those meetings she had apparently expressed the desire to change her life for the better. To that end, he had agreed to help her improve her mind through reading and conversation.

If this is a true account of what took place during their liaisons, then Avril was an amazingly gifted student, for the first 'Reverend Smythe' pamphlet appeared less than three years later. Penhaligon claimed varying degrees of involvement in the Smythe works, but the veracity of his claims could not be established. One thing is certain: he revealed Avril Smithson's identity for the wealth it would bring him, even though they had been in a secret relationship for nine years. He took his payment from the *Herald* and invested it in land around Allcombe. It was a wise investment, if not a moral one: the Penhaligon family still owns large amounts of Allcombe real estate today.

Avril Smithson saw none of the money. Her publishers decided she was in breach of contract, having signed using a false name, and she was therefore told she would receive no more royalties from the Smythe books. But the worst was still to come. The *Herald* revealed, in a triumphant final scoop, that Avril was about to become an unmarried mother. Ernest Penhaligon denied all involvement.

Nobody stepped forward to defend Avril Smithson. Even the Suffragettes, a movement for which she had done much good under her false identity, publicly ridiculed her, in an attempt to distance themselves from any harm to their reputation. She dropped out of public view after a baby daughter was born to her. She raised the child, whom she named Grace, in the bosom of her surprisingly supportive family, and continued to work as a lacemaker until her death in 1911, at the age of thirty-four. She was buried in an unmarked grave, suggesting a possible suicide.

Avril Smithson never did escape Allcombe to lead a better life. Her books and her life have all but been forgotten.

Forty-three

Lena Patten, that's me. And I'll remain Lena Patten. No retreat to the maiden name for me. No divorce, no moving out – but that's not to say no changes. There will be a lot of changes, not least of which will be my decision to no longer care about the crap taking place in the rest of the world.

It was the final day in Allcombe that changed me.

Pru attacked me, held me down, made me realize that I am powerless against her, and against anyone who might choose to treat me that way. But all I could think was I had to save Mrs Smithson.

I couldn't protect myself, solve a mystery or triumph over evil, but couldn't I at least help Mrs Smithson?

As I ran back to the cottage I wondered what I was going to say. Shouting to a closed door was not the same as gently coaxing someone down from a window ledge. I couldn't command Mrs Smithson to put down the pills and step away from the glass of water.

When I reached the door, I opened the letterbox and peered into the short, shadowed hallway, made all the more crowded by the rows of decorative plates fixed to the wall. Mrs Smithson sat on the stairs. The letterbox cut off my view of her head and feet, but I could see her squat torso in that frayed woollen cardigan of hers, a loose tartan skirt and her bent knees partly open to reveal a low crotch to her tan nylon tights, stretched like a trampoline between the thick pillars of her legs. She spoke first, muttering something I didn't catch.

'Pardon?' I shouted.

'Do you want to come in?'

'Can I?'

'Door's open.'

I dropped the flap and tried the handle. It turned smoothly and I stepped into the hall, closing the door behind me. A sense of unreality pervaded the close space. I moved back to the wall and the jutting edge of a plate holder jabbed me in the spine.

'They're going to do me in anyway,' she said. 'Right? They're going to string me up like they did Henry. I don't wanna go that way, if you don't mind.'

'That's very understandable.' I thought back through the psychology textbooks I'd read. Surely some of them had covered suicide attempts, but I couldn't think of a single piece of advice. 'There are other options, though.'

'I told you. I'm not leaving Allcombe.' She shifted her position so that she could hug her knees and rest her head against the wall. 'My family have always lived here. Lived and died here. That's the kind of thing that's important. Roots.' She yawned loudly, not bothering to cover her mouth. I saw a thick yellow coating on her tongue, and felt a moment of revulsion. 'Roots.'

'Well, you'll end up in the ground all right. Is that really what you want?' I'd hoped some realistic words might shake her out of her mood.

'Of course that's what I want,' she said. 'That's what I've been bleeding well saying since you turned up here. And it's none of your business anyway, miss. You concern yourself with your husband instead, or he'll go elsewhere. Go home, look after him, and stop wasting your time out here, running around with that little plump friend of yours.'

A psychiatrist should attempt to keep a distance between the patient and her personal life. 'Well, I really don't think we should be talking about me, given the circumstances . . .'

'S'unfashionable, is it? For the old to tell the young how to behave. You're not going to take a lick of advice from me, but I'm meant to treat every word of yours like gold dust.'

'Stay around and tell me what for, then! Why don't you sort us all out: me and Pru, the teenagers, Penhaligon?'

'I can't sort him out,' she said. 'He always wins. He's always won before. Don't you know that? The Penhaligons always get what they want.' She yawned again and closed her eyes. Her hands slipped from her knees to lie flaccid by her bottom, her knuckles on the worn stair carpet. 'He's family. Bet you didn't know that either. Ancient history, it is. The Penhaligons and the Smithsons. Like that.' But she made no gesture. Her body looked heavy, as if it had sunk into the stairs like a stone ornament that had been in the same place for decades.

She looked ready for sleep. A long sleep.

'Have you . . .?' I said. 'Did you . . .?'

'Took them all, miss. While you were with your friend.'

It was impossible to comprehend. 'Oh my God.'

Her wrinkled eyelids flickered, as if she were trying to open her eyes and found them beyond obeying her instructions. 'You're not going to make a fuss, are you? It's not like anyone's left to care.'

'I care,' I said.

'Lost cause of the week, am I?'

She was right. I cared because I didn't want her to die on my watch. If I hadn't heard the teenagers include her in their death threats, she would be alone with them now, just another old lady left behind. I didn't really want to take her with me. I didn't even like her. I just wanted things to be right.

Pru had seen it. Pru knew me well – better than I knew myself, sometimes. And it was that thought that made it impossible for me to sit back and wait for the pills to take hold.

I left Mrs Smithson on the stairs and went into her damp living room with the net curtains twitching in the breeze through the gaps in the sash windows. Beyond them, on the sideboard, was the cream push-button telephone. I called an ambulance. I was going to prove Pru wrong; Mrs Smithson was going to become my responsibility. Not just for today, but for the rest of her life, whether she liked it or not.

We sat together on the stairs and waited for the ambulance to arrive. She talked about Crystal a little bit: how she had insisted on standing on chairs and singing improvised songs about teddy bears when she was little; how she had won singing competitions during wet weeks spent in holiday camps an hour up the coast. And it was obvious that Mrs Smithson had always wanted to come back home. This town suited her, with its aged terraces and empty arcades slowly sagging into the sea. She would have been lost anywhere else.

I hardened my heart and waited for the ambulance.

Eventually she fell into silence. I resumed talking in the hope of keeping her awake. I don't think I said anything deep, or interesting. I remember mentioning the colour of my sofa at home. I told her not to worry about visitors coming round as I wouldn't answer the door to anyone, not even Pru. Particularly not Pru. And I dropped in the fact that I might even buy a turkey and some mince pies for her for Christmas.

I wonder what Christmas would have been like with Mrs Smithson ensconced in my living room. Would I have been ready to force the pills down her throat myself after a month? Would she have demanded tea and biscuits every hour on the hour? Insisted on watching *EastEnders*, *Coronation Street* and *Emmerdale* every night?

Maybe things worked out for the best after all. Freed from Pru and Mrs Smithson, I watched a documentary about Byron on Christmas morning, served myself salmon for lunch, then ate an entire packet of Jaffa Cakes before dozing off on the sofa. I pleased myself. It was a new experience for me.

I didn't go to the daily get-togethers of the wives either. There was a chance that Pru might attend. It was a shame not to go. For the first time, I actually quite fancied a slice of coffee-and-walnut sponge. In fact, anything sweet became good over Christmas. It took away the cravings for cigarettes and alcohol, both of which I've given up. Food is my new vice, necessarily so. When given no option, it's amazing what a person can achieve.

Take Mrs Smithson, for example. She was convinced that she had no choice but to kill herself, and so that's what she achieved. The ambulance took twenty minutes to arrive, and the trip to the hospital in Barnstaple took another twenty. They pumped out her stomach, and yes, that seemed to go well, but she had a massive stroke, they said, and died less than an hour later. That's determination for you. She'd made up her mind to go. You have to admire that. You can see where Crystal got it from – that, and her suicidal streak. Apparently these things run in families.

I sat in the hospital waiting room for hours, picking at the frayed material on the arm of the uncomfortable green chair, with something called a 'Mocha Chocca' in a plastic cup on the MDF table beside me. It was the end of the worst day of my life. I knew Pru had run away – I'd seen the space on the promenade where the car had been parked while climbing into the back of the ambulance. I was glad of that, at least. It was past ten by the time I was informed that Mrs Smithson was gone, and the buses from the hospital had ceased to run. I was facing a long night with only my Mocha Chocca for company, when a miracle walked past me on the way to the glowing Exit sign.

Mike Tunnell.

I called to him and he turned round immediately, a wide smile on his face, as if he had recognized my voice.

'What are you doing here?'

He pulled up his left sleeve to reveal a small square piece of gauze held in place by surgical tape just above his wrist. 'A graze with a knife. Nothing more.'

'Did you get that from . . . the Royal?'

He shrugged. 'They won't be bothering you again. Are you okay? I thought you'd be back home by now.'

'Abandoned, I'm afraid. Pru left me behind. We've fallen out.'

He took the news as I hoped he would. 'Really? Well, let me help. I'm driving back to Telford tonight. I'd love the company, if you'd like a lift. I don't mind taking you to Lyne-ham

'You're a hero, do you know that? My husband's gone back to Iraq today, you see, so there was nobody I could call.' That quickfire exchange was all it took to get myself a lift, and get myself laid. And I needed both of those things that night.

He was magnificent in the fucking department. He knew how to use his cock, and, call me old-fashioned, but that's what I was craving. I think what it all boils down to is that I don't like to *do*. I like to be *done to*. It suits me better. So, in contrast to my dealings with Phil, I did nothing that night but lie back and let Mike Tunnell wallow in me. He treated me like a sticky dessert that was impossible to resist – he had to consume me like the epicurean he was, with as much care for the preparation as the meal. He went through my under-wear drawer and took out the pieces he wanted to see me in. He bathed me and cleaned my face with delicate wipes of his

263

hand. He brushed my hair and laid it out on the pillow behind me. Only then did he slip between my sheets.

It was not unlike being a human plate again. Only this time, it was my fantasy, not his. I never suspected I would enjoy role-play so much.

After, when I calmed down and looked around me, I realized I hadn't even thought about David, even though I was lying on his side of our marital bed, catching the scent of him every time I turned my head into the pillow. He had lain there only the night before, perhaps with Derek. It was actually pleasant to lie there in his smell, feeling nothing in particular, concentrating on the tenderness of my well-kissed skin against the expensive Egyptian cotton sheets that had been purchased by his mother from our wedding list.

Mike and I didn't talk about Allcombe once on the way to Lyneham. In fact, we didn't say anything much to each other, before or after. Before he left to drive back to Telford we shared a cigarette – the only part of the whole experience I feel guilty about now – and he had a long shower which used all the hot water.

Once he'd gone I cleaned his long black hairs from the plughole and stripped the bed. It wasn't that I wanted to get rid of his memory. I didn't need his memory. It was only ever to be a one-off. And it did make me feel better. I hope it did the same for him.

And then I had a Christmas of extravagance: a new skirt, a jade necklace, maroon leather boots, and, worst of all, at least three packets of Jaffa Cakes a day.

At the time I didn't know why I craved these things. I only found out last week. Until I took the test, I thought I'd learned to be happy alone for the first time. Now I know I'll never be alone again.

The Squadron is coming home on Monday. Everything has been agreed with David and Derek Fairly. I'll have to have the house ready by then.

So this is my last entry in this diary. I'm not going to be a psychiatrist after all. There won't be time, and I've lost the will. Why devote my life to solving other people's problems? Pru was right: it never accomplishes anything. From now on I'm going to concentrate on defending myself and my family. That is all that matters, isn't it? Looking after family.

Forty-four

It was February, a Friday morning, and I was pressed up against Tracey Sharp's radiator, looking through the front window and listening to the television blare out a cheerful tune behind me. The children were silent and the wives were talking in soft tones about what they were going to wear to welcome their husbands home from the desert.

'My black leather jacket, I think,' Melanie said. 'With black trousers and high-heeled boots. I'm having my hair layered this afternoon.'

'Watch out, Suzi Quatro,' I mumbled, but not loud enough to be heard.

'I've made a new dress,' Rachel said. 'I found some lovely material.'

'Great,' enthused Tracey. 'John will really appreciate that.'

I pictured John Pinkett, lankily loping from the plane to be confronted by the sight of his wife swathed in an empire-line nightmare adapted from floral curtains.

It was strange to be on the inside this one last time. The

removal vans were scheduled for Monday, the same day that the men would arrive at Brize Norton with sand in their hair and boots, and I was almost sorry to miss it. But the solicitors were already in the first stages of agreeing the terms of settlement, and Steve had told me through his representative that he wanted things to go smoothly and quietly. Leaving the married quarter early was meant to be proof of my agreement.

Everything at home was in boxes. The daily gathering of the wives was the only way to get a cup of coffee, but more than that, I had wanted to attend, even though sponge was the last thing on my mind. I hadn't been able to think about food since Allcombe.

Allcombe haunted me.

There were things I needed to know, was desperate to know. And I had thought of a way to get the answers I craved. But not yet. Not quite yet.

The television chucked out a high-pitched tune about butterflies, and I found myself humming along.

'I can't wait,' said Karen Mitchell. 'It feels like so long.'

'It will be lovely to have them back,' Tracey said. 'Even if they do make a mess of the house. The first thing Darren will do is dump his clothes in the middle of the hall, and leave a trail of sand through the house as he heads for the PlayStation.'

The wives chuckled in agreement.

'Peter will give the kids a pat on the head, me a kiss on the cheek, and then will settle in front on the telly with a cup of tea,' Karen confided with a small smile. 'I'll get stuck into his mountain of washing. Don't they have washing machines on the base out there?'

The behaviour of the husbands seemed perfectly reasonable to me. I, too, would wear stinking clothes for four months and become immersed in the virtual world of PlayStation rather than hold a conversation with these women.

I turned around and looked at their little group. Yvonne was gone and, just as I had predicted, they were carrying on as usual. It was as if she had never existed.

Before I could think it through, I let myself say what I had always wanted to say.

'Karen, Peter hates your cooking. Always has done. Particularly your scones. He says he throws them at the starlings nesting in the garage roof. Better than an air gun, apparently. And Rachel, your husband has his own wardrobe of designer dresses to wear. He always takes one to the desert, a John Rocha number with a slit up the side, and does a drag act if you get enough Stella into him.' I was on a roll. 'Melanie, Paul doesn't play golf on Sunday mornings. He goes to the Link Centre in Swindon and takes part in fantasy role-playing tournaments. Apparently he's a level-sixteen Wizard called Rufus Carnus.'

'I don't know what you think you're—'

For the first and last time, I interrupted Tracey Sharp. 'And Darren is banging the redhead who works behind the Mess bar at weekends. You can ask anyone. It's been the joke of the camp for months.'

It was quite an experience to see all of them speechless. The children remained glued to the television. The song about the butterfly came to an end and a new song about a whale called Wanda began.

Melanie Watt found her voice first. 'You sad, bitter, ugly, vicious bitch,' she said.

'I know,' I said.

'You come here and you tell all these lies to try and make yourself feel better . . .'

'And that's all it is.' Rachel pointed a trembling finger at me. 'A pack of lies. You can't handle the fact that your husband doesn't want you any more . . .'

'Actually, I left him, I think. In the end. Technically speaking.'

'. . . so you try to make us all unhappy too. Well, it won't work!'

'You mean you are happy? Gosh, I'm sorry, I must have missed the bit where you all got out your party hats, jumped up and down and clapped your hands together with glee.'

'Get out,' said Tracey.

'Right. Bye then. Have a good life with your permanently disconnected husbands and your sedated children. I hope it all works out for you.'

I gave them all a smile, collected my coat from the hall, and closed the front door behind me.

Bare-branched well-trained trees were dotted along the road that ran through the married patch. There was frost, thick on the grass, and the road looked clean in its sheer white slipcase, as if it could lead to somewhere more enticing than the gates of RAF Lyneham. The sudden change from hot to cold made me yawn. I hadn't been sleeping well.

Then I saw it. The symmetry of the closed houses was marred by one swinging door that led into darkness.

Yvonne Fairly's house was open. And that could mean only one thing; the gossip was true and Lena was there, collecting the baby's remaining possessions to take into her own home.

I crossed the street in the intense cold of the February morning. I needed to see her one more time.

Forty-five

'Hello,' I said.

'Hello,' she said.

Normally I wouldn't bother to record such a boring exchange, but it was the only build-up that came before I launched into my ridiculous, mortifying speech. 'So you're going to look after Fairly's baby,' I said. 'That's good, really good of you. Charitable. Do you need a hand moving the cot? I could help. Not just with the cot. With everything. I'd make a great babysitter. Or a favourite auntie. I don't mind.'

Even as the drivel came out of my mouth, I was aware that Lena was not quite as beautiful in her hatred of me as I had expected her to be. Weight had piled on to those cheekbones. Her hair hung lank down her back and strands had been shoved behind her ears, as if she no longer cared what it did. Around her neck was a heavy necklace with a large green stone in an ornate silver setting, resembling a flower; neither the colour nor the style suited her, dulling her emerald eyes and washing the pink blush from her cheeks.

I wondered what I looked like to her. I'd had a haircut for

the first time in years and the weight had begun to slide off me to reveal a Pru who might conceivably be considered attractive, one day. Not that I cared about that, but I thought Lena might. I wanted to ask her, but her expression warned me against opening my mouth again. She looked as though she might scream. I gave her time to compose herself, and she got there eventually, once she'd put the dining table between us.

'Of course, you know that's never going to happen.' The sound of her swallowing was loud in the silence. 'How are you?'

'Oh, fine, you know. Fine.' I laid my hands against the warm wood of the dining table and pictured Yvonne lying there, as dead as the friendship Lena and I had once known. 'You?'

She nodded. 'I've got something I want to give to you, actually. Can I come round to yours? Later this evening?'

'Will you, though? Or are you just saying that?' I sounded petulant, demanding. It took an effort to change the subject. 'What's going to happen to this table, do you know?'

'Going for auction.'

Yvonne's pride, the pedestal on which she made her grand gesture, going to the highest bidder at a bargain price. Once upon a time, before Allcombe, I would have found out when and where the auction was to be held and gone myself to claim it as a memento. Not now, though. I had no need for such things any more.

'I've got something for you too,' I said.

'Later, then. After dinner.'

'Okay.'

I wrenched my eyes from the table and turned to go.

'Oh, and Pru?' The tone was so familiar that I looked back over my shoulder with an impatient quirk to my mouth before I could stop myself. 'Since you're here, you can give me a hand with the cot after all.'

Forty-six

It was dark by five, and although I knew Lena wouldn't come for ages, I got ready for her anyway. I took the suicide note from my jewellery box, the one I had removed back on the first night when I showed her my collection. Then I dug out from the wardrobe the only dress I had that fitted me – a black crossover number that looked okay once I'd put on my best bra and control-top pants – and cracked open a fresh bottle of Mess gin.

Then I arranged myself on the floor, with the gin and two glasses next to me, between the stacks of packed boxes, and read and reread the note to pass the time.

The time went with a little help from the note and the gin. A quarter of the bottle was gone by the time I heard my back door open to admit a rush of freezing air. I folded up the note, as small as I could make it go, and slipped it into my bra. I wasn't ready for her to see it yet.

She came into the room like a character from a melo-drama, and peeled off her long black coat and tall purple boots so that she could sit cross-legged opposite me, in our familiar positions. She retrieved a lipstick from her handbag, next to her on the floor, and applied it. Only when it was thick and bright on her lips did she speak. 'Thanks for your help earlier.'

Carrying the cot to her house had been like old times: an argument about who wasn't pulling their weight, and a lot of swearing when one end dropped on Lena's toe. It had been wonderful.

'S'fine.' I slopped some gin into the spare glass and she shook her head as she dropped the lipstick back into her bag and snapped it shut.

'Not for me.'

'You've given up? I don't believe it. Is this for the benefit of Fairly's baby? Are you going to play happy teetotal families with your borrowed offspring?' I hadn't realized quite how bitter her decision had made me until that moment. The emotion that swirled in my stomach with the cold gin was undoubtedly rejection.

'What's wrong with that?'

I laughed, and lay down on the carpet, moving my arms and legs like a starfish. 'Nothing, Lena. S'lovely. Congratulations. Will Fairly become an honorary Patten too?'

'David and I will live together when the men get back from the desert. Derek will stay in the Mess, as far as the RAF is concerned, but obviously he'll be spending most of his time with us. I'll sleep in the second bedroom, and the baby will be in the box room. We're picking up Jasmine from Yvonne's parents next week.' Her voice seemed distant. 'We'll raise her as a family. That's the plan. And we'll raise the new one together as well.'

'The new one?' I stopped moving my arms and legs and lay still on the carpet. 'What do you mean?'

'I mean I'm pregnant.'

'Wow!' It wasn't quite the right word, but it was the only one that came to mind, so I repeated it. 'Wow!'

'It's early days, so don't tell anyone.'

'Well, you know me, I was going to take out an advert in the local paper, but since you've asked me not to . . .'

'Oh, shut up, Pru,' she said, and it brought tears to my eyes, for all the times she had said it and all the times she would never say it again. I sat up and took a swig of gin. She was tracing a pattern on the beige carpet with her index finger. There was a slight frown, drawing her eyebrows together. 'I couldn't save her. Mrs Smithson.'

'S'nice that you tried, though. I'm sure she appreciated it. I would have, if it was me.'

'God, you make such a sloppy drunk. You're out of practice.' She looked at me with a critical eye. 'We made a terrible team. Right from the word go.'

'Yeah . . .' I had to ask the obvious question. 'So is David the father?'

She gave a smile and a shrug that looked smug to me. 'I don't know. Maybe, maybe not.'

'But he thinks it is his . . .?'

'Does it matter?' She smiled again, a slow spread of secret delight across her lips, and I understood that she was telling the truth, about this if nothing else. It really didn't matter to her who the father was, and what lies she told to her husband. And David would never suspect. He had always thought of her as a goddess, and goddesses don't fuck random weirdos in strange seaside towns.

'So you're leaving,' Lena said. She waved a hand at the boxes and the bare walls.

'Very observant of you, Watson.'

'Getting a divorce, I heard. What will you do?'

'Dunno. Travel. Eat a croissant in Paris and a gerbil on a stick in Peru. Try new things. Maybe even get laid. Sex seems to have cheered you up.'

'A holiday would do you the world of good,' she said with a tilt of her head. 'Go sit on a beach somewhere.'

'Drink Pina Coladas? Get caught in the rain?' An attack of the giggles rushed up over me and wouldn't leave me alone. It only subsided when it became obvious that Lena wasn't going to join in. 'Sounds fabulous,' I said, when I had control of my voice back. 'I'll do it. Book me a ticket.'

'It would probably be for the best if you did go away and try to forget about me. I don't think we should see each other, for a while, anyway.'

'Oh God,' I said. It just slipped out. I tried to recover. 'Get over yourself, you vain cow. You're pretty rubbish company, you know.'

'You'll forget all this, Pru, and you'll be fine,' she enthused. I could tell she had rehearsed this section of the conversation. 'Give it time, you'll see. You have to give it time.'

'Yes, oh Yoda. So right you are. Much to learn from you I have.'

'Well, fine, whatever,' she snapped. 'Just don't stew about things, okay? I know what you're like. You're probably lying awake thinking about stuff. About A-Allcombe.' She stumbled over the word. 'I know I have been. Wondering whether we should try the police again.'

'And say what? You have our word that the most popular man in town tried to have us killed?' I downed my gin and poured myself another thick measure. There suddenly seemed to be no reason not to finish the bottle. 'No, I've come up with a plan. To deal with . . . Allcombe.'

'Really?' She leaned forward. 'What's that?'

'What do you care? You've got your new family to think about.'

She sighed and opened her handbag once more. 'You really don't get it, do you? I only ever wanted to be your friend, Pru. And I could have been a good friend to you if you'd ever trusted me for one minute. Treated *me* like a friend. Maybe even confided in me. I wouldn't have judged you. I had things I wanted to confide in you, too.' She rummaged in her bag and produced the thin blue leather notebook I had seen her scribble in occasionally. 'Maybe this will make it clear to you,' she said. 'I don't need it any more.'

She held it out and I took it. The leather was warm and rough in my hands. I flicked through the fat, crinkly pages; about two thirds of the book was filled with small, neat handwriting in black ink. 'Your diary?'

'Read it if you like. Give yourself a laugh.'

'Thank you,' I said. 'Really. Thank you.' I hugged the notebook to me and stroked the cover.

Lena rolled her eyes as she got to her feet. 'I should go.'

'Wait.'

'I don't think so.' She put her feet delicately into her boots and zipped them up.

'No, please,' I said. 'I told you, I have something for you too. Here. Take it.' I reached into my bra and drew out the folded note. I had never thought to let another person see it, but it wasn't so hard, not after the gin and the gift of the notebook. 'Read this.'

She took it and unfolded it, one crease at a time, until it was open in her hands.

'Read it aloud,' I said.

'I'd rather not.'

'Out loud!' She jumped. I realized she was afraid of me, afraid of the physical power I had exerted over her on Allcombe promenade. She licked her lips and started to speak, reading the words written in faded red pen, one at a time, breathing life into a long-dead message.

Dear Prudence

> *Happy seventeenth birthday. Many happy returns.*
>
> *I never thought we'd make it this far, just the two of us, no help from the world. There were times when I wanted to put a pillow over your head and then throw myself out of the window to save us both from the misery of this world, but it would have been wrong, wouldn't it? You have your own life to lead. I shouldn't rob you of the chance to be happy. It's possible one of us might just manage that.*
>
> *Seventeen. You don't need me any more. How did you put it? All grown up, you said. You can take care of yourself. I should learn to give you space.*

Space is fine, Prudence. Space can be arranged. I've been ready for a long time to give you some space.

Don't do anything fancy for a funeral. Just do well at school and look for a good man. That should be a good life. And hold true to what you said this morning – that you were never going to end up a sad case like me.

Mum

The words were over. Lena had stopped speaking. I found I had something to say.

'Sleeping pills,' I said. 'Lorazepam. Over fifty of them. I didn't find her till the next day. I stayed out all night after our argument. It was the first time I'd dared to do that.'

'Oh,' Lena said.

'But you know what? She was always going to do it and I knew it. It was never an if. It was a when. I couldn't have ever saved her. Do you get it now, Lena? You can't save anyone.'

'Right,' she said. She folded up the note and stared at it, a small white piece of history. 'That makes sense.'

She was piecing me together like a jigsaw and the gin in my stomach rose up to the back of my mouth. I wanted to be sick on her elegant boots. This was exactly what I had always feared: she pitied me, and now I never wanted to see her again. 'You know what, Lena? It doesn't matter. Don't give it another thought. I haven't. Not since I was seventeen.'

She held out the note to me, sympathy horribly alive in her eyes, and I put my hands behind my back. 'Keep it. Call it a trade for your diary. Isn't it time you got going? Lots to do for your new arrivals.'

'Listen . . . if you want to talk before you go, come round.'

'How big of you.'

She put on her coat and slid the note into one of the pockets. I followed her to the back door, where she hesitated, half in, half out of the dark. 'When you read my diary, you'll see that I really do love you, Pru. I really do.'

'That can't be right. Because I really do love you. How can two people who love each other end up saying goodbye like this?'

She shrugged and held out her hands. I wrapped the long cold fingers in my own. 'Allcombe,' she said. 'Allcombe has a lot to answer for.'

I kissed the backs of her hands and she didn't pull away. I let her go and watched her walk back to her house. It was about to become a proper home for the first time, and I silently wished her luck.

Forty-seven

The morning sun was bright when I returned to Allcombe; not as a tourist, but this time as a resident.

The promenade looked different in early spring. I parked the car near the Bosworth Slaughter and walked across the empty road to the iron railings, feeling the serrated teeth of the wet sea-wind on my cheeks. The Christmas lights had been taken down from the lampposts and replaced with heavy multicoloured streamers. Gaudy red and blue painted tubs, some already displaying buds of green, sat under each post. Plans were in place for summer.

To my left the terrace of dilapidated Victorian hotels stretched away. The Royal and the Paradise looked far away: silent, sleeping. The ubiquitous ice-cream van was parked in front of the Paradise. To my right was the pier, the bobbing boats, the fishermen's cottages, and my new home.

I took a slow walk to my front door. The key supplied by the solicitor slid easily into the lock, and the door swung back to reveal a dark, narrow hall that smelled of damp. The carpet bore the tracks of wet footprints – the solicitor must have been there that morning for a final look round – and the small black eyes of the birds on the decorative plates on the walls observed me with keen suspicion. Little did they know that they now belonged to me.

An extra £5,000 for all of Mrs Smithson's possessions had seemed a fair deal. Nobody would appreciate them as I would.

An examination of the rooms reassured me that nothing had been taken. The ancient furniture, the glasses in the display cabinet, even the battered kettle: everything was there, waiting for me. I switched on the central heating at the boiler and filled the kettle with water from the banging pipes. While it grumbled its way up to boiling point I forced open the stiff back door and took a stroll around the garden. Tiny tendrils of weeds were beginning to find Henry's wooden cross, so I cleared them away. It seemed only right.

The teabags were crumbly with age, but I managed to produce a drinkable cup, even without milk to take the edge off it. I took small sips as I climbed the narrow stairs.

At the top of the stairs a door opened onto a utilitarian bathroom with grey-white tiles delineated by black mould, and a bath, stained yellow and with a single shrunken bar of Imperial Leather that appeared to be welded in place. The medicine cupboard over the bath had a cracked sliding mirror serving as a door, and behind that was a wrapped bar of Imperial Leather, a bottle of cheap shampoo for permed or coloured hair, and a half-empty miniature bottle of gin.

'Thanks, Mrs Smithson,' I said as I poured the gin into my tea. A large mouthful made it easier to walk into the bedroom.

There were fewer personal items than I had been expecting: no pictures or photographs hanging on the walls. There was an ancient Teasmade and a stack of well-thumbed romantic novels on a dusty bedside table. The bedspread was a thin patchwork that had been sewn from irregular patches of any number of materials. It looked clean, but hardly warm enough to get through an Allcombe winter.

I lifted the bottom corner and pulled open the divan drawer. There it was, just as I had suspected: four full carrier bags with stretched handles, brimming with dog-eared photographs and yellowing papers. I pulled the nearest one towards me and it toppled over. The contents spewed out, trying to slip back into the safety of the shadows, but I was determined and, after a little scrabbling in the dark, the bedspread was covered with a mountain of Mrs Smithson's past. I took a quick sip of tea, winced against the hit of the gin, and examined my find.

Many of the objects she had chosen to keep seemed arbitrary: a ticket stub from a journey from Exeter St Davids to Bristol Temple Meads, made on Christmas Eve in 1974; a photograph of a blue Wolseley in front of a terraced house with a yellow door; gold wrapping paper, folded neatly but bearing no tag. There was no way to know the significance of these things. It was more difficult to piece together her life than I had expected.

Were these four bags really the best she could do for a treasure trove of memories? Could sixty years be spent on this earth with nothing to show for it but four bags full of tickets and wrapping paper?

And then I put my finger on what had really been bothering me since Lena told me that Mrs Smithson was dead.

There was no suicide note.

Mrs Smithson had just checked out. She had decided not to elucidate.

I scoured the objects, turning over each piece, looking for a few words, anything that could be taken as a message. All I wanted was to see her handwriting, to compare it to all the other examples of penmanship I'd seen in my life, to see if I could divine suicidal tendencies in the strokes of her letters. I was on the point of giving up when I spotted the letter.

It was written on cheap lined paper that had gone grey with age, the corners curling, the marks of the pen faded, and it wasn't so much a letter as a scribbled note.

J
Popped out for milk
T

So I wasn't looking at Julie Smithson's words. Tony Gamberetti was the writer, I guessed, and the note came from the days before Crystal became famous, and Julie was left behind while her boyfriend and her daughter toured the country together.

I was holding written proof of their domesticity.

He'd popped out for milk. He'd fetched milk, and come back again. How happy it must have made her that he came back that time. That was what made this note so precious – it represented a happiness that hadn't lasted. But that didn't mean it hadn't existed at all.

Perhaps the key to life was to take what you could get,

when you could get it. Hadn't Lena written something about that in her diary? A decision to live for the present – that was what both she and Mrs Smithson had in common. They had recognized pleasure and grabbed it.

I had never been that brave.

I curled up on the bed and battled against my emotions – for how long I don't know. The sun was low in the sky and the birdsong coming from outside the sash window had taken on a tired edge when I uncurled. Photographs and pieces of paper had stuck to my hands. I removed them, one by one, and dropped them back into the pile. Then I downed the remains of my tea for the benefit of the gin and thought about what lay ahead.

Things had to change. I'd need to be brave for my plan to work. And that was what really scared me.

Forty-eight

Forty hours later, in the cold brilliance of an early morning and with my plan in place, I took up my position by the iron railings in front of the Paradise.

Strangely enough, and for the first time in my life, luck was with me. It wasn't the teenagers who came out to meet me just before midday.

It was Penhaligon.

'You look well,' he said, his eyes roaming over me. He held out his big pink hand. The fleshy part of his thumb was covered by the long sleeves of his dark blue overcoat that nearly brushed the ground. I had forgotten how short he was.

I took his hand and shook it hard, certain he could feel my fear through my fingers. 'Thanks,' I said. 'You too.' But it wasn't true. He looked older than before. I noticed wrinkles around his mouth and eyes, and the skin on his hand felt rough. I stepped back and looked up at the dark windows of the Paradise. 'Business booming?'

'What do you want, Ms Green?'

'Lena's left me,' I said, surprising myself. This wasn't part of the plan.

His blue eyes widened. 'But you weren't a couple.'

'Not technically, no. Still. I'm on my own now. And there's some things that I have to know.'

'Even though this is one instance where the sea air definitely wouldn't be good for your health?'

'Was that a threat?' I said. Everything he said was delivered in such a pleasant tone that it was difficult to tell. I couldn't equate this gentleman of business to the psychopath with the knife.

'I was prepared to drop the matter,' he said. 'You, apparently, aren't. I hear you've moved into one of the cottages by the pier. Do you think that will make you a local?'

'It makes me a concerned resident.'

He gestured around the promenade: at the empty expanses of concrete, the barbed wire on the bandstand, the long stretch of railings punctuated only by the lone ice-cream van. 'Do you see anybody else voicing concern?'

'Crystal Tynee did.' I watched his face for signs of danger. I was ready to run for it if I had to. 'And she's dead. Just like the old ladies you look after.'

'Not quite like that,' he disagreed with a smile. 'The residents of the Paradise die of old age. Crystal Tynee committed suicide. It's common knowledge that she took pills.'

'Of her own accord?'

'I'd consider it quite an achievement to force someone to swallow a mountain of tablets and then make them sit quietly for a couple of hours while it took effect. It certainly would be beyond me.'

'I don't believe that,' I said.

He leaned in close to me. 'It was suicide. I promise you. Was that what you had to know? Do you think you can let the matter go? I have things to do today, and it's too cold to stay out here chatting any longer.'

'You threatened me,' I said.

He shrugged. 'You were trespassing.'

'You had a knife.'

'As I said at the time – it needed sharpening. I was taking it to get that done.'

'You locked us in a basement!'

'I detained you until the police could arrive. It's called a citizen's arrest. You can look it up, since you're so keen on the law.'

He had an answer for everything, but I had one more card to play. 'You locked us in a basement – with a dead body.'

Penhaligon's full wet mouth twitched. 'Don't be so absurd, Mrs Green.'

'Gladys Little was in that bin bag, wasn't she?'

'You didn't take the opportunity to check?'

'Wasn't she?' I was desperate. 'Wasn't she?'

'Goodbye.'

He turned away and I grabbed his arm. He reacted instantly, putting one hand on my breastbone and forcing me back against the railings. My breath deserted me; I had to fight to make a sound. 'Listen to me,' I forced out, 'I can't drop it until I know. I can't forget it and go away unless you tell me. Gladys was killed by one of your cronies, wasn't she?'

I thought I saw a glint of admiration in his narrowed eyes: I had surprised him. 'And if I tell you, Prudence, will you leave? Because I find I want you to leave and be happy, if you can manage it. Somebody, somewhere, should be happy, don't you think?'

This sudden talk of happiness was like the dropping of a mask; his voice was different – as high as a boy's. I had not thought him capable of goodness, but it came as a shock to learn that he was not unaware of the existence of goodness in the world. I really did believe at that moment that he wanted happiness for me, even if he didn't have a clue how to help me get it.

'If you tell me, I'll leave. And I'll be happy.' I wetted my lips with my tongue. 'I mean, I'll try my best to be happy.'

'Very well.' He nodded once, as if that was the best he could expect. 'The answer is no. No, Gladys Little was not in that bin bag in the basement.' He stepped in close to me. 'It's easier to give them an overdose of medication. They die natural, peaceful deaths and are taken away to the local hospital. It's easy to arrange.'

'Why?' I whispered. 'Why do this?'

'Money. Once the personal savings of these little old ladies run out, there's really no more use for them. And I do have two ex-wives, five children, and a liking for fois gras to support, you know.' His smile held the contemptuous tenderness of a long-term lover.

'But that's not really the reason, is it? Can that really be it? Or is it because . . . you like it?'

I saw no answer in his flushed face.

'What was in that bin bag?'

'I really don't know. Would you like to go down there and check?'

I shook my head too quickly and he laughed.

'So why did you lock us in the basement?'

'Isn't it obvious?' He shrugged. 'I was going to have you killed.'

'And is this the truth?' It was never going to be enough. There was no proof, nothing to show to the police. No way to stop him. 'How do I know if you've told me the truth?'

'You don't.'

I felt myself crack into pieces in front of him. He stroked away my tears with his thumb. Then he took three steps back, slid his eyes over me one last time, and strolled into the Paradise.

Forty-nine

And here I am at the end.

I stayed up all night to get this down on paper. It's the hardest work I've ever done in my life, tackling exhaustion, stopping only for toilet breaks and the occasional sip of disgusting tea. But now I'm done. I feel proud of myself.

The sun hasn't come up yet, and I can hear voices outside the house. I peeked out of the window and saw the lads, sitting on their car: the little one flicking his lighter, the big one kicking his black boots against a jerry-can by the rear wheel.

On the bed, sitting on the damp bedspread beside me, are three objects. One is the note Mrs Smithson had kept all those years. The second is Lena's diary. The third object is a bottle. It contains approximately two hundred Lorazepam tablets.

Why am I writing this down? Because this is the first suicide note that explains everything, from the beginning to the end. If you're reading this, you know it all. And I'd imagine you agree with me that there's no reason left for me to be alive.

But there is another reason. Just like Crystal and her FRIPL, I'm leaving a message in the hope that the person who ends up with this note – and, who knows, maybe you bought it to add to your own collection – will succeed where I have failed, and find some way to stop Mr Penhaligon.

So now, in the house I bought in the hope that Mrs Smithson's memory would give me the courage to take my pills, I'm going to die.

Or, at least, Prudence Green, inveterate pessimist and friendless fat cow, is going to die.

Because I've discovered in the last few days I don't need Lorazepam to make that happen. How did Lena's diary put it?

> I think sadness is a road that you commit to, a road
> that never goes anywhere. It stretches onwards into the
> night, and if you decided to turn round you would see
> dawn on the horizon behind you, but you don't dare
> look over your shoulder for fear of seeing something in
> your past, something that you imagine pursues you.
> Maybe it does, maybe it doesn't – but Pru will never
> know. Because she never turns round.
>
> All it would take is a decision. Why won't she turn
> round?

I did turn around, Lena, only a few days ago, while sitting on Mrs Smithson's bed. I looked behind me and saw a vision of my mother. But she was an old lady, and old women are easy to get rid of. I've learned that from Mr Penhaligon.

So somebody new is going to be born – somebody who isn't a slave to her mother's genes, somebody who doesn't collect pills and suicide notes. No, the new Pru will have a different sort of collection: positive words, letters and accounts of happy times, and the first items in her collection are Lena's diary and Mrs Smithson's note. I've decided that those two possessions will be the start of a new person. They are all the hope I need, until I find happiness.

Now all I have to do is get out of this house, slip past Dead Vegetation, and escape this horrible seaside town. That shouldn't be too hard.

Time to finish this suicide note. There's a strange smell in the air. I think something downstairs is burning.

Acknowledgements

My grateful thanks to the following people for helping me to whip this book into shape: Will Atkins, Emma Dunford, Michelle Spring, John F. Griffiths, Neil Ayres and everyone at the best writing website in the world, www.ukauthors.com.

Also, thank you to Jane Gregory, Sophie Portas, Karolina Sutton, Simon Trewin and everyone involved with the New Writing Partnership's Escalator Scheme.

Finally, my thanks to Busy Bees Crèche, who gave me the time to write, and the Buzz Stop Coffee Stop, who provided me with toast.